RAVENSDALE.

A Romance.

BY ELLEN T——.

LONDON:

PUBLISHED BY G. PURKESS, COMPTON-STREET,
SOHO; STRANGE, PATERNOSTER-ROW.

PREFACE.

THAT novelist is said to deserve the best of society, who enlists the charms of fiction in the cause of morality, and renders the intricacies of his plot subservient to the best interests of mankind. Such a writer may inculcate the most valuable lessons while the feelings of the reader are carried away by the actors in the mimic scene; and though his fanciful personages, like the phantoms in Macbeth,

"Come l'ke shadows, so depart,"

yet their influence on the heart and the intellect, may be lasting and beneficial.

If such are admitted to be the proper objects of a writer of fiction, the authoress of the following pages may claim the merit of "holding the mirror up to nature" with unshrinking fidelity; "showing vice its own feature," with no sparing hand; and presenting in the ultimate happiness of more estimable characters, the proper reward of purity of mind, and consequent propriety of conduct. No one, it is hoped, can rise from the perusal of the work without a deeper abhorrence of immorality, and a stronger attachment to virtue.

The writer has already enjoyed no small share of popularity, and if public approbation should also be bestowed on the present effort of her pen, she will have been successful to the utmost of her desires.

London, November, 1847.

RAVENSDALE.

BY ELLEN T——.

CHAPTER I.

Who has not heard of the vale of Cashmere,
   With its roses the brightest that earth ever gave
Its temples, and grottoes, and fountains as clear
   As the love-lighted eyes that hang over their wave.
Oh, to see it at sunset, when warm o'er the lake,
   Its splendour at parting a summer eve throws,
Like a bride full of blushes, when lingering to take,
   A last look at her mirror, at night ere she goes.—MOORE.

HE lines of the poet just quoted well apply to Ravensdale, when viewed in all its pristine beauty, during the latter part of the last century; and even now that the noble mansion has fallen to decay, and the spacious and splendid grounds attached to it are overrun with the long, rank grass, and the crystal lake that meandered in such soft beauty through them is dark and sluggish, and the willow that erst drooped in such graceful beauty now dips her long branches deep into the stream, as though mutely mourning the sad change that time has wrought on that once sweet sequestered spot, yet there is beauty still—a soft, tranquil beauty, that tunes the heart to a deep and thoughtful interest in all the scenes that were once enacted within the now crumbling walls, where the clinging ivy seems rather to give than to receive support.

In the year 1794, Ravensdale was perfect in beauty; nothing was wanting to render it attractive to the eye of the beholder. Situated but a short distance from the metropolis, it was yet so rich and splendid in scenery, and the views from every window of the princely abode were fraught with such romantic beauty, rendered more perfect from a touch of wildness that mingled with it, that the spectator might well imagine himself to be many miles removed from the great city of London.

This sweet habitation had belonged to the family of the Claverings for many generations; they had once been a large and flourishing family; but, as is frequently the case with the high and noble born, had gradually dwindled till but three of the name were left,—the Dowager Countess of Clavering, her daughter the Lady Grace, and her son, the heir of this vast domain, the young Earl of Clavering, who now, at the commencement of our narrative, was daily expected to return to Ravensdale, having been absent the last few years upon his travels.

The dowager Countess had been left a widow in early life with two children, from which time, she had withdrawn herself from the gay world, and lived in quiet seclusion at Ravensdale; here her children were educated, and grew up amid the surrounding beauties of nature, fair and lovely, both in person and in mind.

High born, proud, and haughty, the countess yet possessed a kind and tender heart. Arthur her eldest child, she literally doated on. Every thought and hope for the future was garnered up in him, "her dear, handsome, noble boy," as she was wont to call him; and fondly and proudly did the mother exult over the budding charms of her only son. She certainly loved Grace, a merry, romping girl, who shared in all her brother's sports—frequently to the great vexation of the countess, who had no notion that young ladies had any right to use their time so, or take that bracing exercise which is as natural—ay, and as necessary too—for the youth of one sex as the other. Grace early scorned all control: light-hearted and joyous as a bird, she likewise emulated it in freedom. In vain did the countess scold and lecture Grace on the impropriety of young ladies scampering through the park. Grace would droop her head in silence at her mother's reproof, which, the next moment, was forgotten, or, at least, unheeded: for espying her brother in the distance, with a shout of merriment, Grace would bound across the lawn with the fleetness of the deer, and, as her wild laugh sounded far and near, the countess would sigh and say, "Poor child! nothing on earth can tame her exuberant spirits I wonder what will become of her." And then glancing at her boy, the mother's heart would swell with proud exultation, and Grace for the time would be totally forgotten.

When the young earl had attained his eighth year, the countess's only sister, who, like herself, was a widow, and in very delicate health, came to reside for a time at Ravensdale, accompanied by her little Edith, a fair, gentle girl of six. Mrs. Mannering's complaint was consumption; she had been ailing a considerable time; indeed, ever since the birth of Edith (which occurred two months after the death of her husband, who, too, was a victim of the same fell disease), her health had been on the decline; but no alarming symptoms had presented themselves, till, unfortunately, a cold, caught by exposure to a sudden change of atmosphere, settled on her lungs, and resolutely bade defiance to the skill of a physician, whose aid was resorted to in vain.

Change of air was strenuously recommended, as likely to produce a salutary check upon the disease, and if not efficient to save life, might, at all events, prolong it.

In obedience, therefore, to the advice of the medical attendant, Mrs. Mannering prosecuted a journey to Ravensdale by easy and pleasant stages. The countess received her sister and niece with warm and truthful affection; and under her kind and unwearying care, the invalid for a time appeared to grow almost well again.

Indeed, Mrs. Mannering so far recovered as to begin to flatter herself that her physician had been mistaken in the cause of her illness, and warmly and eloquently would she discourse with her sister on the future, which their imaginations painted in rainbow tints.

Frequently, when the sisters were seated side by side under the friendly shade of the willow, while the clear pellucid stream murmured gently at their feet, their children, rich in infantile beauty, would pursue their sports with all the hilarity of youth and health and hearts which, as yet, knew not what care or sorrow meant.

The dark clustering curls of Arthur, and his soft hazel eyes, contrasted sweetly with the golden ringlets of the fair, blue-eyed Edith.

And as their parents marked, with approving looks, the tenderness which evidently existed between them, they fervently and fondly hoped to see those two loved beings one day united to each other. And the countess would tell her son that Edith should be his wife, and Mrs. Mannering would bid her little daughter kiss her husband, and tell her that if she were a good girl, she should, when she grew a woman, be the Countess of Clavering; and Grace would laugh right merrily, and clapping her dimpled hands, inquire who was to be her husband, and then the countess would bid her take pattern by Edith, and she should likewise some day marry a lord.

Fancies such as these impressed upon the minds of mere children, are seldom if ever beneficial, and still more seldom are they ever realised.

When the summer had sped, and hoary winter came on apace, Mrs. Mannering's disease, which all this time had slumbered, not been extinguished, now burst forth with renewed vigour. In vain she endeavoured to persuade herself it would again abate; it baffled all attempts to mitigate its severity; and earnestly and ardently as she longed to be permitted to live to see her darling child grow to maturity, she felt that she must die—must quit this mortal scene, and all that seemed to invite her stay, to descend to the dull, cold tomb. Alas ! it was sad to see how much she clung to earth. Scarce five-and-twenty summers had passed since she first beheld the light; in the comparatively short space of ten years, she had passed from the frolicsome child to the proud, high-minded woman, had been a gay and delighted bride, a proud and happy wife, a joyous and affectionate mother, a sad and weeping widow. —all—all in those few short years; and now she was stretched upon the bed of death, The summons had come to call her hence, but she heeded not its voice.

"I feel quite well, dear Grace, with the exception of this tiresome cough, which prevents me taking that repose which, I feel convinced, would fully restore my strength," said the almost dying invalid to her sister, as she hung in sorrow over her couch.

Tears choked the utterance of the countess, and she could only bend her head in token of her acquiescence.

"The weather is now so cold and changeable," resumed the invalid, "that it affects my constitution, which you, my sister, well know has ever been delicate; and I really cannot expect to get entirely rid of my cough before the spring, which will soon be here; only a few months, and then I hope to be thoroughly restored to health. Speak, Grace," she continued, with a show of emotion; "do you not think that when the warm weather returns, I may confidently hope to recover. You know how well I was when I first came here?"

"Yes, love, I do," replied the countess, striving to conceal her emotion from her sister, "but it will be long before the summer comes again, and I tremble to think what great progress your complaint may make in the interim."

"Fie, sister," said the invalid, endeavouring to speak gaily, "you are but a poor Job's comforter. You should strive to keep up my spirits; but, alas! you have infected me with your own gloomy apprehensions;" and she sighed heavily.

Still, spite of the hope she fondly clung to of ultimate recovery, Mrs. Mannering daily, nay almost hourly, grew worse. Yet she struggled hard against the grim tyrant, persisting almost to the very last in encouraging the belief that she should be restored to her usual health. Bitter, indeed, were the emotions of her sister, as she watched her, day by day, sinking slowly into the tomb; and yet so far from turning her thoughts to another and a better world, she clung to this with a pertinacity that was truly astonishing, and most painful to witness.

It is sad for the young to die—it is mournful to see the flower that has scarcely opened wide its delicate petals, drooping in premature decay. When the flower has bloomed brightly through the summer, we weep not to see it drop its leaves, and bow its head as winter draws nigh. We feel assured that at the approach of spring it will again start into a new existence, once more to delight our senses with its sweet perfume and delicate tints.

Thus when, with the eye of faith, the departing spirit looks beyond this gloomy sky, and even yearns to take its flight to the realms of bliss, where all sorrow and sadness will for ever flee away, and sickness shall be known no more, then, with words of hope upon our lips, and an unclouded brow, we can soothe and sustain them to the end, and at last yield them without regret, knowing they are but transplanted to a more genial clime, where they will bloom with redoubled beauty. But painful and sad, indeed, it is to witness the slow, but certain decay of those who resolutely cling to this world and all its enjoyments, which they must shortly quit for ever—to see them, as it were, torn from life, while their every thought and desire tends to earth. And this was the mournful task of the countess; bitter as it was to resign an only and tenderly loved sister, it was dreadfully aggravated by the knowledge that she herself wished earnestly, oh! how earnestly, to remain.

With tender love, the countess strenuously sought to prepare her sister's mind for the sad and inevitable termination of her illness; but Mrs. Mannering seemed determined to deceive herself, and heeded not the gentle admonitions of her sister, and even hinted that it was unkind of her to speak so despondingly.

CHAPTER II.

The hand of the reaper
  Takes the ears that are hoary;
The voice of the weeper
  Wails manhood in glory;
The autumn winds rushing
  Waft the leaves that are scarcest;
But one flower was in flushing
  When blighting was nearest.—SCOTT.

IT was a saddening sight to the countess to gaze upon her sister, as she sat wrapped in a loose dressing-gown, in her easy chair, drawn close to the blazing fire, discoursing of the future like one who may reasonably look forward to many years yet to come; while the hectic flush upon her cheek, her quick dry cough, and laboured breathing, told a fearful tale. Oft when Mrs. Mannering gave utterance to some light, playful remark, her sister was forced to turn away her head in order to conceal the tears that came thronging to her eyes.

"What ails you, Grace?" inquired the invalid, in a peevish tone, as she observed the rising emotion of her sister. "You really grow quite childish; here is my little Edith," fondly drawing the child towards her, "setting you an example you would do well to follow; see how cheerful she looks."

"She does, poor child," returned the countess, impressing a kiss upon the sunny brow of her niece; "but, alas! my sister, she knows not the anguish that presses upon my bosom, swallowing up every other thought in its intensity."

"You allude to my indisposition," replied the invalid, with a more serious expression of countenance than she usually wore.

"I do, I do," returned her sister, sobbing; "the physician that came from London to see you this afternoon——"

"Yes," replied the other, catching her breath, "tell me—I meant to ask you his opinion of my complaint, but till now had not courage to do so. I guess, from your emotion, that it is unfavourable for my recovery; still keep me not in suspense, tell me—tell me all."

"Alas, my dear sister," replied the countess, "he has but confirmed the fears I have so long entertained, that it is utterly impossible to eradicate the disease which has taken such strong hold of your constitution."

Mrs. Mannering made no reply; her delicate and wasted frame shook convulsively; and she clasped her attenuated hands before her face. A sense of suffocation seemed to oppress her, which at length found relief in large pearly tears, which forced themselves between her small and almost transparent fingers, and then one by one dropped upon her knees.

Who can tell the bitterness of the young mother's feelings, who, up to this moment, had confidently encouraged the hope of recovery? The countess could only gaze upon her in agonised silence; she dared not comfort her with words of hope she knew could never be realised; and her own tears gushed forth as she witnessed the agony of her only sister, and knew that she would ere long be torn from her embraces.

After some minutes of uninterrupted silence, Mrs. Mannering raised her head, and removing the traces of tears from her countenance, fixing her eyes, which shone with an unwonted brightness, on her sister's face, inquired if she thought it were not possible the physician might be mistaken.

The countess threw her arms round the invalid, and enfolding her in a tender embrace, replied,—

"Would to God! dear love, I could encourage such a belief, but, alas! it is impossible."

"Oh, Grace," returned her sister, weeping on her bosom, "it seems so sad to die; at the thought of a speedy and final separation, all things wear a brighter aspect, and seem to bind me still closer to earth. The flowers we have loved and cherished will bloom again, but I shall not witness their beauty. Sweet spring will return and clothe the earth afresh in verdure. The summer's sun will shine again as brightly as in days gone by; but no more will it gladden my heart, and bless my longing sight. I must descend to the dark, cold grave! Oh, say, Grace, is it not sad?"

"It is, my sister," said the countess, in a gentle, soothing tone, "but let it not affect you thus. Were it not for our dear children, who could not spare us both, methinks I would gladly quit this world, and join our best relatives who have gone before us to a better and purer state of existence."

"Death at a distance, Grace," replied the invalid, "is like a summer cloud; but when it is hovering over us, ready and waiting to mark us for its own, our spirits faint and tremble at its approach;" and for a moment she shuddered, but instantly after resumed in a firmer tone, " I will endeavour, dear Grace, to bow me in submission to the stroke, knowing that it is God's omnipotent will alone that points the arrow and permits it to descend."

"Oh! bless God, for those words," said the countess, earnestly, "never fear, dear love, but he will sustain and comfort you to the end."

From this hour, Mrs. Mannering abandoned all hopes of recovering from her illness, yet she steadfastly avoided any allusion to her death; she became more thoughtful, and frequently desired to be left alone; beyond this, her manner was unchanged.

"Remember, Grace," she said one evening, as she was seated alone with her sister, "that Arthur is to be the husband of my Edith. Ever encourage the affection that now exists between them, and they will grow up, united in mind and disposition."

"Dear, dear Edith," said the countess, " I pray that my boy may prove worthy of possessing such a dear and gentle creature; I wish Grace more strongly resembled her."

"Grace," replied the other, " is a bright, merry child; her lot, I feel assured, is doomed to be one of gaiety, and lively happiness. Edith, I trust, will also be happy, but her happiness will be of a calmer and more thoughtful kind."

The countess assented to her sister's remark, but she felt that it was impossible to look upon a child, and foretel in what current its future life should flow.

The winter was one of unusual severity, and though carefully defended from even the lightest breath of air, yet the invalid rapidly declined in health. Each day found her growing weaker, till, at length, she could no longer bear the exertion of rising, and she was confined wholly to her couch.

At her own request, the children were admitted every day into her sick room; and then she would call her nephew to her side, and tell him ever to love Edith, and remember that, when he grew a man, Edith was to be his wife; and the little fellow, who displayed sensibility beyond his years, would promise never to forget, and voluntarily assure her that he could never love any one half so much as his own dear cousin.

Many weeks of exhausting weakness did Mrs. Mannering bear with uncomplaining fortitude; but at length she was so worn down with illness, that she confessed herself desirous to "be at rest."

" I am willing to go, dear sister," she whispered, as the countess hung in sorrow over her; death has lost all its terrors: I can now gladly welcome him as the harbinger of peace. Kiss dear Edith when I am gone, but do not talk to her of death; she is too young to understand the meaning of it, and it might produce a baneful effect upon her mind. Farewell, sweet sister, for the present; hereafter we shall meet again," and resting her head upon the pillow, she calmly breathed her last, so calm that death might well have been mistaken for his brother—sleep.

Thus bereft of her only sister, the countess devoted herself entirely to the care and education of the three children, of whom she was their sole surviving relative. Next to her darling boy, Edith held precedence in her heart. Grace was so wild and untameable that the countess felt less affection for her than the other two. Edith was by nature mild, yielding, and loveable; whole hours would she spend by the side of the countess, who calling by the endearing name of mother, her young heart would never have known that she bore not in truth that near relationship; while Grace was sporting on the lawn, or roaming the fields in search of wild flowers.

As the children gradually approached towards maturity, they were strictly a family of love. Rich in youth and beauty, their hearts were as one, differing much in mental as well as personal qualifications; yet their minds blended so sweetly together, that they had not a wish beyond their own little circle.

When Arthur had attained his eighteenth year, the few friends whose advice the countess valued, strongly advised that her son should travel; and though she dreaded the separation which must be an inevitable consequence of his so doing, yet as the youth himself seemed anxious to visit other climes, and a favourable circumstance afforded him an opportunity of journeying with the son of an old and esteemed friend of the countess, she yielded a somewhat reluctant consent.

Many tears were shed at parting, and promises exchanged of frequent correspondence, and the countess failed not to impress upon the mind of her son the engagement that existed between himself and his fair young cousin. With vows of never-dying affection, the youth fervently pressed her cheek, and bade his mother love and cherish her till his return. Edith then but sixteen, little more than a child, was yet possessed of so much sensibility that her girlish affection was given entirely to her cousin, whom from infancy she had been taught to love and regard as her future husband. Before they parted, Arthur presented her with his portrait, and, oh! how greatly she valued it; he himself placed it round her neck, and there she constantly wore it in his absence, and how many times in the day did she draw it forth, and gaze with tearful eyes upon his parting gift! As weeks and months flew by, the half childish love with which she had been wont to regard her absent cousin, gave place or rather changed into the warm and truthful affection of the tender woman.

Edith and Grace loved each other with the fondness of sisters. Grace, who retained all her infantile exuberance of spirits, was far from feeling any envy for the preference with which the countess regarded Edith. It was so natural for Edith to be loved; she seemed by nature formed to win all hearts to herself. Fair and slight made, even to fragility, the blue veins perceptibly meandered beneath her transparent skin; her golden ringlets waved luxuriously over her fair and beautifully-formed forehead; her eyes matched the soft tints of the violet, and were shaded by snowy lids, the long, deep fringe of which cast a shadow on her cheek. Altogether, she was a sweet and lovely being; in spirits, "not violently lively," but stealing on the senses "like a May-day breaking."

Grace, on the contrary, was a perfect Hebe—a creature of mirth and joyousness; two years younger than Edith, she was still a child. Indeed, she was one of those light-hearted, frolicsome creatures who appear children all their lives. Thoroughly good tempered, she loved and admired the excellent qualities of her sister Edith, as she invariably called her; the countess would frequently desire her thoughtless daughter to endeavour to imitate what she owned she admired; but Grace would playfully shake her head, and declare that it was impossible.

"I never could, dear mamma, even if my life depended upon it, mould my face into that pretty, demure look that suits so well the features of Edith; neither would it become me if I could; all are not possessed of the same gifts, and I must be content with what has fallen to my share."

"And a plentiful share you have, dear Grace," said Edith, kindly. "I love to hear your merry laugh, and should be sorry to see you less gay."

"I really believe," replied the countess, laughing, "that you girls praise each other by mutual consent."

"We love each other dearly," said Grace, throwing her arms round Edith, who warmly returned her embrace.

And as the two were thus enfolded in each other's arms, the aunt and mother regarded them with tearful eyes, breathing at the same moment an earnest prayer for their future happiness.

CHAPTER III.

"To love an absent one for years,
    To pray for his return,
To shed the tears of bitterness,
    And day and night to mourn:
To spurn all other proffered love,
    For that far distant one,
And turn all thoughts, all hopes, to him,
    The young heart's summer's sun:
Yet this has been, still is, nay more,
    It oft again will be;
For this is woman's truest love,
    And woman's constancy."

THREE years had Arthur been absent, but still was he unforgotten by the fond and faithful Edith. We say he was not forgotten, but he was treasured in her young heart's core, as the being whom she all but idolised. Oh, how earnestly did she count the days and weeks that were likely to elapse before his return; how every expression in his letters, as far as related to herself, were read and re-read twenty times a day!

"And will he love me as dearly as when we parted? Shall I be all to him that I then was?" were questions with which she constantly tortured herself; and frequently, when unseen, would she weep, lest he should love her less.

"Silly Edith," exclaimed Grace, when, discovering her in tears, she inquired and learned the cause. "You absolutely have no real occasion for a single anxiety, so you endeavour to conjure up some fancied word on which to expend your sighs and tears. Well, every one to their fancy; but, tears are far from pleasing to me. I am very desirous for Arthur to return, because, when you are married, mamma tells me that you must, as a matter of course, have a house in town; and there, at least, we must spend part of every winter, and go to balls, theatres, and all sorts of fashionable places. Will not that be delightful? I declare that my head is almost turned, even at the thought of so much happiness," and humming a merry air, the lively girl turned from the room.

"Where are you going Grace?" said the countess, who met her at the door.

"Nowhere in particular, mamma," she replied. "What, is that a letter from——?"

"Your brother, child; I was seeking for Edith, in order to impart to her the contents."

"This way, mamma," replied Grace, leading her into the room she had just quitted. "Pray tell me the news, is Arthur coming home soon?"

"Edith, my love," said the countess, giving no heed to her lively daughter, "Arthur is now in London, and to-morrow will be here, dear noble boy, how I long to see him again;" and her eyes shone with maternal pride.

"Oh, that is indeed, capital news," exclaimed Grace; "I am delighted beyond everything. We shall no longer be immured in this dull place all the year round, but go to town and enjoy ourselves. I see no good in being rich, if we ——"

"Hush, Grace," said the countess, "I wish you would leave off such childish talk, and be a little more woman like. I am sure you are by no means fit to mix in fashionable society; your manners are perfectly hoydenish; I don't know what your brother will say to you."

Grace scarcely allowed her mother to finish these remarks before she bounded from the room, and the countess, alone with Edith, was surprised to observe that she trembled violently; her colour had flown and it was evidently with difficulty she repressed the tears that were thronging to her eyes."

"Edith, my love," she exclaimed," to what can I attach this emotion? You are not, my child, grieved that your destined husband is soon about to return."

"Oh! no, no, my mother," replied Edith, hiding her blushing face in the bosom of her aunt; "but I tremble lest Arthur should regard me less tenderly than when I last beheld him. He has travelled, and must undoubtedly have met with others more attractive in person and manners than myself. Alas! if I should disappoint his expectations."

"Foolish child," returned the countess, smiling kindly; "Arthur will be surprised indeed to observe the great improvement three years have made in your person. How proud I shall be to present you to him."

Edith felt gratified at her aunt's remarks, and yet she trembled for fear he in whose eyes she alone desired to appear lovely, should regard her as wanting in personal charms. How many timid glances she cast towards the mirror, and each time how dissatisfied she felt with the reflection it exhibited on its polished surface; and yet, to all other eyes but her own, how transcendently lovely did she appear!

The countess had said truly that her son would be surprised at the improvements that time had effected in the fair Edith. When the youthful earl alighted at the home of his childhood, and was received into the extended arms of his proud mother, who gazed upon his high and noble brow with the delight a parent alone can feel, after the first gush of fond exultation was over, the countess turned towards the spot where Edith had stood the moment before, but she was gone. At the first intimation of his arrival, she had flown from the apartment, dreading with her natural timidity the first meeting between herself and her destined husband. The impression she made upon him in that interview after their long separation would most probably colour the whole of her future life. No wonder, then, that while her heart yearned for, she yet shrank from that meeting.

"My sister Grace," said the young man, turning to embrace her, "I should have known your merry face anywhere. You are, indeed, but little altered."

"I can say more for you, then," replied the young girl, laughing, "for you have grown so tall, and moreover so handsome, that I can scarcely recognise you as my boyish playmate of a few years back."

"You are, indeed, dear Arthur, greatly improved," said his proud mother, as she gazed upon him with renewed exultation.

"You will make me quite vain with your flattery," said the young man, smiling; "but where is my cousin Edith?"

"I will seek her," returned the countess. "Silly girl, she is so fearful, Arthur, that you will not regard her with the tender affection you acknowledged before you left home."

A shade of anxiety passed over the handsome features of the youthful earl at these words, and he said hastily.—

"What reason can Edith possibly assign for indulging such a supposition?"

"None whatever," returned the countess; "but she is so devotedly attached to you, and sets so high a value on your regard, that it makes her dread the slightest diminution in your attachment; consequently, let me warn you, Arthur, to receive her with unbounded tenderness; her mind is so peculiarly sensitive, that she would note a change in your manners that might probably be imperceptible to all others."

"I confess that I am most desirous of again beholding her, and rest assured that I shall receive her kindly."

The countess instantly left the room in search of Edith, and during her absence Grace noted an expression of sadness in her brother's face, for which she could not account, and which caused her heart, for almost the first time in her life, to throb with a sensation akin to anxiety. She loved Edith so dearly, that even Grace, with all her thoughtlessness, trembled lest the sadness depicted in her brother's countenance boded aught of anxiety for her gentle cousin.

The young man was roused from a fit of seeming abstraction by the entrance of his mother leading Edith by the hand.

Instantly all shade of anxiety vanished from his brow, and tenderly embracing his affianced wife, he seemed for some minutes lost in astonishment at her extreme loveliness.

"Dear Edith," he said, kissing her blushing cheek, "my own sweet cousin, I am delighted to see you once more. Speak, love, are you not glad that I have returned?"

Edith replied only with a look; but it was a look of such fond devotedness, that it spoke more fully than words.

Grace breathed more freely. She could not doubt that her brother loved Edith. And yet, in the course of the evening, she observed that when Arthur was seated by the side of his cousin, and even while listening to the music of her voice, the smile upon his lips frequently gave place to a look of extreme dejection, and his thoughts seemed wandering from his fair companion; and, on the plea of feeling fatigued, he begged to be allowed to retire early. Assent was readily bestowed and the countess, with her daughter and niece, sat conversing together for some time after her son had retired.

"Now, my love," said the countess, addressing Edith, as soon as they were alone, "I trust you are convinced how utterly groundless were your fears regarding Arthur. He is surely devotedly attached to you. And now you have both met, my child, to part no more on earth."

"I hope so, indeed, dear mother," replied Edith; "and, if he but loves me with the same truthful affection I nourish towards him, we shall indeed be blessed."

"You must and will, my child," said her aunt, solemnly. "I am almost tempted to regret that your sainted mother lived not to witness this day. How greatly, Edith, would she have rejoiced!"

"Dear Edith," said Grace, drawing closer to her side, "may you be happy as you deserve."

The two young girls mutually embraced, and then parted for the night. Grace laid her head on her pillow with a painful foreboding, that, if her cousin married Arthur, she would not be blest with that happiness which she so richly deserved.

"I will speak to Arthur seriously on this subject," was Grace's mental resolve. "Better that Edith should sacrifice the hopes she so fondly nourishes, than be made wretched hereafter."

In fulfilment of this determination, Grace rose early, and, tapping at her brother's door, solicited his company in a walk round the park before breakfast. He replied in the affirmative, and, in a few minutes, joined her below.

"Arthur," said Grace, after a few common-place remarks, "I observed last evening a sadness in your face, for which I could not account; but it made me, who has ever been thought wild and inconsiderate, thoughtful and anxious. You are not angry with me, Arthur?" she continued, seeing his brow darkened. "I wish to inquire into the cause of your sadness and frequent abstraction, from no idle curiosity, nor a wish to pry into affairs you may desire concealed, but from love to Edith."

"Well, Grace," said her brother, "what then? I also love Edith with passionate warmth."

"Do you, indeed?" replied Grace; "then I have done. From your manner last night, I was almost led to doubt it."

"Indeed, Grace!" returned her brother, laughing, "then you judged very erroneously; but as yet I doubt not you are little skilled in such matters. When you become acquainted with love yourself, you will be better able to discern the symptoms of it in others; and, as for my sadness that you noted down so carefully, fatigue, I should think, would well have accounted for it, which a good night's rest has entirely banished."

Her brother spoke so gaily, that Grace felt convinced she had been mistaken in her ideas, and laughing merrily at her own want of discernment, she soon forgot the circumstance altogether.

CHAPTER IV.

"They gave her away to be his bride,
  For the light of her bloom and beauty's pride,
  And bade her love with the warmth and truth
  Of a heart in its fond confiding youth.
  And I saw her pass in bright array,
  With loved friends round her glad and gay;
  Where the joyous dance and song swelled high
  The note of mirthful revelry.

And my glance from the charm of that fair face stray'd,
  To gaze on the choice that her heart had made;
  He leant on his arm as seeking rest,
  While her small white hand in his own was prest."

PREPARATIONS were speedily set on foot, in order to celebrate the marriage of Arthur and Edith Mannering. The countess was all life and gaiety, superintending every arrangement. Grace was in her highest possible spirits. Smiles, soft and beautiful, sat upon the blushing face of Edith; and Arthur, in the presence of the fair being that he was so soon to call his wife, seemed incapable of any feeling but joy.

So far, all went well; still Edith, as well as Grace, observed that he resolutely avoided all allusion to any circumstance that had occurred in his travels, and, whenever conversation chanced to turn towards that subject, he invariably changed it to some other topic.

" I think," said the countess to her son as they were consulting about the friends whom it would be advisable to invite to the wedding, " it will be a proper mark of respect to ask your young friend Edward Villiers."

The young man seemed confused at this question, and answered with a show of hesitation,—

" I scarcely know, he is an entire stranger to Edith, and it will doubtless be more agreeable to her feelings to——"

" Oh, do not think of me, Arthur, I am sure any friend of yours will be gladly welcomed by me," said Edith, kindly.

" Your having travelled together, and been in daily companionship for three years," said the countess, " it would be a marked discourtesy not to write to him on such an important occasion."

" Well, if you think so I will write to him, and solicit his company."

His mother cordially approving of this proposition, the invitation was sent, and an answer speedily received signifying that it was accepted.

Edward Villiers, to whom allusion has just been made, was the only son of a highly respectable, but not over wealthy merchant, who, having a large family of daughters to provide for, destined his son for the counting-house.

The elder Mr. Villiers, was the youngest son of a baronet, and the family estates going with the title to his eldest brother, and coming to live a life of dependence, he had, with a small capital, embarked in commerce, and success had crowned his praiseworthy efforts. The Countess of Clavering had long known and esteemed his worth, and when he determined that his son should travel for a few years, she eagerly embraced the opportunity that offered for Arthur to accompany him.

Edward Villiers at the time we desired to introduce him to the reader, had just entered his two-and-twentieth year; was tall and well made. He possessed likewise, that index to the mind, a speaking countenance, on which every thought and feeling was plainly expressed.

He was fair, with remarkably bright blue eyes, an open forehead and dark brown hair that waved in clustering curls around his brow, which seemed to scorn even the semblance of deceit.

He was naturally of a mild and conciliating disposition, tenderly attached to his family, but more especially to his mother and sisters, in whom he could not see a fault.

This young man arrived at Ravensdale the day before the one appointed for the wedding of its master; he received a kind and cordial welcome from the ladies of the family, but there was a slight restraint in the manners of her son towards him that the countess was puzzled to understand.

Arthur was so engrossed with Edith and the countess in preparing for the morrow, that the task of entertaining their guest fell to Grace, and he surely had no need to desire a gayer companion. Indeed, it is wonderful how well two young persons of opposite sex will contrive to get acquainted if left entirely to themselves. An hour thrown upon their own resources for amusement, will make them more familiar and better acquainted than months spent together in the presence of others.

The day being fine and warm, Grace proposed a walk round the park, and off they gaily started arm in arm, chatting with the easy familiarity of old friends.

" I am glad to escape from my brother and Edith," said Grace, laughing, " lovers are no company for any one but themselves, and it appears to me uncommon dull work to be sitting still all day talking about love."

Her companion smiled at the *naivete* of her remark, as he answered,—

" I conclude you have had no experience in such matters as yet, Miss Clavering, or you would, perhaps, think differently.'

" So my brother tells me," returned Grace, " but if love must of necessity render me dull, I would rather be excused making its acquaintance."

" Your brother seems attached to your cousin," said the young man in a tone of inquiry.

" Oh, yes," replied Grace, eagerly, " you surely cannot doubt it."

" I doubt the possibility of loving two," said the other, as though forgetful of the presence of his companion, he was thinking aloud.

" Of loving two," reiterated Grace, in astonishment, " I am at a loss to understand you."

"Pardon me, Miss Clavering," replied the other hastily, "my thoughts at the moment were wandering, or believe me, I had never given utterance to that remark; yet having aroused your suspicion (though I assure you unintentionally), I deem it an act of positive justice to acquaint you with the cause that gave rise to that thoughtless speech, for fear it should make a more serious impression on your mind than there is any occasion for. It is simply that your brother appeared much attached to a young lady we were introduced to on the continent, and whom I should have thought it was impossible he could so speedily have forgotten. Having imparted to you thus much, (I cannot in honour more), I am assured Miss Clavering, that you will confine it entirely to your own breast, to do otherwise——"

"Oh, do not fear," said Grace, interrupting hastily, "the secret, if secret it be, will never, through me, be known to any but ourselves; but what you have told me accounts entirely for much that appeared strange and unaccountable in my brother; but I trust he loves Edith; alas, if he is only fulfilling what he conceives a duty in marrying her, and when it is too late, Edith discovers that he does not love her, it will break her heart—it will indeed!"

And sorrow was so plainly depicted on the countenance of poor Grace, that her companion began bitterly to reproach himself for having communicated intelligence calculated to throw a shade of sadness over her usually joyous spirits.

"Dear Miss Clavering, I must entreat your forgiveness for my thoughtless speech, though in truth I cannot forgive myself."

Grace smiled brightly as she replied, "let us think no more about it, Edith is too lovely, too amiable, not to be fondly and tenderly regarded. To-morrow," she added with her wonted spirit, "I shall be at a wedding, for the first time in my life, and I am resolved to be unusually gay; weddings, you know, are the merriest things in the world."

"Are they?" replied her companion, smiling.

"To my thinking," said Grace, in the same lively strain, "there are but two extremes of happiness and misery—weddings and funerals. There are, of course, many gradations of each, but they centre in these two points."

"I shall not obtain much sympathy then," said the young man, "when I tell you that I think myself very unhappy in being forced to leave you so soon; I have found in you so agreeable a companion that——"

"Well," said Grace, seeing he hesitated, "it will be your own fault if our acquaintance is not speedily renewed; in a month I shall come to London, and there——"

"Alas!" said the young man, "we shall then be as much removed. You will, of course, mix with the light and gay, in frequent assemblies, from which I shall be excluded; and this reminds me of what your affability had caused me totally to forget, and I have been all this while addressing you as Miss Clavering, instead of Lady Grace."

"For which almost unpardonable rudeness, I insist upon inflicting a penalty," replied the young girl, laughing.

"Name it," said the other, catching a little of her gaiety, for mirth is always infectious.

"That, for the future, you shall simply call me Grace; and, remember, I expect implicit obedience."

"Dear Grace," said the young man, warmly, "you honour me more than I deserve."

The wedding morn dawned with unusual splendour. It was the beautiful month of May, and a fresher, fairer morning, had never beamed upon this earth.

The bridegroom was up betimes, impatient for the hour that was destined to unite him to her who had from infancy been his affianced wife.

There are few, if any, young persons at nineteen, that could not, with the aid of dress, be made to look pretty on their wedding day. And Edith, always lovely, looked transcendently so in her bridal dress, and Arthur gazed upon her with unbounded delight, as she entered the room, leaning on the arm of his mother, who presented her to him, with fond exultation. Grace, too, all smiles and good temper, the very picture of youthful vivacity, was on this morning gayer than usual, and the smiles that mantled round her dimpled mouth, attracted the gaze of Edward Villiers far more than the warm blushing ones that dwelt upon the fair face of the bride.

All were assembled in readiness for the ceremony, which was to take place in the drawing-room of Ravensdale. Bright eyes glanced in all directions, and whispered voices spoke in praise of the beauty of the bride, and the noble form and manly bearing of the bridegroom. And surely a more noble pair never met to plight their faith to each other. Edith, all gentleness and soft delicacy, offered a pleasing contrast to the firm and dignified bearing of Arthur, who repeated the few simple, but solemn vows, in a clear, audible voice, while Edith's voice trembled, and she looked up to him, as it were, for support, when she gave utterance to her part of the ceremony; and, when the benediction was pronounced, the tender, warm-hearted Grace, was the first to offer her congratulations on the happy event, and warmly embracing Edith, wished her every joy and happiness. And the countess, likewise, was not slow to welcome Edith as her daughter. And congratulations, warm and affectionate, were showered from all sides on the youthful pair, til Edith was so overcome, that tears usurped the place of smiles.

"Dear Edith, why do you cry on a day so joyous?" whispered Grace. "It should be the gayest of your life."

"It is the happiest, dear Grace," replied the young bride; "but gaiety and happiness are not always so inseparable as you appear to think them."

"They ever should be inseparable if I could will them so," returned Grace, laughing.

Young Villiers, who had become greatly prepossessed in favour of Grace, contrived to withdraw her from the company in the course of the evening, and together they wandered round the beautiful grounds which were attached to the house—conversation naturally turned on the new married pair, and at Grace's request, he imparted to her a few more particulars, respecting the young person for whom her brother had evidently conceived an attachment while away from home; and Grace, in her turn, expressed her determination, carefully to watch over the happiness of Edith.

"You have a kind heart, dear Grace," said the young man.

"If you knew Edith as I know her," she replied, "you would be equally as anxious for her happiness, and as fearful aught should occur to interrupt her felicity."

"To-morrow I shall leave you, Grace," resumed her companion, without heeding her last remark, "but with the hope that we shall soon meet again."

"Oh, yes," replied Grace, "in a few weeks I shall visit London and then—"

"And then" repeated the young man, "I shall look forward to the joy of again seeing you."

Grace, felt flattered by the attention and evident interest she had unintentionally awakened in the breast of the stranger. Grace had been so excluded from society; treated so much like a silly, thoughtless child, that she was delighted at meeting with one, who regarded her as a sensible, and attractive woman, and as such experienced a pleasure in her company, which now, for the first time, was eagerly sought for by one of the opposite sex.

No wonder, then, that she parted with such a companion with regret, and looked forward, at least, with equal pleasure with himself, to a speedy meeting in London.

CHAPTER V.

" Love is oft a fatal spell—
    A garland of the cypress tree;
  A weeping willow wreath, may well
    Its emblem be."
" An April day, of sun and shower,
    The glow, the chill, of hopes and fears.
  An ague of the heart—a flower
    That blooms in tears."

THE sun shone fair and bright, illuming with its sweet reviving rays, all people, and all things, carriages with rich trappings, attended by servants in gorgeous liveries, dashed through the principal streets of Paris; and all the fashionable carriages were crowded with fair ladies, whose bright faces and splendid toilets, contesting with the numberless military uniforms of the gentlemen, gave the place an appearance of enchantment. All looked gay, and in keeping with the beauty of the scene.

In the midst of all this gaiety and bustle, a young lady, neatly, but plainly dressed, might have been seen quietly pursuing her way through the crowded streets. There was a languor in her step, as though she had lately suffered from ill health; and her eyes "dark and intricate," lacked the lustre of health and happiness. Lovely she certainly was, in no light degree, and her raven tresses waved in rich profusion over her high and commanding brow; there was a peculiarly intellectual expression beaming on her countenance, which was pale and thoughtful. A large shawl completely enveloped her figure, but the outlines which were plainly perceptible, were replete with grace and beauty; she was tall, beyond the generality of her sex, but withal, so elegantly proportioned, and so graceful in her carriage that she was entirely free from an awkwardness that is apt to accompany an undue height.

That she was suffering from unhappiness, as well as ill health, was clearly perceptible by the saddened expression of her eye, as she glanced towards the group of happy faces that surrounded her.

Suddenly the colour mounted to her cheek, and she quickened her step, at the same moment dropping the veil she had thrown aside to enable her to enjoy more fully the sweet refreshing breeze.

This was evidently occasioned by the presence of some person she had wished to avoid, but it was unsuccessful; she had been seen, and recognised by a young man who formed one of the many idlers that were whiling away their time in the gay streets of Paris; and without a moment's hesitation he approached, and addressing her by the name of Miss Montravers, inquired kindly after her health. She stopped abruptly at the interruption, and with an air of cold reserve, answered his inquiries, and then wishing him good day resumed her walk. "Miss Montravers—Catherine," said the stranger, "excuse the liberty I take in forcing my company upon you, but I cannot leave you thus."

"The poor and dependent," she returned with dignity, "are accustomed to have liberties taken with them; and, since I may not exercise the feminine right of commanding, allow me, at least, to beg of you no longer to intrude your company upon me."

"Alas, Miss Montravers," replied the other sorrowfully, "what have I done to deserve such cold, not to say unkind treatment?"

"Then why do you wish to injure me," she exclaimed, "by persisting, whenever you chance to meet me abroad, in walking by my side when you know that my character has already suffered in consequence of your so doing?"

"I believe, Miss Montravers," he replied, "that my greatest fault is that of loving you, I do, Heaven knows, in sincerity and truth."

"The world does not, and never will give you credit for such feelings; neither, indeed, can I, were it possible that," and she hesitated a moment, and then she added, "but this is useless; if, in truth, Mr. Moreton, you entertain the slightest regard for me, you will show it most effectually by leaving me to pursue my walk alone. I have already been severely censured for encouraging your attentions, and——"

"Encouraging my attentions," said the other, in a tone of surprise. "You must surely be joking, Catherine?"

"No, sir, I am in no humour for joking; we have been seen together, and my character, as I before said, has materially suffered in consequence. I have been threatened with dismissal if I was ever known to speak to you again. I have been accused of endeavouring, from sordid motives, to ensnare your affections; I have—but, enough, you must spare me the mortification of repeating all that I have borne for, and through you."

"Good God! Catherine," exclaimed the young man, in a tone of saddened surprise. "Is it possible that you have borne all this, and yet you refuse, as you have ever done, even to listen to my suit? I swear that I have not a thought that is dishonourable either to you or myself. I would, Catherine, make you my wife, and remove you from this life of toil and dependence that you now lead. A mind so highly cultivated as yours——"

"Stop!" she interrupted, somewhat affected by the other's earnestness. "If I have judged you erroneously, I am sorry for having done so; still be your wishes regarding me ever so honourable it cannot, it does not alter our relative positions. The high and wealthy Mr. Moreton, is removed far beyond the humble and dependent Catherine Montravers. Now, sir, let us part; I know not, but we may have been seen, and in that case, I shall be deprived of the means of earning an honest livelihood."

"Yet, Catherine, one word more," urged the young man."

"Not one, or I shall find it difficult to credit the truth of your assertion that you feel an interest in my welfare. I have been absent from Mrs. Porter's the last fortnight through extreme ill health, and I am now returning thither. You know how strict she is, and will readily believe that if she learned I had met and conversed with you this morning, it is most probable she would refuse me admittance."

"Farewell, Catherine," returned her companion, "dearly as I love you, I will not force my company upon you when I know it to be disagreeable;" and without waiting her reply, he turned away, and was soon lost sight of in the crowded streets, and the young lady pursued her walk uninterrupted, till at length she stepped before the entrance of a fashionable hotel, and, bowing to the porter, to whom she appeared well known, she proceeded up the broad staircase, and turning to the left, entered a front room on the third story; it was vacant, but from the number of books that were scattered carelessly about, a pair of globes that stood near the window, and a harp and pianoforte, the latter of which was open, and music placed in front of it—from all these minute signs, it was easy to perceive that the room was appropriated to study. And Catherine Montravers threw herself on a chair that was placed near the table which occupied the centre of the room, and covering her face with her hands, remained for some time perfectly silent, during which interval her bosom heaved in painful throbs, and she seemed to be the prey of some violent and almost uncontrollable emotion. Suddenly the opening of the door startled her, and rising hurriedly from her seat, she curtsied politely, and somewhat humbly to a proud and portly dame, who might well be described as "fair, fat, and forty," and who scarcely returned the salutation of her dependent.

"I am very glad you have returned, Miss Montravers; a fortnight is a long absence—a very long absence; and I am much surprised that you should have taken advantage of my kindness, to remain away for so long a period; many ladies would refuse to receive you back again."

"Excuse me, madam," replied the young lady, in a tone of deep humility; "but you are aware that nothing but extreme ill health would have detained me so long."

"You were well enough when you left here," interrupted the first speaker; "and out of kindness I permitted you to visit a person with whom you informed me you were acquainted when you were last in Paris."

"All that is perfectly correct, madam; at the house of that friend I have been confined by severe indisposition ever since; this is, indeed, the first time I have left it; anxious to return to my usual duties, I seized the earliest moment of convalescence to hasten back."

"Your illness must have been very sudden and unaccountable. May I inquire the nature of it?"

"Oh, surely, madam," replied Catherine, eagerly, and a burning blush sat on either cheek; "my illness arose, in the first instance, from cold—a severe cold."

"I have had a very severe cold myself," returned the lady, haughtily; "but I have not deemed it necessary to confine myself to the house; but, however," she added, after a moment's hesitation, "you are now perfectly recovered, I hope."

"Yes, madam," replied Catherine.

"I was very much shocked," returned the lady, "to observe, in your absence, what very little progress Miss Porter has made in music; she ought now to be perfectly competent to play waltzes. Mrs. Norton's eldest daughter, who is two years younger than Miss Porter, and has not learned music more than three or four years at most, plays divinely, and makes me quite blush for the backwardness of my own daughter; and then," continued the lady, without giving Catherine time to reply, "Miss Matilda's drawing is very indifferent, which is the more vexatious, as the child possesses a natural talent for drawing, and consequently the fault must lie with yourself."

"I am very sorry, madam—" began Catherine, but the lady interrupted before she had time to proceed.

"Mr. Porter was very much amazed last evening, by discovering that Master Alfred is wholly unacquainted with history, and if you remember, I particularly specified that I wished all the children to be well versed in history, as I consider that to be the ground-work on which to rear a good, solid education."

"I am very sorry, madam," again resumed Catherine, "that you should have occasion to find so much fault, but——"

"Oh! that is not all," said the lady; "Mr. Porter desired I should speak to you concerning Charles's writing; it is absolutely vile."

"Charles is but six years old, madam," urged Catherine, gently.

"I had almost forgotten to mention," continued the lady, without heeding her remark, "that Jane stoops terribly. I am surprised that you have allowed her to contract so bad a habit. Prevention in all cases is a great deal better, and likewise easier than a cure; but as you have been utterly regardless of the one, you must set about the other instantly."

"I will do my best, madam," said the poor governess, whose head was nearly bewildered with the multiplicity of duties that daily fell to her share.

"There is one thing more," added the lady, "and this I am induced to mention out of true kindness and consideration for yourself."

And here the lady paused, as if to impress the truth of what she had just stated on the mind of the unfortunate governess, who, thinking she was expected to make some reply, merely gave utterance to the accustomed "Yes, madam;" and this time it was said rather faintly.

"I have observed," resumed the lady, with emphasis, "that Mr. Moreton has passed and repassed this hotel very frequently in your absence, and he appeared to have by some means gained an idea that you were not here."

"He learned it not from me, madam," said Catherine, who was rather puzzled by the incongruity of the other's speech.

"I am not supposing that he did," replied the lady; "but I trust I may not infer that you have given him any encouragement."

"Oh! no, no, madam," said Catherine, and the blood again rushed tumultuously to her cheeks.

"Then I trust you will be very cautious and guarded in your conduct for the future, as you cannot, for an instant, suppose he can entertain any but dishonourable intentions towards you ;" and she laid particular emphasis on the personal pronoun. And having said thus much, she swam out of the room, highly satisfied with the part she had taken in the foregoing conversation, and perfectly enraptured at her own kindness, in deeming it worth while to give a word of advice to so inferior and dependent a person as the governess of her family; and never even dreaming it possible that her last remark was calculated to wound her feelings. Indeed, it had never entered her head to suppose that such persons as governesses had feelings, and if such had been hinted to her, she would have deemed that they had no right to possess them. Sentiment and feeling, in her ideas, belonged exclusively to the rich, and here we cannot refrain from saying, that we fear Mrs. Porter was by no means singular in her ideas. Many there have been, and with sorrow be it said, still are, who, though they would doubtless be shocked if accused of entertaining such opinions, yet act towards their dependents in a manner every way calculated to induce them to suppose that they are regarded as wanting in that tenderness of feeling and innate refinement which so peculiarly marks an intellectual and sensitive mind, and which is as frequently found among the suffering sons and daughters of toil, aye, if not more so, than among those who are brought up in the lap of luxury, and have no wish or hope ungratified.

Catharine Montravers was possessed of a mind formed by nature for noble and exalted feelings. She was not, in manners, calculated to please any and every beholder; no lively sallies, or merry jests ever, on her part, contributed to the mirth of others. On the contrary, she was naturally possessed of that luxurious melancholy which is born of genius; and in intellect she soared far above all with whom she came in contact; and, though chained down to the common drudgery of a school, her mind, pure and unshackled, disdained to be enslaved thereby, and, in the few moments of freedom she obtained from her unruly pupils, she would contrive to forget her sorrows, and revel for awhile in the sweets of poetry and romance; for she had that true poetry of soul which instantly appreciates and enjoys the beauty at once of language and exquisite imagery with which some of the works of our own poets abound.

By birth and education an Englishwoman, she had acquired, with the greatest facility, every accomplishment that it is desirable for a woman to know, though with no thought that it would ever be necessary for her to turn them to account. But misfortunes, to which all are liable, had deprived her at once of parents and fortune, and threw her, with an only sister many years younger, entirely upon her own resources.

Catherine instantly exerted herself, and, having provided an asylum for her sister in the house of one who, she was assured, would carefully watch over the tender charge, she sought and obtained a situation for herself, as private governess in a gentleman's family. In doing so, she prepared herself to expect toil and anxiety in return for the small salary (scarcely more than a servant's wages) which was deemed amply sufficient for the accomplished and intellectual governess. But, alas, poor Catherine had not prepared herself for the constant mortification to which she was exposed; still she curbed her proud spirit, which rebelled against the almost insulting hauteur and disrespect with which she was treated. An object of pity to the servants, she was likewise an object of dislike, because she shrunk, with an instinctive delicacy, from the coarse familiarity with which they would otherwise have approached her. Catherine, in the midst of affluence and grandeur, was an unhappy and isolated being, till one gleam of sunshine lighted and cheered her path.

> " Blest power of sunshine, genial day,
> What balm, what life, is in thy ray !"

Thus felt and thought poor Catherine, when she loved, for the first time, with all a woman's fond devotedness. How sweetly that love cheered and blest her hitherto sad and dreary heart! How bravely it enabled her to bear every humiliation to which she was daily and hourly exposed; how little they were heeded or cared for now! Her heart revelled in the sunshine of love, which threw a bright halo on all which surrounded her; how content she was to suffer on, forgetful of all beside that one sweet sunny spot of happiness which she treasured deep in her heart's core! Oh, judge her tenderly! Deem not harshly of her, if, perchance, her love was won too easily; if she weighed not accurately her own position and station in society, but allowed the balance unjustly to preponderate in favour of love. Remember, in that balance she cast her all of happiness, and—but the tale is an old one—"woman's love is ever true; it blooms even amid despair." And so did Catherine's. She pressed to her bosom the viper that was doomed to destroy her, and yet she still encouraged hope and faith in him, though he had left her to pursue her sad and solitary career alone. Storms and clouds had eclipsed the light of that love which shone so brightly on her; it was, in truth, but a meteor's ray, "brief e'en as bright." Let us, then, touch but lightly on this part of her character; for the poor governess has claims upon our sympathy—who, indeed, more so? Inferior in mental acquirements to none, she is yet regarded as at least a grade below her employers; receives, in return for services which in themselves are invaluable, a pittance so trifling, that it admits of no prospect of her ever being enabled to retire from the arduous duties of her profession.   No, she must struggle on, year after year; and, far from being deemed an object of sympathy, she is considered by most persons as very fortunate if she continues to procure situations, as her pupils, one after another, no longer require her services; and if, which is unhappily but too often the case, her health and strength give way before her wearying and harassing employment, alas! what is to become of the unfortunate governess?

When Catherine Montravers was left once more alone in the school-room, she sank again upon the chair, from which she had risen on the entrance of her proud and unfeeling employer. Bitter indeed she felt the humiliation she dared not resent; she passed her hand across her fevered brow, but though her eye-balls burnt and throbbed, they had no tears; tears, the sweet dew of the mind which invigorates and refreshes the feelings, when scorched and parched with feverish heat, were denied to her, who so greatly needed their softening influence.

"Alas!" she exclaimed, half aloud, as she leant her aching head upon her arm, which rested on the table, "alas, and is it in truth impossible for any one to regard me with an honourable attachment," and her lip trembled; "if he should forget me now that he is far away—but, no, I will not harbour a suspicion against him, which is, which must be groundless. Unless he really and truly loved me, he could never have looked such deep fond love as I have read in his eyes, which though they passed all others coldly by, yet ever beamed with tender love and unutterable affection upon me. And then his voice, those tones so deep, and full of tenderness—deceit could never lurk beneath such a winning exterior. No, no, it is surely impossible."

Catherine's meditations were here interrupted by the entrance of her pupils, six in number, whose clamorous voices and noisy mirth engrossed for the time her whole care, and though weak from recent illness, and sad and thoughtful, from a variety of causes, she exerted herself to go through the routine of her irksome duties, endeavouring to counteract the faults of which their mother had made such bitter complaints.

CHAPTER VI.

"To watch o'er all his happiness,
        To weep if he but sigh;
To mourn, if paler be his cheek,
        Or lustreless his eye.

To still the trembling of her hand
        If it by him be prest,
To treasure all his kindly words
        Within her aching breast.

To see him wed another,
        And yet calm her aching heart,
And strive to bid all other,
        Save a sister's love depart."

WHEN Edward Villiers quitted Ravensdale, and started on his journey to London, he felt a depression of spirits, such as he had never before experienced; in vain he endeavoured to shake it off, it clung to him with a tenacity that surprised even himself; he had often before heard people complain of *ennui*, but he had never been able to comprehend the meaning of the word, for till this moment he had never been troubled with the slightest depression; he was never in a very gay mood, but he was likewise equally removed from all sad and sombre thoughts; blest in his own circle, loving and beloved by all, marriage had never once occurred to him; he was not certainly of the number who sneer at, and affect to pity, those who enter into its bends, nor was he in the habit of vaunting the superior enjoyments of a bachelor's life, still though he had never decried matrimony, he had never seriously thought of it as regarded himself, but now, strange to say, it was uppermost in his thoughts, though this might probably be accounted for by his having so lately witnessed the ceremony, which united two fond hearts, and he began to think with Grace, that a person's wedding-day must of necessity be the gayest of their lives. At least, he was convinced, that were it possible he could win the fair hand of the lovely Grace, that day would be to him the happiest and sweetest he had ever known.

But arousing himself from these thoughts, sweet though illusive, he strove earnestly to cast them from his mind.

"Pshaw!" he exclaimed, "this will never do, I am positively in love, and with whom? Ah,— he continued, "there's the rub;" had it been any one but the Lady Grace, daughter of the high-born and haughty Countess of Clavering, he could at least have entertained a hope of winning her, but he dared not raise his thoughts so high, and therefore determined to forget her; but he found to his sorrow, that it was a more difficult task than he had at first imagined.

On his arrival once more at his own home, he was gladly welcomed by his mother and sisters; his father was engaged in the counting-house, and to avoid the numberless inquiries of his sisters,

he gladly joined him there, and by plunging at once deep into the books, endeavoured to forget all things else. But he found his thoughts—thoughts which are so free, and will roam where they please, wandering back to Ravensdale, and the merry laugh of the frolicsome Grace sounded anew in his ears, and the pen dropped from his fingers, and for a while he abandoned himsel to a long fit of musing on her who was now all in all to him; and when the day drew its slow length to a close, and he entered his mother's dining-room, where he had often spent so many happy hours with the dear relatives who so lately possessed his entire love, he could scarce conceal the lassitude that oppressed his spirits; his mother and sisters, no very great ob-server saw not the sadness that was hovering over him, but there was an eye that marked it

No. 3.

all, and longed to inquire the cause, but timidity chained her tongue, and she could only endeavour by quiet and thoughtful interest, to banish the gloom without seeking to know from whence it sprung.

Helen Thornton was the orphan daughter of an old and esteemed friend of Mr. Villiers, and on the death of her parents had been by him kindly received into his family, where she had now dwelt for years, loved and cherished by all; her temper was so mild and gentle that she won the affection of Mrs. Villiers and her daughters without an effort; and though, at the time we introduced her to our readers, scarcely seventeen, she was so active, so clever in every arrangement, that the management of the house was chiefly under her direction; who so happy, so bustling, as Helen, while superintending the domestic concerns? under her skilful hands all went well. It was Mrs. Villiers proud boast that Helen could do everything, nothing came amiss to her, no pies or puddings could compare with those which were made by her fairy little hands, and no sewing could by any possibility be brought into comparison with hers.

In short, Helen was the cleverest, neatest, and withal the prettiest little housewife that was anywhere to be met with; she could both draw, and play the piano, equal to any lady in the land, and yet she did not disdain to darn a stocking, to sew calico, to make pies, to iron a frill, or in short, to make herself useful in the thousand little occupations that appertain to the duties of a good housewife.

Mrs. Villiers had always encouraged the hope that her son would marry Helen.

"She is just the very wife for you, Edward," the good lady would say, when conversing with her son on this subject; "she is a fortune in herself."

The young man would invariably acquiesce, bestow many commendations on the object of her praise, and think no more about it.

True, young Villiers was not blind to the merits and many attractive qualities of their fair inmate, and as he was always ready to show her kind attentions, and, before he went abroad, was accustomed to sit her on his knee, and call her his little sweetheart, Mrs. Villiers and her daughters regarded it as a settled thing, that in due time, Edward would marry Helen; and if the truth must be told, Helen encouraged the same hope herself. She loved Edward, though scarcely aware of it, and fully believed he loved her in return; and the young man, without intending it, had certainly done much to confirm such a hope as the young girl nourished; for on his return from his travels, she had been the first object of his anxious solicitude. All were remembered, and presented with some little gift in token of it, but to Helen was awarded a gift more costly, and in presenting it, he had claimed in reward a kiss from her ruby lips.

Edward Villiers meant not for an instant to awaken even a thought of love towards himself in the gentle bosom of Helen, whom he regarded as a dear and cherished sister; he acted entirely from thoughtlessness—but what a fatal thoughtlessness it proved. Helen possessed a good share of feminine delicacy, and with a little thought on the part of the young man, that delicacy would have prevented her from entertaining a passion for one who neither sought or desired to kindle it; but she laboured under the erroneous impression that she was beloved, and when she now for the first time observed a cloud on his brow, her heart throbbed with anxiety, though she naturally attributed it to any but the right motive.

"Now do, Edward," said his youngest sister Jane, and who was about Helen's age, drawing her chair close to her brother's, "do tell us all about the grand wedding; how was the bride dressed?"

"Is she pretty, Edward?" said Eliza, manifesting an interest on the all important subject which her sister was anxious to bring into discussion.

"Yes, very pretty—and as for dress," he added, smiling, "of course, she was dressed as prettily as it is possible to be."

"Was there much company?" said Elizabeth, who being the eldest of the family, was more matronly than the others.

"Yes, a great many were invited to the wedding; but the first day we were quite alone."

"Of course, they received you very kindly," said Mrs. Villiers.

"Oh, very; and the grounds attached to Ravensdale are so beautiful that I could have wandered about there for ever."

"La, brother!" replied Fanny, who was the most sentimental of the family, and prided herself upon it; "I am surprised to hear you say so; and but just returned from Italy."

"The countess has one daughter, I believe," said the elder Mr. Villiers, joining in the conversation at this juncture.

"She has, the Lady Grace; and the most beautiful creature I ever beheld—and such spirits—so gay—with such a beautiful, clear, ringing laugh!"

Helen turned pale at these words; but she found courage to inquire if the young lady was fair.

"No," returned Edward, "that is the bride, now the young Countess of Clavering, who is a perfect blonde, with golden hair; but Grace is rather dark, with eyes that I could only describe as being large, languishing, dark, and yet so full of soul that—that——"

"That," interrupted Jane, laughing; "they seem to have made a great impression on you."

"I suppose," said Fanny, "that she is very proud."

"Not in the least," said Edward; and now that he was conversing about Grace he had regained all his wonted animation. "She is so amiable and unobtrusive in her behaviour, that in conversing with her you quite forget her rank."

"How very condescending of her," replied Jane again, laughing.

"I should so like you all to see her," continued her brother without heeding her remark. "You would be so delighted with her—I am sure you would."

There was a silence for a few minutes, after Edward had given utterance to these words. No voice re-echoed the wish he had expressed—on the contrary all felt sorry he had become acquainted with the apparently fascinating Lady Grace.

Helen was the first to speak, and in a timid voice inquired whether Lady Grace was so very beautiful.

"She is, indeed, dear Helen," replied the young man, "and I hope some day you will be able to judge for yourself; and then, I am sure, you will love her." And he little thought how deep a pang his words inflicted on the mind of his hearer.

And surely beauty, in a great measure, is ideal, for in a sober truth Grace scarcely deserved the high encomiums Edward bestowed on her personal charms. She was dark in complexion, and was possessed of a redundancy of jet black tresses, which waved in natural curls over a particularly clear, and sunny brow; her face was oval, and her mouth set round, with dimples which certainly lent a witchery to her countenance; and her eyes, on which he had bestowed so much praise, were black and roguish, and gave token that the owner was given to merriment, as the reader is aware she was.

Helen listened with a beating heart to the high encomiums Edward bestowed upon the titled beauty; for the first time in her life she was conscious of a feeling of envy; how grieved she felt that she so little resembled Grace in personal attractions. Never before had Helen coveted beauty, or been dissatisfied with her own appearance, which was, at least, prepossessing.

Rather fair, though by no means a blonde, she was possessed of an healthy, beaming face, and her chestnut hair was arranged in lustrous bands on either side of it, which afforded a pleasant relief to a face that might otherwise have been considered rather too long; her eyes were grey, and in expression mild and pleasing; slight made and somewhat below the middle height. And yet, with these slight recommendations, Helen was regarded as a beauty by the villagers. Yes, one and all looked upon her as perfection. How true it is that when we love a person for their mental perfections they are handsome in person, at least to our eyes.

Mrs. Villiers, with feminine tact, adroitly changed the subject of conversation to a totally different topic, but her son no longer manifested any eagerness to join in it, after replying once or twice to direct questions put to himself, he relapsed into a thoughtful mood.

Music was proposed in the course of the evening, and Edward showed a little more animation, as he listened to the simple ballads which were sung by Helen, for no one could play or sing as well as her, and she strove earnestly on this particular evening to excel her usual efforts. If aught can chase away gloom it is surely sweet sounds, that ever fall so softly and pleasantly on the ear, as for the time to claim our undivided attention. Edward felt this as he smiled approvingly on the singer, and during a temporary cessation, he requested Helen to play a piece that Grace had told him was a favourite with herself; gratified at the prospect of pleasing him, she instantly complied, accompanying it with her voice.

"I think you must have omitted some part, or played it incorrectly," said Edward, as she concluded.

"Oh, no!" she replied eagerly, and pointing to the music, she commenced afresh, as she added, "see I am perfectly correct."

"It sounds very differently then;" he returned, "Grace must have played it more——"

"Gracefully," said Helen, and she bent over her music to conceal a tear, that the fulness of her feelings had brought to her eye.

"No," returned the young man, "I did not intend to say that, but——"

"But you thought so," said Jane, laughing; "come, Edward, acknowledge I have finished your sentence accurately."

"I shall acknowledge nothing of the sort," replied her brother, making an effort to recover his usual spirits, as he observed the serious expression that sat upon the face of his other sisters, and the sorrowful one of Helen's.

CHAPTER VII.

" ' Tis sweet to hear the watch dog's honest bark
    Bay deep mouthed welcome, as we draw near home ;
'Tis sweet to know there is an eye, will mark
    Our coming, and look brighter when we come ;
'Tis sweet, to be awakened by the lark,
    Or lull'd by falling waters ; sweet the hum
Of bees ; the voice of girls, the song of birds,
    The lisp of children, and their earliest words.
But sweeter still, than this, than these, than all,
    Is first and passionate love—it stands alone."

A FORTNIGHT has elapsed since the marriage of Edith to her cousin ; a fortnight of sweet uncontrollable happiness to that fair and gentle being. Her life appeared to her, now, one continual sunshine of happiness ; there seemed nothing left for her to desire : united to him whom from childhood she had been taught to love, and which love had grown with her growth, and strengthened with her increasing years, till it had swallowed up every other thought and feeling. And she sometimes trembled at the excess of her own happiness, fearing lest aught should wither or destroy it ; but such thoughts as these were but few, and like summer clouds which shine themselves away. And fondly would she creep close to the side of her husband, and sliding her hand softly into his, would gaze upon his noble brow, with that mingling of love and reverence which woman alone can feel. And Arthur would tenderly smile upon her, and bending down to kiss her forehead, inquire what made her so sad.

"Sad, dearest," she would reply, " alas ! you cannot tell how blessed I am."

But Arthur Clavering could scarcely understand such deep, thoughtful happiness as was experienced by the fond and faithful Edith. He knew when Grace was happy, for her clear ringing laugh would assure him of the fact, and her lively spirit threw a brightness on their little circle which to him would have been otherwise dull and solitary. If Edith were happy, he would ask himself, " what made her wear such an expression of sadness on her countenance ?" forgetful that Edith's face was naturally of a pensive cast, and that happiness manifests itself very differently in one person to what it does in another.

And there were times when Grace perceived an expression of anxiety on her brother's countenance, and feared (not perhaps wholly without good reason) that his thoughts were wandering back to her whom he had left behind, and for whom, she was assured, he had professed an attachment.

Early one morning Arthur started on a shooting excursion, and the countess being engaged in her own apartment, Edith and Grace were left entirely alone.

Grace's thoughts turned towards London, which she hoped soon to visit, and warmly expressed to Edith the pleasure she anticipated in doing so. Edith was swayed by different feelings, and by no means looked forward to the proposed visit with the joyful anticipations that filled the breast of Grace.

"There is no one with whom we are acquainted in London," said Edith, " and we are so utterly unused to gay scenes, that I fear we shall not find them so agreeable as you imagine."

"We shall very soon have plenty of friends, I have no doubt," returned Grace ; "and now there is at least one we know—an unimportant one, if you like—still he must be reckoned as one."

"One we know ?" said Edith ; " I am at a loss to understand you ; perhaps you will have the goodness to enlighten me ?"

" Then you have really, totally forgotten that pleasant and agreeable young man, Mr. Edward Villiers," said Grace, laughing merrily.

"It seems you have not," replied Edith ; " and, in truth, I think you are the only person who discovered him to be so very pleasant and agreeable ; for myself, I scarcely spoke a dozen words to him, and Arthur has told me, since his departure, that he is not anxious to continue the acquaintance."

"And why not ?" inquired Grace, in a tone of surprise.

"That, I did not consider it necessary to inquire. I was perfectly satisfied with what he said, and did not trouble myself concerning his motives, which I am sure are good ones."

"I," said Grace, " am by no means so assured of the excellence of his motives, and should consider it decidedly necessary to hear them, before I resigned the acquaintance of a young man whom I find both pleasant and agreeable, though others have failed in making the like discovery."

"Why, Grace," said Edith, in a tone of great surprise, "how warmly you speak in favour of one, of whom you know comparatively nothing. You should remember," she added, in a more conciliating tone, "that your brother, my dear Grace, can be actuated only by kind feelings towards yourself, in choosing or forbidding an acquaintance."

"He may choose your's, Edith," replied Grace, in a firm voice, "but he has no right to, neither shall he exercise such——"

"Oh! hush, Grace," said Edith; "dear Grace, think what you are about to say, you quite alarm me."

"There is no occasion for any alarm, Edith," replied Grace, "and I love Arthur dearly; still, I cannot allow him to exert so arbitrary a power as you appear to think he is warranted in doing."

"Not an arbitary power, dear Grace," said Edith, "but," she added, smiling, "we have been foolish enough to allow ourselves to be betrayed into an unusual warmth concerning a person for whom neither of us have the slightest regard. Is it not absurd, Grace?" she added, laughing.

Grace laughed too, but this time her mirth was somewhat constrained, and she gladly had recourse to laughter to hide the blushes and confusion Edith's remark had created; for Grace was conscious of a tell-tale feeling in her, which pleaded strongly in favour of the handsome young stranger from whom she had so lately parted.

At this moment the servant entered, carrying a silver waiter, on which lay a letter.

"For me, John?" said Grace, hastily; and, recovering instantly her confusion, she rose, and advanced eagerly towards him.

"No, my lady, it is for the earl,"

"Give it me, John," said Edith, "and I will present it to your master on his return."

"Stay," said Grace, quickly, as the man made a motion of handing it to his mistress; "let me look at it, for I feel assured it is for me;" and, snatching it from the waiter, she glanced momentarily at the address, which was written in a small but beautiful hand-writing, evidently that of a female; and then, without the slightest hesitation, tossed it into the fire, which (for the mornings were still cold) was burning brightly on the hearth.

"Grace! Grace! are you mad," exclaimed Edith, endeavouring to snatch it from the blazing element, but her efforts were unsuccessful, and Grace, with a self-satisfied countenance, watched it till the last atom had disappeared, and then mentally exclaimed,—

"May every effort to cause uneasiness in the bosom of my gentle sister perish, as this has done, as easily and as effectually."

But Edith for the time was seriously displeased.

"I feel assured, Grace," she replied, to her pleading for forgiveness; "that letter was intended for Arthur, and you had no manner of right to destroy it."

"How know you that?" said Grace, gently; "suppose I had good reason to know that mischief-making people were endeavouring to sow the seeds of discord in the mind of Arthur, against me, his only sister, and that letter——"

"Pardon me, dear Grace," interrupted Edith, kindly, and fully restored to her usual placid mood, "if there is one thing I more heartily detest than another, it is an anonymous letter, and I am glad, nay, thankful, that you have destroyed it. I will not ask, dear girl, for a knowledge of how you obtained a clue to this letter, which, but for your promptitude, I tremble to think, might have been the means of rendering us all unhappy; now it is utterly powerless to injure us—how fortunate we were quite alone."

"It could not possibly have arrived more opportunely," returned Grace, smiling. "I verily believe everything happens for the best."

"But, dear Grace," said Edith, "suppose another letter should come, it might not arrive so apropos."

"No more will come," replied Grace, firmly; "there is not the least fear of that, Edith, so think no more about it;" and then running to the piano, which was open, she commenced playing a lively tune, as though determined to banish all sadness both from herself and cousin.

In a few weeks from this period, Arthur and Edith, accompanied by their sister Grace, left Ravensdale for London. Edith endeavoured in vain to persuade her mother to join them; she had been for so many years accustomed to perfect seclusion, that her entreaties availed nothing, and Edith, with tearful eyes, bade her adieu, for the first time in her life. Grace was only too glad to escape from the solitude of Ravensdale, and felt nothing of the anxiety that filled the breast of Edith; her brother, too, seemed pleased with the prospect of mixing with the gay world, and they arrived at their town residence, situated in one of the fashionable squares, with a reasonable prospect of happiness. Their company was soon eagerly sought for, and Arthur was gratified to perceive that his lovely wife, and pretty volatile sister, created quite a sensation in the *beau monde.* There was something in the light, unsophisticated spirits of Grace that perfeetly bewitched the gentlemen, and she had lovers sufficient to have contented the heart of a much more exacting beauty; and yet, sooth to say, she was not contented; which proved her heart was capable of receiving a more lasting impression than any would have guessed, judging from her wonted volatility of mind; but those who appear the most light and frivolous are often-times possessed of deeper and more constant affection than they receive credit for. And thus it was with Grace. She had been in London an entire month, and during that time had visited almost every fashionable place of amusement; and though everywhere her eye had earnestly sought for that one whom she had already learned to love, yet she had seen him not.

Can he entirely have forgotten me? was a question that she frequently asked herself; and most young ladies of the age and inexperience of Grace would have felt no hesitation in answering it in the affirmative. But Grace was a more close observer of men and things; and she, there-fore, made no hasty conclusion, but pondered it deeply in her mind, and the result was, she felt satisfied she was still unforgotten in the heart of him she so tenderly remembered. "Edward Villiers," she would say to herself, "loves me; but he is proud, and, thinking that he might not be kindly received by my brother, he keeps at a distance, and endeavours to forget me. Poor fellow!" And then Grace would sigh, and think him deserving of her most compassionate feelings.

Still Grace went into society, laughed, and danced with any who sought that honour, and seemed so full of spirits, and her eyes glanced so merrily, that none suspected the secret she kept so cautiously confined to her own bosom.

CHAPTER VIII.

" The heart which may be broken; happy they!
    Twice fortunate! who of that fragile mould,
The precious porcelain of human clay,
    Break with the first fall; they can ne'er behold
The long year link'd, with heavy day on day,
    And all which must be borne, and never told;
While life's strange principle will often lie
Deepest in those who long the most to die."

CATHERINE MONTRAVERS is seated in the school-room, on the very same chair on which we last left her. How much of deep anxiety and corroding care she has experienced in the short space of a few weeks (which is all that has elapsed since her return to her wonted avocation) may be guessed from her pallid cheek and sunken eye. But now, for a moment, a passing moment, a rich carnation hue sat upon her cheek, and her eye sparkled with unwonted brilliancy, as she glanced at two letters with which the servant presented her. Her lip quivered, and her hand shook like an aspen leaf, as she received them, and glanced with a painful scrutiny at the separate envelopes.

Alas! what can thus have moved her? A sudden and death-like pallor has chased away every vestige of bloom from her countenance!—her eye, the instant before so bright, has become glazed and dim; and sinking back on her chair, she seems on the point of fainting. Oh! for some friendly arm to support and cheer her. She casts a searching look around, as if in hopes of meeting some sympathising eye, or hearing some gentle voice whisper one word of consolation. But she is alone, without a single friend to cheer or sustain her sinking spirits; and with the full returning consciousness of her utter loneliness came also the power of self-support. Drawing one deep, long breath, and wiping the cold damp from her forehead, she tore open one of the letters, and perused its contents. As she did so, what terrible agony was depicted in her face— what an utter abandonment of every other feeling in an inexpressible misery, that seemed to take possession of her entire soul. She dropped the letter, and clasped her hands, wan and wasted, before her face, as if to shut out the world, and all things else, from their bewildered gaze; yet how silent was her anguish; no tear bedewed her cheek, not a sigh heaved from her breast; she nearly hid her face in her clasped hands, and bowed her head as if in resignation at that fell stroke which separated her at once from all that she treasured so fondly. Alas! if hearts could break, hers must have perished in that speechless agony of grief, fearful even to witness— how much more dreadful to endure; the dream of bliss she had so long cherished, was flown, leaving nought but misery to show where it had once been.

Presently she raised her head, and carefully folding up the fatal epistle, endeavoured to collect her thoughts, and consider calmly the contents. "He is married, then," she exclaimed; "another calls him husband, and I, whom he swore to love, whom he vowed most solemnly he would make his wife, and whom, if eyes can speak, if actions can tell of love, he once fondly, truly loved—and can he so soon have forgotten me? No, no! Love may sink by slow decay, but by sudden wrench, hearts can never thus be torn asunder. By marrying another, he has wronged me, himself, and her to whom he has given the dear and holy name of wife. I must still live on, regardless of the bitterness of my fortune; my heart, though wrung with anguish, must still, though bleeding, beat. And I must control this fond passion, which still clings to him in spite of the cruel wrongs he has heaped upon me. Alas! why is my heart so true? why cannot I cast him from me, as unworthy even of a thought? would that it were possible, but it is not, I know and feel that it is not."

Unhappy Catherine! Who could do otherwise than commiserate her unfortunate lot? Alas! none should judge unkindly of her; if she has fallen into error, she has suffered a commensurate amount of punishment, as woman ever does when she sins; none but her own heart knows how severe has been the temptation; how merciless, and yet how alluring the tempter; nor how long and successfully he was resisted; nor how unprotected and lonely her situation. The world knows and takes into account none of these, and numberless other circumstances that may be urged in extenuation of her sin. Many a noble heart is oftentimes wrung anew with anguish, and sorrow heaped upon a head already weighed down with grief, through the cruelty and oppression of a cold and unfeeling, yet ever meddling world; to whom it is as nothing what pangs those who have erred may suffer. "Ay, let her suffer, she deserves it all," is language we frequently hear, when words of kindness and sympathy should fall from the lips of those who thus wantonly condemn the sufferer.

Catherine had considered herself, and justly so, unhappy, in being forced to procure a subsistence by a life of constant mortification and self-denial; but now all was gone, to return no more. Her last hope had perished—her last dream had fled—the one sunny spot in life's desert had been robbed of all its beauty and freshness, and she stood alone, amidst the wreck of her former happiness; the very breeze that had lent its aid to fan that bliss into a genial warmth had now strewn its ashes over the ground.

"Alas! alas!" she exclaimed, as she thought upon the past, "that I should have lived to bear this weight of grief—this burden of bitter sorrow. Would that I had died before we met, then—then—none would have missed the unhappy Catherine."

So overwhelmed was she by the sad news contained in the letter she had perused, that the second one had been allowed to fall unregarded to the ground; indeed, her anguish was so severe that she had totally forgotten it, till her eye accidentally wandered towards the spot where it had fallen; and the sight of it instantly recalled her scattered senses, and reaching it from the ground, she opened it, and with a smile of pleasure perused the contents.

"God be praised," she said, warmly, "that on me alone hath misery fallen. My sweet sister, you are happy, and will be. He upon whom you have bestowed your young affections is entirely worthy of them, and his respected parents will be pleased and proud to receive you as their daughter. I will, then, no longer murmur. In witnessing your happiness I cannot be wretched; there are yet some drops of comfort infused into my cup of bitterness, and for that I will bless God, and bow in resignation to my own sorrows. I promised our dying mother to shield you from every ill. And, oh! my sister, I have so far succeeded in procuring your happiness, and gladly would I seal it, even at the expense of my own." She was here interrupted by the abrupt entrance of her employer, and hastily concealing her letters, she rose, according to her custom, to receive her.

"I have come to acquaint you," said the lady, in her usual haughty manner, "that it is my intention to return to England immediately. That is," she added, "as early as arrangements will permit."

"Yes, madam," simply replied Catherine, and then humbly waited what further she had to say.

"My object in mentioning this determination to you," continued the lady, "is to request that you will have the goodness to see to the packing of the children's wardrobe."

But although she used the word "request," the tone in which the words were spoken, was that of giving an order, not of asking a favour, for the packing of the children's wardrobe formed a part of Catherine's duties; still, she replied, unhesitatingly,—

"Certainly, madam, I will do as you wish."

"That will do," replied the lady, turning to leave the room.

"May I be permitted, madam, to inquire what day you propose quitting Paris?" said Catherine, summoning up courage to put the question, though not without misgivings as to how it would be received.

"For what object do you make such an inquiry?" replied the lady, turning round, and surveying the governess with a suspicious air.

"In order, that I might ask, as a favour, madam, that you would, if possible, spare me for an hour, to call upon the friend who so kindly attended on me during my late indisposition," said Catherine, in a tone from which she in vain strove to banish all embarrassment.

"I scarcely know how it is possible for me to do so," replied the lady, still surveying her with a suspicious aspect.

"It would appear so ungrateful," urged Catherine, "for me to leave Paris without calling to bid her adieu, and tender my last thanks for the kindness I have experienced from her."

"You would be almost sure to meet Mr. Moreton," replied the other, "for in spite of my orders to the contrary, he is constantly on the watch; I am surprised at his impertinence."

"Indeed, madam, it was wholly unknown to me," returned Catherine.

"So far, I have pleasure in commending you," replied the lady, in a patronising manner. "Ever since you have been in my service," (how the word service grated on the ears of the governess,) "I have no hesitation in saying that you have conducted yourself in a manner every way becoming your situation."

"Then I may hope, madam, you will not consider it necessary to refuse my request."

"I am too indulgent to refuse a favour that I can with any possibility grant," said the other, "and on condition that you are absent but a very short time, you may go this evening."

Catherine curtseyed her thanks, and her employer withdrew, fully persuaded that she was now one of the most kind and considerate persons that could possibly be met with. It is surely difficult, very difficult, to form a correct opinion of ourselves, and the knowledge that it is so easy to deceive ourselves into the belief that we are more amiable and meritorious than we really are, should induce us to exercise great caution before we draw our conclusions. And we may all say with the poet,

> "Oh, wad some power the giftie gie us,
> To see ourselves as ithers see us."

And this would certainly do more towards enduing us with the sweet grace of humility than aught else on earth.

Catherine possessed a firm mind, and was capable of curbing her feelings, and keeping down thoughts that would otherwise have overpowered her; thus she was enabled, with an apparently tranquil heart, to go through the regular routine of her scholastic duties; there was indeed, a deep and unfathomable sadness in her dark eyes, painful to witness, had any been interested enough in her to heed it; but who thought or cared for the apparent melancholy of the friendless Catherine? There was indeed one who heeded it, and generously longed to withdraw her from the humiliation and hardship to which she was exposed, but so far from his affection having benefited poor Catherine, or mitigated the sorrows of her condition, it had, unintentionally on his part, been the means of making her situation more irksome and painful to bear, for it was the constant source of admonition and reproach on the part of her employer.

CHAPTER IX.

> "OH, my lov'd mistress, whose enchantments still
> Are with me, round me, wander where I will,
> It is for thee—for thee alone—I seek
> The paths of glory, to light up thy cheek
> With warm approval; in that gentle look
> To read my praise as in an angel's book,
> And think all toils rewarded, when from thee
> I gain a smile worth immortality.
> How shall I bear the moment, when restor'd
> To that young heart where I alone am lord?
> Though of such bliss unworthy, since the best
> Alone deserves to be the happiest.
> Oh, my own life! why should a single day,
> A moment, keep me from these arms away?"

EDWARD VILLIERS had read in the morning papers, among the fashionable arrivals in London the names of the youthful Earl and Countess of Clavering and their sister, Lady Grace, at whose very name his heart beat quicker, and his pulse throbbed with pleasure. Sweet Grace! dear, artless, witching maid! his first impulse was to hasten to thy side, to read anew in thy dark eyes the secret of thy love for him; but the next moment brought with it more sober thoughts.

"No," he inwardly exclaimed, "I will not dear Grace, seek to win a heart so pure—I will not ask you to unite your brilliant fortune with one so lowly as mine. Oh, would that we had never met, or that I could even now forget.

How sweetly bless'd we might have been,
Had not fate frowned so dark between!'

Hadst thou been born in the same humble station as myself, I could then with honour have sought thy hand, as the dearest and sweetest boon of existence; but now alas; there's madness in the thought; and though I can never hope to love thee less, yet I will not cause a shade of sadness to hover over thy dear spirit, which has never known what sorrow meant."

Thus nobly resolved Edward Villiers, and thus he doubtless he intended to act; still he could no longer conceal from his dear home-circle the depression of spirits under which he laboured. All saw the sad change which had "come o'er the spirit of his dream," and all did their best

No. 4.

to chase away the unwonted gloom; but Helen strove more earnestly than the others to cheer and enliven him when, after the labours of the day, he returned to them. And Edward could not possibly be wholly insensible to the kind and soothing attentions of one for whom he had ever entertained a tender brotherly regard, and well did Helen consider her efforts rewarded by an affectionate smile, a fond pressure of her hand, and sometimes he would even bestow a kiss. As Mrs. Villiers and her daughters observed these tokens of love, which were freely given to their pretty inmate, they began to hope he might be induced to make the industrious little Helen his wife, and frequently the good lady would urge her son on this subject.

"Helen, I am sure, loves you," she would say, "and I am certain will make you a truly excellent wife. You have the advantage of knowing her character more thoroughly than you could any other woman's, and she is so amiable and deserving, and withal so great a favourite with all of us, that, in short, I am convinced, my dear Edward, you could not possibly do better than marry Helen."

"But would it be right, mother, to marry Helen when, if the truth must be confessed, I love another?"

"Helen, I know, will gladly accept you, even though you acknowledge to her that you have been impressed in favour of the Lady Grace, whose rank places her at so remote a distance from you, that I am sure your regard for her will never cause Helen a moment's uneasiness."

"Well, my dear mother, I cannot decide at present; marriage is a solemn thing, and I would not rush lightly or heedlessly into it. Had I never seen Lady Grace, I should, perhaps, have found no difficulty in loving Helen."

"But, my dear Edward," urged Mrs. Villiers, "as it is impossible you can marry the Lady Grace, I should think that——"

"I do not love Helen," interrupted her son, "as I ought and could love the woman I would make my wife. I do not even feel that decided preference for her which would justify me in offering myself for her acceptance; on the contrary, I am, heart and soul, devoted to another."

"I trust," replied Mrs. Villiers, "that reason, and your natural good sense will lend their aid to subdue this ill-fated passion; in that case——"

"In that case, mother," returned the young man, "I will not hesitate to seek the hand of Helen; I may then with honour do so, but at present it is impossible."

Mrs. Villiers was satisfied with this assurance, and doubted not that in time he would forget the object of his now ardent passion. The heart of Helen too, beat responsive to the hope that animated the heart of her kind patroness; and, even Edward himself began to reflect upon the advisability of marrying Helen; she would certainly be a more suitable match than the young and beautiful, yet thoughtless Grace. But how dearly he loved her; yet the thought of being coldly and proudly repulsed by the haughty countess, determined him to keep aloof from her fascinating daughter; and though the image of Grace filled his breast, yet he remained firm to his resolve, and carefully avoided any opportunity that offered itself of even so much as seeing her.

This praiseworthy determination was not, of course, persevered in without great self-denial and sacrifice of his dearest wishes; but he felt that it was for Grace alone he made that sacrifice, and she was worthy of it all. Thus passed the first six weeks after Grace had been in London, when one morning as young Villiers was vainly endeavouring to fix his attention to the duties of his office, the postman, whom all are ever glad to welcome, entered, and presented him with a letter, the very hand-writing of which made his heart palpitate with joy; to tear it open and devour the contents was but the work of a few minutes; it ran thus:—

"You will doubtless think me very bold, in thus again forcing my acquaintance upon you, but the fear that I have unknowingly given you offence, has induced me to break through the barriers which custom has prescribed, in order to seek the cause that has prevented your keeping the promise you voluntarily pronounced, that when I came to London, we should meet again.

"Yours, GRACE."

"P.S.—I shall be at the opera with my brother and Edith this evening."

The reader must conceive with what transport this *billet* was perused, and how rapturously the young man carried it to his lips—how fondly each little word was treasured in his memory. Oh! 'tis sweet to trace, in the letters of those we love, the soft breathings of a spirit that yearns for our return, to whom all things are as nothing while we are not. Thus felt Edward Villiers, as he read with a throbbing bosom the letter that was penned by Grace, her whom he was seeking to forget; and though her true sentiments towards him were concealed beneath the veil of feminine modesty and true purity of feeling, he saw sufficient to convince him that he was loved—that he had inspired her with no transitory or evanescent passion for himself, but a love that bade defiance to all obstacles, that was no more easy to be extinguished than the flame that was likewise kindled in his own breast.

Never, surely, had any day seemed so long as this. How many anxious glances Edward cast towards the sun, which, on the recept on of the letter had scarcely attained its meridian height —how happily and hopefully he watched its decline, for that eve he was destined once more to gaze upon the enchanting face of Grace, his first and earliest love—how tedious each moment seemed that kept him from her side.

The evening found him among the earliest of the arrivals at the opera, and carefully did he scan each party as they entered, in the hope of finding among them her whom alone he wished or cared to see; for some time his hopes were vain, but at last, when he began almost to despair of seeing her, and to fear that some unforeseen circumstance would prevent their attendance, he recognised the earl and countess, and the never-to-be-forgotten Grace, entering a box facing the one he himself occupied; instantly he observed that Grace cast an anxious and searching look round the house, while a shadow of disappointment for a moment overspread her countenance, the next he saw that he was recognised, and a smile at once kind and reproachful chased away the gloom, and the colour upon her cheek deepened to a richer glow. Edward thanked her for these mute signs of affectionate interest on his behalf, by a look of the tenderest regard; and then concealing himself from the observation of the earl and countess behind the curtains of his box, he waited with a heart throbbing at his own happiness, the conclusion of the opera, to the performance of which he was wholly blind; he had no eyes for aught save Grace; she alone engrossed his every thought, and he felt that to gaze upon her thus was in itself delight, and he would have been well content to remain thus employed the entire night; her presence alone banished all weariness.

The moment the curtain dropped he hastened from the box, and stationed himself in the lobby, through which he knew Grace and her relatives must pass, and in a short time he beheld the earl approaching the spot where he stood, with one of his fair companions on either arm.

"What, Villiers, is that you?" said the earl, as he recognised his friend and fellow traveller.

"The same, my lord, and your poor servant ever," replied the young man, promptly and gaily.

"I see you have not forgotten your old favourite, Shakspere," returned the other, laughing.

"No, and I hope I never shall; but," he added, with a slight hesitation in his manner, "will you allow me to release you of one of your companions, the crowd here is too great to permit you to take care of both?"

"Willingly," replied the earl. "Grace, give your hand to Mr. Villiers."

The blushing girl instantly complied, and Edward felt her hand rest tremblingly on his arm, and rapture filled his breast! and as he conducted her towards the carriage, he found an opportunity to press it to his lips.

"I was afraid, Mr. Villiers," said Grace, "that you had entirely forgotten me."

"My dearest girl," returned the young man, "you have not been absent from my thoughts an instant. I have been wretched."

"Why?" said Grace, in a tone of surprise.

"I cannot explain all to you, now. This is no time or place to enter into details, suffice it, Grace, that I love you."

At these words he felt her hand tremble yet more, but she offered no reply.

"You are not offended with me, dear girl," resumed Edward. "I am sure you would not be if you knew how I have struggled against the passion I could not extinguish."

"No, no, I am not," replied Grace, hurriedly.

"We are none of us capable of controlling our feelings, Grace," replied her companion. "Yet, had it not been for the precious letter I received from you this morning, I should never have gained courage to declare my sentiments; but in that letter, dear Grace, I fancied I could trace feelings that beat in unison with my own."

"And you were not mistaken," replied Grace, frankly.

"That being the case, dear girl, I will no longer hesitate to avow to your friends the love with which you have inspired me."

At this moment the carriage drew up, and Edward was obliged to place Grace by the side of the countess, without giving utterance to another word. As he did so, the earl cordially invited him to enter, and accompany them home. As he hesitated for a moment, whether or not to accept it, Grace bent down and whispered hastily,—

"Not to-night, but to-morrow. To-morrow, in the morning, I shall be walking near the park."

Edward immediately understood the assignation, and pressed her hand in token that he did so; and then politely taking leave of the earl and countess, he wended his way towards his own home, his heart filled with joy at the anticipated meeting with Grace, on the morrow.

CHAPTER X.

" How sweetly does the moonbeam smile
        To-night, upon yon leafy isle?
        Oft, in my fancy's wanderings,
        I've wished that little isle had wings;
        And we, within its fairy bowers,
        Were wafted off to seas unknown,
        Where not a pulse shall beat but ours—
        And we might live, love, die alone!
        Far from the cruel, and the cold—
        Where the bright eyes of angels only
        Should come around us, to behold
        A Paradise, so pure and lonely."

WITH a thoughtful, though happy heart, young Villiers repaired the following morning at an early hour to the park, where Grace had signified her intention of walking; nor did she keep him long in suspense, for he had arrived at the appointed rendezvous but a few minutes when he espied Grace approaching. In a moment he was by her side, and,

"This is, indeed, kind of you, dear Grace. You have afforded me an unhoped for opportunity of imparting to you my sentiments, and the desires I am bold enough to entertain," were the first exclamations of the young man, as he drew the arm of Grace gently through his own.

"Mr. Villiers," said Grace, smiling, "do not talk of boldness, or I shall fear you intend to censure the freedom I have displayed in my manners towards yourself."

"Censure you, dear Grace!" replied her lover, in a tone of surprise, "when, in truth, I know not how to express my gratitude. You have raised me from the depths of despair, and, by your kindness, placed me on the very pinnacle of hope."

"Mr. Villiers," returned Grace, "I have ever been a decided enemy to all deceit; consequently, you must not suppose, that in thus appointing a secret interview with you this morning, I have the slightest desire to conceal the attachment I have avowed for you, from my or your friends."

"You have greatly honoured me, dear Grace, both by the tender regard you declare you entertain towards me, and the frankness which has given me courage to sue for your hand, a boon so precious, that the consciousness of my own inferiority would otherwise have prevented me sueing from your rightful guardians; even now, I dread being coldly, if not rudely repulsed. In that case——"

"In that case," returned Grace, "I shall not feel myself bound to abide by their decision."

"Dear Grace," replied the young man, "how can I ever hope to repay your kindness? but without the consent of your friends, I could not, my dear girl, feel myself justified in withdrawing you from the bright and happy circle in which you now move, in order that you might share my comparatively poor and humble fortune."

"Edward," said Grace, in a tone of slight reproach, "I have confessed that I love you, and, therefore, need not blush to own that even the poorest lot, if shared with you, would be far sweeter, and more preferable than the most brilliant destiny, if purchased at the expense of happiness, and happiness apart from you is out of the question."

"You think so, dear Grace," replied Villiers, "and were I given to vanity, I should be easily induced to believe that it might prove so; but Grace, I should never forgive myself, if I were to place you in a position you might hereafter repine at."

"Can you think so meanly of me!" returned Grace, evidently hurt at the implied doubt of her lover.

"Not meanly of you, Grace; that would indeed be impossible; but you have never known what it is to have a wish ungratified; every comfort that my limited means would afford, dear girl, would be ever yours."

"Stop one moment, before you proceed further," replied Grace, warmly. "I will not, like a romantic girl, deny the value of riches, or be foolish enough to expect happiness to go hand-in-hand with poverty and want; at the same time, I must and do think that those persons are the happiest who are at once removed from the two extremes of wealth and poverty."

"If, dear Grace, you could content yourself with my humble lot, I can, at least, promise you a kind and warm reception into my family. My mother is already aware of my love for you, and has chided me for daring to raise my thoughts to one so far above me. How proud I shall be to present you to her as my promised bride."

"And I," said Grace, "shall love her as a parent, for your sake, and we shall, I am sure, be blest."

Her lover reiterated the fond wish, yet knew more of the world and its rough usage than Grace, who had never yet had to encounter its buffets, and he trembled, not for his own, but her happiness; never till this moment had he coveted wealth, or rank, but now he would gladly have been enabled to make a more ample fireside for the fair girl who was about to become his wife. On his arrival at home, all saw that he wore an unusual thoughtfulness upon his countenance, and all were eager to learn the cause; but when the secret was told, not one was ready to offer him congratulations on the important event; and the blanched face of Helen, who strove in vain to sustain her usual composure, struck sadly on the young man's heart, and for the first time he was sensible of a feeling of sorrowful regret, that he could not return the regard she so evidently nourished in her gentle breast, and he forebore to expatiate upon the happiness he expected in the proposed union of himself and the lady Grace. His mother, to whom he had ever been accustomed to award implicit obedience, even to her lightest wish, looked sad and sorrowful, and though she endeavoured to express a hope that his suit would meet the approval of the lady's friends, yet there was a total absence of that tender cordiality that usually characterised her tones; and, even while speaking she cast a sympathising glance towards the unfortunate Helen, whose pallid countenance and anguished look filled the heart of Edward with the keenest sorrow. Strange and incomprehensible are men! He whom a few hours before had been devoted entirely to the warm and fascinating Grace, and would have discarded with anger the suggestion that he might be impressed in favour of another, now felt that he could at least award a portion of his affections to one who was so sincerely attached to himself, and earnestly did he long to pour into her bosom the balm of consolation; but now he felt that such sympathy would be wholly misplaced; any attempt to offer it would be looked upon as a mockery; in silence, therefore, he regarded her with a kind and thoughtful look, which sufficed to restore the lost bloom with redoubled brilliancy to her countenance.

Poor Helen was too unsophisticated, too little versed in the intricate windings of a man's heart, who feels himself flattered by a love which he cannot return, and yet desires to retain his own, perchance from no better feeling than the gratification of his own vanity. We were saying Helen was too unsophisticated to attempt to conceal the state of her feelings; when, being accidentally left alone with young Villiers on the following day, he contrived to lead the subject of conversation to his own expected union with Lady Grace Clavering.

"Come Helen," said the young man, in a half-laughing tone, "you have not even wished me joy, or even happiness in the marriage I am about to form. This is a neglect I little anticipated from you; for, I had flattered myself, you felt an interest in my welfare."

Helen's heart throbbed almost audibly, and a sense of suffocation for the moment impeded her utterance; and it was with difficulty that she contrived to offer an apology for having forgotten to wish him that happiness which she, of all others, was most anxious he should experience.

"Dear Helen," replied Edward, kindly taking her hand, "You must not suppose that I seriously meant to chide you for an omission which I am perfectly aware was unintentional. I have ever loved you (Helen started and turned pale at these words)—as a kind and tender sister," added the young man, after a moment's hesitation, and Helen again started, and sighed, though she scarce knew why.

"You do not speak, Helen," resumed Edward, after both had been for a few minutes silent, "neither do you appear to feel so deeply interested, as the occasion, I think, might demand."

"Edward," replied Helen, turning her soft blue eyes full upon him, "do not blame me if I cannot feel so deeply interested in the object of your attachment as you may naturally expect and desire of me, whom you have for years ever associated with all your hopes and plans for future happiness, till at length—(here Helen hesitated, and then, averting her glowing face, and fixing her eyes on the carpet, said, with a *naivete* that at once charmed and reproached her hearer) "You are yourself in love, Edward, and will therefore make some allowance for the confession I am about to make, and which it is necessary for me to do, in order to free myself from the imputation of unkindness towards you."

"Alas! Helen," replied the other, "I dare not construe your speech as my vanity would, perchance, lead me; but no, there is too much of misery in knowing that I am loved at the very moment when I can no longer with honour seek to win your heart. Tell me, Helen, that it is another, and not myself, who——"

"Spare my blushes," returned Helen, without daring to raise her eyes from the floor. "You have said rightly, you alone are the object of my regard; and now never let us again name this painful subject; knowing that you are engaged to another, it will be at once my duty and earnest desire to conquer a love that meets no return."

"I am destined to be miserable," returned the young man. "Had I known sooner that you loved me, sweet Helen, (pressing her hand to his lips) how blest we might have been, but now, alas! there's madness in the thought," and releasing her hand, he covered his eyes and feigned the deepest sorrow and emotion at the discovery he pretended to have made; whereas, the reader is well aware that his mother had long since acquainted him with the affection that Helen entertained for him. Not so her. She, poor girl, implicitly believed that till her own blushing confession, Edward knew not of her love; and now that she witnessed his apparent distress, her gentle bosom throbbed with the soft emotion of pity that ever makes its home in a woman's breast, and with all her sex's tenderness she sought to win him from his sorrow, and with kind and gentle words make him forget his woe; and (for who is so generous as a woman when she loves,) she even mentioned Grace, and bade him, for the love of her, to rein in the sorrowful feelings which she had unwittingly given rise to.

"Dear Edward," said Helen, endeavouring to remove his hands, which were clasped before his eyes, "for the sake of Grace, her whom you have confessed you so fondly love, I beg—I entreat of you, forget, if possible, all that has past between us this morning; if it will in any measure add to your happiness, I will endeavour for the future to regard you only as a dear and affectionate brother; and as a visitor, surely, even Grace, your affianced wife, will receive me kindly, and perhaps permit me to love her as dearly as I shall still regard you."

"Dear noble, generous girl," exclaimed the young man, removing his hands and clasping her fondly to his bosom. "Helen, I love you, as you deserve to be loved; listen to me one moment, my girl." Helen raised her head, which had reclined for one brief moment on the bosom of him she loved, and fixed her eyes upon his face, while he thus spoke,—

"I have gone so far with the Lady Grace, that it is impossible for me to retreat; but I have told her, that marry her without the consent of her friends, I dare not; consequently, if they refuse to receive me as her husband, I am with honour freed from my engagement; then, Helen, you will not refuse to accept my hand—to become my own dear wife. Promise me this, love, and for the present I am content."

"Nay," said Helen, wildly, "you love Grace—she returns your affection—you must be her's, and her's alone."

"But if, as is most probable, I am with honour free to marry whom I choose, you will not, my love, surely allow any foolish fancy to stand in the way of our mutual happiness. Had I known sooner your real sentiments, never would I have been thus unhappily entangled. I early became aware of the favour with which the Lady Grace regarded me, and dazzled by her rank and beauty, I offered her my hand, a step I now bitterly regret."

"Oh, do not say so; enough that I am unhappy; the friends of Grace will undoubtedly give their consent, when they learn that her happiness depends upon it; and before I unfortunately disclosed my affection to you, your love was all her own. Forget me, or rather think of me as a sister, and with her you will be happy."

"It is unlike my own candid Helen, to withhold a promise that cannot be productive of harm to either, and which I have assured you will materially add to my happiness. Say," he continued, drawing her towards him, and imprinting a kiss on her cheek; "say that you consent to accept me, if I am refused by the Countess of Clavering."

Helen hesitated, she knew that it was wrong to give her promise, under such circumstances, and yet, did not like to pain him whom she so fondly loved, by refusing to grant what he so urgently desired, and therefore reluctantly complied, and likewise still more reluctantly consented to conceal all that had past between them from his mother and sisters.

CHAPTER XI.

" Oh! grief, beyond all other griefs, whose fate
    First leaves the young heart lone and desolate
    In the wide world, without that only tie
    For which it loved to live, or feared to die:
    Lone as the hung-up lute, that ne'er had spoken,
    Since the sad day its master chord was broken.''

ALAS! how sad and lonely was that long, long day, to Catherine Montravers, on which she received the letter that dashed her long and fondly cherished hopes to the ground, that engulphed her in the wide sea of sorrow, over which she cast her eyes in vain for one green and sunny spot, on which she might rest secure amid the rough storms that now encompassed her: there was none even to share, much less soothe her sorrow; not one to whom she could tell the weight of anguish that pressed so heavily on her young heart. No, she was a lonely and isolated being; she must endure all, struggle through all, alone! Can any heart conceive a more painful destiny, the very word "alone" strikes on the ear as the knell of all that binds us to earth; the flowers of summer may bloom as brightly o'er our path; they may fling their rich perfume in renewed sweetness on the soft balmy air; music may seek to gladden us, with its light and joyous tones, or pour upon our once delighted senses the depths of its rich and full revealings; but these avail nothing, if there are none to share them with us. When warm hearts are flown, oh, who would inhabit this bleak world alone? All of us would prefer a wintry sky, if shared with those we love, to the warmth and brightness of the summer's sun, whose power sheds such brightness on our hearts, that had the world no joy but this, to sit in sunshine calm and sweet, in converse with those who are dear to our hearts, it would be a world too exquisite for man to leave for the gloom, the deep cold shadow of the tomb. Catherine felt that she must henceforth pursue a solitary career, more sad and solitary, because it must necessarily be pursued amid the busy scenes and strife of this noisy world; had she possessed means that would have enabled her to retire to some sweet secluded spot, where, unknowing and unknown, she might have passed her days in peaceful serenity, being a spectator, not an actor on the stage of life, then much of the bitterness that was infused into her cup of sorrow had been removed; she would have drank, at least unrepiningly, the draught that had poisoned her happiness, but this consolation was denied her; she must wear a tranquil brow and smiling aspect; must, with unruffled temper and ever patient placid demeanour, pursue an occupation wearying and harassing to the mind, while she was made accountable for every failing that was manifest in her pupils. Surely nothing can be more unjust than to visit the faults of the instructed upon the teacher, and yet this is almost invariably done, sometimes we are ready to admit, thoughtlessly, but such thoughtlessness should be carefully guarded against, as it is an act of cruelty and injustice. Next to the toil-worn needlewoman, no class of persons have so much claim on our tenderness and compassion, as those who earn their bread by imparting instruction, in some respects indeed their claims stand prior to the first-named, inasmuch as the governess must be elegant, ladylike, well informed, and highly accomplished, to qualify her for such an office, in addition to which she must be possessed of an aptitude to impart what she is herself well versed in (no easy matter). And when we take into consideration the high and intrinsic value of her services, we think there are none who will not readily admit that money alone can never repay the benefits that are derived from this class of the community; kindness, tenderness, and gratitude for their labours should ever be awarded, not as concessions but as their due; instead of this they are more often treated with cold neglect, or unfeeling disdain. And poor Catherine felt deeply the wrongs to which she was subjected; there were, indeed, moments of gloom when she was tempted to give up all in despair, but other and better thoughts gained the mastery, and she resolved to suffer on, to seal up in her own bosom the story of her woes, so cruel and unmerited; they could not be breathed even to her sister without reflecting shame upon her head.

"Alas!" thought Catherine, "into what a vortex of misery has not his unfaithfulness plunged me;" and then she rested with something like satisfaction on the anticipated return to England, and she was sensible of an ardent and yearning desire once more to behold her sister, to witness her happiness, and draw some refreshing strength from the same pure stream.

In the evening of this day, she visited and bade a parting adieu to the only friend she had in Paris; this done the remaining days that intervened before their departure were fully employed in preparations for the journey; there was so much that required doing, and none could do so well as Catherine, that but little time was left her for thought, or even the slight preparations the journey might be supposed to involve as regarded herself.

And when all was in readiness, and they were at length started on the journey, all the care, and consequent anxiety of the children devolved on her, and Catherine reached the termination of it, harassed and exhausted, both in body and mind.

Mrs. Porter loudly complained of her own fatigue, and thought the children looked pale and weary, but it never occurred to her that the governess might possibly be more tired and weary than either her or them.

Poor Catherine laid her head on her pillow, sad and thoughtful, and arose in the morning weak and dispirited, and but ill-fitted to encounter mental exertion; but her employer was anxious that no more time should be lost, and desired Catherine to commence the usual course of studies immediately.

"Miss Porter has an excellent voice," said that lady; "it only wants training. You must, therefore, take more pains to cultivate it. Your own voice is perfect, so you cannot do better than accompany her, and give her all the time you can spare from other matters; do not forget her sister's drawing; I wish her to sketch as much as possible from nature. And——" but we spare the reader the infliction of all that the inconsiderate lady so urgently pressed upon the unfortunate governess. Suffice it, that Catherine promised to do her best, and besought in return, that she might have an opportunity afforded her of visiting her sole relative. It was several days before this most reasonable request was granted. In the meantime, Catherine felt tempted to write and acquaint her sister of her arrival in London. But no, she would surprise her by unexpectedly appearing in her presence; so long and fondly she dwelt upon the joy of a sudden meeting, as far as her sister was concerned, that it grew at length into a promised happiness.

"Yes, yes," she repeated to herself, over and over again. "I shall witness her joy—shall hear from her own lips how sweetly blessed she is. This is a happiness of which none can deprive me. Dear sister, rather than thy tender bosom should ever know a pang, I would gladly ask my wounds again——for thee, thou art formed for happiness. Sorrows, such as I have encountered, would break thy gentle heart. Let me, then, be thankful that on me alone they have fallen. I am better fitted to bear trouble, and will not repine while thou art blessed." These thoughts stimulated Catherine to renewed exertion, and uncomplainingly she pursued her avocation.

The day preceding the one on which Catherine had obtained leave to visit her sister, Mrs. Porter expressed a desire that she would accompany the elder children to the Opera, she having received the offer of a box for the evening; but having an engagement herself, she was anxious they should avail themselves of it. Catherine, as a matter of course, felt bound to declare her willingness to comply with the lady's request; and in the early part of the evening, accompanied by her young charge, entered the box assigned them for the occasion.

Catherine was possessed of a fondness for music, amounting well nigh to a passion; and as its witching sounds stole upon her delighted senses, with all the aid of scenic representation to render the effect more perfect, she sat as one entranced; forgetful for the time of her own sorrows, and the cruel wrongs she had sustained; but as the play proceeded, it developed a tale of woe, strangely similar to her own eventful history. The heroine, beautiful and accomplished, loved with a fond intensity, "not wisely but too well," one whose rank and wealth placed him in a station of life far above her, whom he afterwards cruelly deserted for another. The tears swam in Catherine's eyes, for she (perhaps the only one in that large assembly) could fully appreciate the bitter sorrow, and soul-sickening anguish of the betrayed and deserted heroine. No heart can throb for another's woe, like one that has been deeply wounded itself; and as the barbed arrow of grief still rankled in the breast of Catharine; she was acutely sensible of the seeming sorrows of another; indeed, she half forgot that it was merely fictitious woe.

So far her attention had been given exclusively to the stage, but as the curtain fell upon the conclusion of the first act, her eye for one moment glanced listlessly round the house; at the same instant she started with a convulsive movement, her heart seemed to suspend its motion, and her face assumed the hue of death: for seated opposite, with a calm, unmoved exterior, contemplating her, even with a smile of recognition, was he to whom she had plighted her first vows of love, who had sworn to make her his bride, who had won from her all that makes life sweet and precious, and repaid her trusting love and faithfulness with that refinement of cruelty, which to the last moment of his marrying another, cheated her with words of passion, and renewed promises he never could fulfil. Oh God! that such things should be; and yet how often are young, fond, warm hearts thus crushed; how many a fair and tender blossom, whose sweet scented leaves attracted the hand of the spoiler, are reft of their perfume, and left alone to wither, droop and die.

Catherine's first feelings, at this unexpected meeting with him from whom she had parted not many months before, in the hope of a speedy reunion, when they they should be united never more to sever—was that of the keenest anguish, for, seated by his side, was a fair young being, whom she had no difficulty in discovering to be his new-made bride, who filled that position she had so fondly hoped she was herself to occupy; but when he, who had so cruelly wronged her, perceiving that he was recognised, bowed with the air of an old acquaintance, the indignant blood mounted to her cheek in a deep and burning glow, and averting her eyes, she resolutely avoided meeting his gaze. Yet, when the curtain again drew up, and she endeavoured once more to turn her attention to the stage; she found it utterly impossible, the, charm was broken, and the music had no longer the power to interest or enliven. The remainder of the performance was to her a blank; her whole thoughts were painfully occupied, yet not for herself alone, she now began to experience even a keener pang, such as she had never known before, and was rendered doubly severe in coming from a quarter in which she had never looked for misfortune; for, seated in the same box with him who had so injured herself, engaged in paying marked attention to a young and beautiful girl, was the very man whom she had considered engaged to her sister, and to whom she knew that sister's affections had long been given. "Oh, surely, surely," was her inward exclamation, "Helen, as well as myself, is not doomed to bitterness and sorrow."

The play ended.   With redoubled anguish Catherine returned to the stately mansion of her employer. A gay and brilliant party was assembled beneath its roof. Glad music lent its aid to enliven, and all was mirth and hilarity. How little thought the many happy hearts that beat responsive to the gaiety and pleasure by which they were surrounded, that one fair young

being, formed for happiness equally with themselves, was sinking beneath that very roof, under the load of sorrow that oppressed her, and not one to whom she could look for support or consolation.

Mirth and sorrow, joy and anguish, oftentimes reside in the same dwelling, and yet the occupants know it not.   Very few persons trouble themselves to dive deeper than the exterior; if that wears an appearance of contentment, they seek not to inquire farther, and little think that the face may smile when the heart is breaking.

No. 5.

CHAPTER XII.

" Oh! you that have the charge of love,
    Keep him in rosy bondage bound,
As in the fields of bliss above.
    He sits with flow'rets fetter'd round.
Lose not a tie that round him clings—
    Nor ever let him use his wings,
For even an hour, a minute's flight
    Will rob the plumes of half their light,
Like that celestial bird—whose nest
    Is found beneath far Eastern skies;
Whose wings, though radiant when at rest,
    Lose all their glory when he flies."

WHEN Edward Villiers solicited the fair hand of Grace of her brother, the young Earl of Clavering, he manifested the greatest surprise, which indeed was only exceeded by his displeasure, but when he learnt from the young man that he was authorised by the lady herself to sue for a boon he would otherwise have never gained courage to seek from him, the earl violently pulled the bell, and ordered the servant to inform the Lady Grace that he desired her presence instantly. She came, but not as he anticipated, pale and trembling for the result, but firm and erect, ready and eager to ratify the choice her heart had made.

In reply to her brother's angry interrogatory as to whether she had given Mr. Villiers the encouragement he averred, she answered proudly,—

"He has spoken truth, Arthur; nay," she added, "he has not told you one-half I have expressed towards him; for I love him so truly, that I am willing to forsake my nearest and dearest friends for him."

"And you have told him so?" returned her brother.

"I have told him so," re-echoed Grace.

"Pardon me," said Edward, addressing the earl with a show of indignation, "but I cannot allow you to think me mean enough to accept even this precious gift," and he took the hand of Grace, and raised it respectfully to his lips, "much coveted as it is, without the full and free consent of all her friends."

"Which you came here this morning, doubtless, fully prepared to meet," replied the earl, sarcastically.

"Scarcely so," returned the young man, with an air of modesty; "I am so fully alive to my own inferiority, that but for the assurance of Lady Grace, that her happiness as well as mine depended upon the issue of this interview, I never should have sought what I felt myself unworthy to obtain."

"Brother," said Grace, seeing the earl was about to reply, "listen to me before you say a word more. I wish to convince you, beyond the possibility of a doubt, that I love Mr. Villiers, not with a silly, girlish affection, but a love that will endure, if need be, suffering and hardship cheerfully for his sake."

"Such sentiments," replied her brother, "are merely those of a romantic love-sick girl, who is ready to fall into the arms of the first man who wooes her, no matter what his rank or station in life may be."

"I am sorry," said Grace, and indignation coloured her cheek to a crimson glow, "that you should entertain so poor an opinion of me—your only sister. But argument is useless; I am myself assured that I love with an affection such as a woman can feel but once;" and turning to her lover, she stretched out the hand he had previously released, and with a look of trusting devotedness, she exclaimed,—

"Edward, here is my hand; it is yours, and yours alone, if you deem it worthy of acceptance."

Notwithstanding the presence of the earl, which offered a check to the impulse of his heart, Edward could not refrain from clasping the fair girl in his arms, and pressing the first kiss of love upon her lips, till now unbreathed upon.

"Arthur," said Grace, as with instinctive modesty she released herself from her lover's arms, and turned her blushing face towards her brother, "to prove to you that my love is not, as you termed it, a weak romantic affection, that can be matured or crushed at will, I shall make no attempt to set at nought your authority, or endeavour to escape to Gretna Green. On the contrary, if you are still determined to oppose my marriage with Mr. Villiers, I shall be content to remain single till I am of age to judge and act for myself, and then, depend, I shall walk into the first church and give my hand to him who alone will ever possess my heart."

"I have, as yet, expressed no such determination, Grace," said the earl, in a milder tone; "indeed it is not for me to accept or decline Mr. Villiers' offer; I am willing to call your mother's attention to his proposal, and also your own wishes on the subject; if she approves, I of course shall do the same. This, I trust, will satisfy you both."

"Perfectly," replied Grace, smiling. "I know I can speak for Mr. Villiers as well as myself.'

The young man pressed her hand in token of approval, while he expressed to the earl his full concurrence in this arrangement.

The dowager countess consequently was appealed to on the subject, and was far from manifesting that aversion to the match Grace was prepared to expect. A letter of her own had accompanied her brother's to Ravensdale, in which she perfectly exhausted every tender persuasion and inducement to gain her parent's consent, and she was likewise aided by Edith, who the instant she learned from Grace the tender love she had conceived for young Villiers, warmly espoused his cause, till even the earl began to consider the matter in a more reasonable light. Directly Edith interested herself, everything began to wear a brighter aspect, and at the close of a month, Edward Villiers was received at the earl's as the accepted suitor and affianced husband of the Lady Grace.

Preparations too were going on for that ceremony which was to unite them for life to each other; and never had Grace laughed so merrily or looked so bright and beautiful. A change had come o'er her lively spirit, but it was a sweet and happy change; she seemed at one step to have passed from girlhood, and become at once the gentle, animated, and withal, dignified woman; and never had woman loved with truer devotedness than Grace Clavering; every thought and hope centered in him her heart had chosen; he was woven and entwined with every feeling till he had become, as it were, a part of herself.

The dowager countess was the more willing to consent to the union of her daughter with Edward Villiers from his father having been so many years an established and confidential friend of the late earl, her husband; leaving therefore every arrangement to her son, she merely stipulated that the marriage ceremony should be performed at Ravensdale.

"How long the lawyers are, drawing up the settlements," said Edward Villiers. "I so ardently long to call you mine that I am afraid, Grace, you will think me impatient, and not sufficiently grateful to you for your kindness."

"Say not so," replied Grace, kindly; "in one month I shall be your wife, and then——"

"And then, dearest!" exclaimed the young man, catching her in his arms, "I shall ask for nothing more; my cup of happiness will be full, even to the brim. But, oh! Grace," he added, in a melancholly tone, "I sometimes am possessed of such strange and unaccountable fears, that——"

"Stop!" said Grace, placing her small white hand over his mouth, "do not infect me with your silly fears. Come, now, you shall accompany me to the Opera, and try the effect of sweet sounds that I think will banish all gloom."

"Your presence alone, dear Grace, is sufficient to do that; it is the intensity of my love for you that will sometimes make me fear your being snatched from me; but forgive me, love," he added, seeing she looked sad, "I meant not to make you uncomfortable—let us forget this."

"Yes," replied Grace, eagerly, "let us forget it, and now for the Opera," she added, laughing.

The ensuing morning the ever kind and watchful Edith noticed a shadow upon her husband's brow, and—alas! how quick-sighted is love—at the Opera, the evening before, she had noticed his eye wandering too frequently in the direction of a neighbouring box, in which was seated a woman, young and beautiful, but whose dark eye so far from manifesting any sign of pleasure at the notice she attracted, had been turned away in evident anger and disdain. The earl, Edith fancied, had felt piqued at conduct so unusual; and now, this morning, he was apparently nervous and uncomfortable, and replied to her tender inquiry after his health in a tone less kind and gentle than he usually assumed towards her; this sufficed to make Edith at least anxious and restless, and when, in the course of the morning, he left home for the first time since their marriage, without first apprising her of his intention, she felt really unhappy, and without any fixed purpose she entered the library. The earl's desk was open, and glancing her eye casually towards it, she perceived a letter folded, but not sealed. In the hurry of his departure, her husband had evidently forgotten it, and without a thought of unkindness, or even idle curiosity, she drew it from the envelope, believing that it was intended for his mother, for she knew that he had scarce any other correspondent.

It did seem that, by a conjunction of unfortunate circumstances, Edith was to become possessed of the contents of that ill-fated letter. It ran as follows:—

" DEAR CATHERINE,—That in a measure I deserve your coldness, I am willing to allow, but that
your love should have turned to contempt and hatred, I cannot conceive. I wrote to you immediately preceding my marriage, in which I explained to you the unfortunate circumstances that
induced me to form a union with my cousin, and conveyed to you my assurance that none would
ever fill your place in my heart. I love you still, Catherine; but, if you believe it not, grant
me an interview. For your sake, as much as my own, I am induced to make this request; you
will not surely refuse. After all that has passed, I might almost seek it as a right, but I would
rather ask it from you as a favour. Ever yours,   CLAVERING."

Edith carefully refolded this epistle, and restored it to its envelope, with but scarcely more
than a half-dreamy consciousness of the bitterness of its contents, from which she dreaded to
awaken to the cruel reality; and yet true love is so unselfish, so truly prefers the happiness of
the being loved to its own, that Edith's first regret was for her husband.

"Alas, Arthur," she uttered half aloud, "then I, who love you so dearly, have stood between
you and happiness; but for me, you might have been united to the object of your affection—her
for whom your heart even now yearns. I am indeed unfortunate—wretched; for I have, without
knowing it, made you so."

At that moment, she was roused by the sound of her husband's footsteps, and, before she had
scarce time to command her feelings, or assume a look of unconcern, he entered.

"Ah, my love—you here!" he said, but hastening at the same time to his desk, on which
lay, apparently untouched, the letter he had forgotten; observing which, he seemed relieved, and,
placing it carelessly in his pocket, he approached his wife, and, tenderly kissing her cheek, bade
her for the present farewell, saying that he should meet her at dinner. Edith in silence returned
his greeting, then sought retirement, to weep, not for her own, but his unhappiness.

CHAPTER XIII.

" In vain my lyre would lightly breathe
        The smile that sorrow fain would wear,
But mocks the woe that lurks beneath,
        Like roses o'er a sepulchre.
" Though gay companions, o'er the bowl,
        Dispel awhile the sense of ill;
Though pleasure fires the madd'ning soul,
        My heart, my heart is lonely still."

IN one of the gay salons at Paris three fashionable young men were engaged in the varied
manners which their fancy dictated, killing time, or at least making it pass as quickly and use-
lessly as possible.

"I say, Ernest, my boy," said a pale and sickly-looking young man, who could scarcely have
attained the age of twenty, and yet, sad to say, he had evidently, at that early age, been already
familiar with excesses of every kind. His face said as much to even a casual beholder, and his
emaciated frame betokened the existence of an insidious disease, induced, most probably, in his
case, by a life of indolence and excess. He was fair and well-formed; symmetrically so; indeed,
it gave him somewhat the appearance of effeminacy. His light brown hair hung in loose curls
over a forehead as white as alabaster; his eyes were of a pale but lustrous blue; a mouth that
seemed formed for smiles, and displayed to advantage teeth even and white; a slightly-curled
moustache decorated his upper lip; and, had it not been for the sickly pallor that overspread his
countenance, and the look of exhaustion and anxiety that was stamped upon his young brow, he
might well have been considered remarkably handsome; as it was, none could gaze upon him
without feeling a strong interest awakening in their mind on his behalf.

The person whom this youth had addressed as Ernest was some years his senior, utterly different to himself in every respect. He had, apparently, attained the age of five-and-twenty, was
tall, well made, and handsome. He roused himself from a seeming reverie at the sound of the
other's voice, but merely answered with the monosyllable " Well."

"Why, hang it," replied the first speaker, "how confounded out of sorts you do seem, and,
in fact, I feel somehow devilish queer myself. I am tired of everything;" and stretching his
hand towards a decanter that stood near him, he poured out a tumbler of wine, and drank off
the contents at a draught, but he was too accustomed to wine to experience therefrom the exhi-
larating effect he desired.

"That's right, Christopher, push the bottle this way, if you please," said a tall, stout, handsome-looking man, but with such a bold, bad expression of countenance as entirely to conceal his good looks. He had a large, black, cunning-looking eye, that it would appear impossible to make quail; it seemed as though the possessor would be deterred by nothing, however base, in the accomplishment of any design he might purpose.

The youth, with an air of extreme lassitude, did as he was desired; and then stretching himself at length upon a couch, gave himself for the time to unpleasant thoughts, which appeared to have gained the mastery over him.

"Curse it," he exclaimed at length, as he turned over on the couch, with an air of restless impatience, "I am always in some bother or other. I wish I had never seen the girl. I say, Ernest, will you help me out of a scrape?"

"What is it, Christopher?" said the other, bending on him a look of pity. "You do, indeed, seem to be always in trouble, but the reason, I must think, rests with yourself alone."

"Confound it, no!" replied the youth, rising to a sitting posture. "The fact is just this:—I took a fancy to a pretty little girl, and found but little difficulty in gaining her affection, and —and——"

"Yes," returned the other.

"Well, and as I was saying, I found no difficulty in winning her affection, without, of course, meaning anything serious, and now——"

"That you are tired of her, I suppose," returned the other, "you wish me to advise you as to the best mode of ridding yourself of one who has no longer the charm of novelty to please. Excuse me, I beg; Lawton," looking towards the third party, "is more capable of advising you on this subject than myself."

"Who, I?" exclaimed the person appealed to, with an oath that we will not stain our pages by transcribing. "Oh, I have advised him so often, and he is such a devilish inconsistent fellow, that he begins to be weary of my counsel and——"

"Confound it, no," replied the youth, dropping back once more into a recumbent attitude; "but this is really such a very unpleasant dilemma, that curse me if I know how to get out of it—there's the case, and advise on it, there's a good fellow, Ernest."

"If you have injured the girl," replied the young man thus addressed, "I can only advise you to do her all the reparation in your power."

"But she refuses money. I have offered her to name her sum."

'Money!' replied the other, in a tone of disgust. "Can money purchase back the innocence and purity of feeling of which you acknowledge to have deprived her."

"Curse me if I know what would purchase back that which is destroyed for ever. Money, I believe, is generally considered an equivalent."

"Not for that which is beyond all price."

"You talk exactly like the girl herself; it is a horrid nuisance to think that nothing will satisfy her."

"Is she, then, so very unreasonable? Bethink yourself, Christopher, is it not in your power to restore her lost happiness, and if not her innocence, at least the semblance of it?"

"'Gad, I am sure I don't know," replied the youth, with a yawn; "the fact is, latterly I have discovered it to be almost too great an exertion to think."

"It is all very well, Ernest, for you to preach," said the young man, whom his companion had addressed as Lawton, "but we well know that upon occasion you can be as bad as any of us."

"What is it you say?" replied the other, with a clouded brow.

"That you are devilish sly, that's all," said Lawton, with a laugh; "but come, my good fellow, don't be angry."

"Your remarks are extremely offensive, and I am likewise at a loss to understand to what they allude."

"Nothing more," returned the other, with a shrug of his shoulders, "than spite of all your wise counsels, you can love a pretty girl as well as us gay fellows who do not pretend to be better than our neighbours."

"I can love, but not in the way you pretend to imagine."

"You forget the dark-eyed governess, whom you so unceasingly pursued."

"You mistake—I do not forget her; I loved—I love her still, not with the selfish, evanescent feeling that cruelly pursues an object till it is gained, and throws it aside as utterly valueless. I loved in a different—an entirely different—manner. Though, as you say, a governess, I would gladly have made her my wife."

"Made her your wife?" said the youth, starting in astonishment from his recumbent position.

"Ay, and should have been proud to have done so, but——"

"But, what?" said Lawton, eagerly.

"I am not ashamed to avow that she resolutely refused my proposal, though I repeatedly urged it upon her notice."

"Is it possible," said the youth, "that a girl could be silly enough to refuse so excellent an offer?"

"Not one, but doubtless many.   You, Christopher, though so young, I am sorry to say, have been more acquainted with the darkest shades of a woman's character—you have seldom, if ever, experienced her truthful affection, and warm devotedness.   If you trample on a worm, can you wonder if it turns against you; neither can it be a matter of surprise if, after you had lured a woman to sin and sorrow, that she may ultimately prove a thorn in your path."

"Quite a sermon, I declare," said Lawton.   "What a pity there are not more admiring listeners.   What say you, Christopher?"

"'Pon my soul, I don't know what to say," yawned the youth.   "I dare say it is all very excellent, only I can't exactly appreciate it."

"Bravo, Christopher—that is exactly the case with me; but as for this governess, whom Mr. Moreton would persuade us is a perfect paragon of perfection——"

"Stop," cried Moreton, in a voice of anger, "I will not even hear you breathe her name—a name too spotless and pure."

"Moreton," interrupted the other, " 'pon my soul the girl deceived you, for I heard from her own lips that she was by no means backward or shy in receiving the advances of the Earl of Clavering."

Moreton was about to reply, in anger, to the imputation cast upon one he so fondly loved, but he was interrupted by the entrance of the waiter, closely followed by a female figure, muffled in a large mantelet, and a black veil folded thickly over her face.

"Who, in God's name, have we here?" said Lawton, in a tone of surprise.   "Your servant, madam," approaching the veiled figure.   "I trust the honour of this visit is intended for me," and he motioned the servant to withdraw the moment the door closed behind him.   The lady sprang towards the couch on which the youth reclined, and, dropping her disguise, displayed a face and form of exquisite beauty; her hair, which was remarkably fair, hung in rich and sweeping folds over her neck and shoulders, reaching well nigh to the slender waist; a faint pink on either cheek, offered a sweet contrast to the ivory whiteness of her forehead; eyes of heaven's own blue, soft, dove-like and bewitching.

"Marie," said the youth, gazing on her with astonishment.   "What has brought you hither?"

"Christopher, dearest Christopher," she returned, and casting herself on her knees, before him, and taking his thin white hands in her own, she bathed them at once with tears and kisses.

"What is it you want, Marie?" said the young man, in a somewhat petulant tone, as he endeavoured to withdraw his hands.   "Tell me, at once, your object in coming here."

"Alas! Christopher," replied the girl, raising her tearful eyes, which were large and bright, and fixing them with an earnest yet tender expression on his face.   "And is it possible you can be otherwise than glad to see me, your own Marie, whom you have so often assured of your fondest love; and—and——" she hesitated, and perceiving no sign of pleasure on his countenance, but, instead of the warm and ardent gaze that had once so fondly greeted her, he wore a look of coldness and evident vexation, she gave vent to her feelings in a flood of bitter tears, which for a time completely choked her utterance.   Up to this moment, Moreton and his companion had remained silent spectators of the scene, but Lawton appeared to think it was now time to interfere; he therefore approached the girl, and endeavoured to raise her from her kneeling attitude, while he addressed her as follows:—

"I am sorry, madam, that you should thus have forced yourself into the presence of Mr. Warden, when I informed you only this morning, that at present he was too indisposed to receive the visits of any but his own immediate relatives.   I likewise, I believe, had the honour of informing you that he would be happy to listen to any request, so that you made your wishes known through myself."

"Yes, yes," replied the girl, rising and casting him from her, apparently without an effort. "You did tell me all that, ay and more, but I believed you not.   Christopher," she added, melting again to softness, as she once more turned her exclusive attention to the youth, "this man wished me to believe that my presence had grown distasteful to you, that you no longer loved or even cared for the poor girl, whose heart and affections are entirely your own; but I refused credence to the foul imputation. I will not, cannot, think you capable of scorning me at the very time I most require your love and protection."

"What can I do," said the youth, with an air of extreme lassitude; "Lawton has said truly that——"

"What can you do?" interrupted Moreton; "act as your heart, I am sure, must dictate; do justice to this poor girl."

"Oh, bless you for those words, the first that have ever been urged in favour of one who, I must with shame confess, scarcely deserves them."

"Say not so, Marie," replied Moreton; "you have sinned only for him, and through him, and he alone can restore you to your own and his esteem, and if he hesitates to do so, he well deserves to be branded with shame and infamy."

"Marie!" said the youth, rising once more into a sitting posture, and giving no heed to the remarks of Moreton, "I desired my friend here to inform you that I was most anxious to meet your wishes as regards providing a home for you, and the necessary accommodation, you tell me, your situation requires."

"But, Christopher," replied the girl, sobbing, "did you likewise desire him to tell me, that I must consent to be at a distance from you?"

"Yes," returned the young man, "and if you regard it as a sacrifice, remember that my health requires it."

"Oh! Christopher, you know not how dearly I love you, or you would not demand so terrible a sacrifice. If you are ill, who would attend upon you more tenderly or carefully than myself? I ask only to be near you, to nurse you in sickness, to enliven your hours of sadness, to whisper words of hope and comfort, to cool your fevered brow, and fan your burning cheek,—can you, dearest, refuse me this?"

"You know not what you ask, Marie," said the youth; "this is no place for you, neither is it customary at a public hotel to be attended by a female. I have offered suitably to provide for you; if you refuse to accept it——"

"What then?" interrupted the girl, eagerly.

"I can do nothing more; and, as to allowing you to be constantly with me, it is out of the question. I cannot entertain such a thought for an instant."

"Marie," said Moreton, scornfully, "renounce all his offers at once and for ever. He is unworthy of that deep tenderness you nourish in your heart for him. Confide yourself to my care, and I will see that you want for nothing."

"Choose, Marie," said the youth, with more warmth than he had hitherto betrayed. "You hear Mr. Moreton's proposal, and you have heard mine; choose between us."

"Alas!" replied the girl, clasping her hands; "and is it come to this? Am I so lightly regarded by you that—that——" and again she was overcome by the acuteness of her sorrow.

"I must of necessity interfere," said Lawton, addressing the weeping girl. "You have gained nothing, Marie, by forcing yourself into the presence of Mr. Warden; he is, as I told you, willing to make a suitable provision for you, and your expected infant; he is now in delicate health, and I have orders from his physician to keep his mind perfectly undisturbed; when he is sufficiently recovered, he will, I make no doubt, be happy to renew his intimacy."

"Yes, yes," replied the young man, "you have stated the case exactly; now, Marie, on those terms will you consent to accompany Mr. Lawton to the apartments he has provided for your reception."

"If my absence will in any way tend to your recovery, I will go, Christopher, with pleasure —say that you still love me, and I shall go happy."

"I do, Marie, I do indeed," replied the youth, somewhat moved; "let me kiss your cheek, (drawing her towards him), there, now go at once."

"I am ready," replied the girl, "one more kiss, dear Christopher; only one more," and she pushed back the clustering curls from his ivory forehead, and fondly pressed it with her lips. "I feel, I feel," she added, as Lawton endeavoured to withdraw her from the couch, "that we shall meet no more, that I shall never again look upon the face I have only loved too well. Oh, never more, but in dreams of bliss shall I hear the voice that has been, nay, still is, in my ears, the sweetest music. Christopher," she added in a solemn tone, "we part for ever. I feel it, I know it, there is a boding chill creeping through my veins that tells me all is over for us on earth. We shall be united only in death."

"You are mad," said Lawton angrily.

"Stay, I feel as though she spoke truth," said the youth, "and —— but no, Marie, you must go with Mr. Lawton."

"Farewell, dear Christopher, sometimes think how fondly I love you, and how tenderly would have watched over you. And now," turning to Lawton, "I am ready to follow you."

"One word more," said Moreton; "think better of your resolve, break with this unhappy connection. Christopher refuses to do you justice; cast him off, I beseech you, from your heart. When I have informed my mother of your——"

"I know what you would say," interrupted the girl. "Your mother, amiable and excellent, would countenance even me, fallen as I am; but I cannot listen to you; my destiny is linked with him I love, and while he survives, I must implicitly obey his wishes." And with a look fraught at once with love and sadness, she turned and left the apartment, closely followed by Lawton.

The youth seemed for a moment overcome, and veiled his eyes with his hands; the next moment he turned to address Moreton, but he, too, was gone, and he was left entirely alone, with nought but his own sad thoughts for a companion. He became restless and uneasy, till the return of Lawton, when, hearing from him that he had left Marie contented, and in a measure happy, with a female who had willingly undertaken the charge of her for a suitable remuneration, he turned his attention once more to his own ailments; and, throwing himself in an easy position on the couch, he was soon fast asleep.

CHAPTER XIV.

"How am I chang'd! my hopes were once like fire,
I lov'd, and I believ'd that life was love;
How am I lost! on wings of swift desire,
Among Heaven's winds my spirit once did move;
I slept, and silver dreams did aye inspire
My liquid sleep: I woke, and did approve
All nature to my heart, and thought to make
A Paradise of earth, for one sweet sake."

ERNEST MORETON is already known to the reader as the ardent admirer of Catherine Montravers, whom he earnestly desired to make his wife; nor is it likely that the unfortunate governess would have been so totally indifferent to his many attractions, and his honourable overtures, had not her heart unhappily been previously prepossessed in favour of another, upon whose faith she had placed the strongest reliance, nor dreamed of the cruel deception which he practised towards her. On the morning following the events recorded in the last chapter, Moreton again and still more urgently pressed upon the mind of Christopher Warden the claim that the young girl Marie had upon his love and honour. For awhile the youth listened with respectful attention, and Moreton half hoped that he might succeed in inducing him to do her the tardy justice of making her his wife, and becoming the father of her child; but the counsels of Lawton, who had obtained a strange ascendancy over the youth, induced him to set at nought the advice of one who would have proved himself a truer and better friend.

Moreton had casually become acquainted with Christopher and Lawton, through residing at the same hotel, and had instantly felt a deep interest awakening in his mind, on behalf of the youthful invalid; at the same time he could not conquer a proportionate dislike for his friend, even before he became acquainted with his character, and nothing but the desire he felt to benefit, if possible, the younger man would have induced him for an instant to tolerate his companion, the more especially when he discovered the many vices to which he was addicted, and for which he had succeeded in inspiring a taste in his youthful companion, who was now fast sinking into the tomb, the victim of those very vices. The contemplation of this was so dreadful to Moreton, that he regarded Lawton with the deepest abhorrence, and could scarcely conceive how the youth was so blinded as to regard him with the warm friendship he evidently entertained.

Christopher Warden had been from infancy a petted and spoiled boy; he had never known a father's ruling care, whose eyes had been closed in death ere his own began to shine, and he had pressed a widowed mother's breast. No wonder that this treasured gift—this image of her departed spouse, was nurtured with the fondest love. Alas! how many hopes were garnered on his brow—how many prayers breathed for his future happiness. He had early been taught to lean upon his mother's fostering care; her arm had shielded him from every ill. Educated beneath her own eye, he had never had occasion to combat (as boys most certainly should) with the world, or been pushed about in the bustle of a public school, which would undoubtedly have fitted him to encounter life as a man, unsupported, save by his own stability of character.

Mrs. Warden had reared her boy in strict retirement, to his sixteenth year, when her own health began to fail, and she felt that her days on earth were numbered, and having no friends and but few acquaintances, she knew not to whom to confide her precious charge.

About this time, John Lawton, the child of her only sister, who, many years before, had married and settled abroad, arrived in England, bearing with him credentials of his identity, and was kindly and gladly received by Mrs. Warden.

The father of Lawton having a large family, and his means being but limited, had sent his eldest boy to England, on a visit to his rich aunt, in hopes that it might—to use his own words, "be turned to his advantage." It was turned to his advantage, but to the utter ruin of the treasured child of Mrs. Warden; she, poor woman, was short-sighted, knew but little of the world, and was but too ready to judge from appearances. Lawton possessed a natural shrewdness, and consequently found no difficulty in imposing upon the credulity of his aunt; while he took the earliest opportunity of ingratiating himself into the favour of his cousin, who listened to his description of men and manners with pleased amazement, and longed to enter upon the world, and take his part in society.

Her nephew being a good eight years the senior of her son, and, moreover, his only relative, to whom he seemed much attached, Mrs. Warden unadvisedly constituted him the guardian, both of himself and fortune, never doubting the step to be at once wise and considerate; her son, too, most cordially approved of the choice she had made, and though she lived for nine months after his arrival in England, so carefully did young Lawton guard his conduct, and so skilfully act his part, that she died happy and satisfied that he would be a proper and tender guardian for her son.

No. 6

Immediately after the death of Mrs. Warden, her son, under the direction of his cousin, broke up the quiet establishment of his deceased mother, and entered at once upon a life of gaiety and pleasure.

Emerging, at one step, from the even tenour in which his days had hitherto been spent, and plunging into all the revelry and dissipation with which London abounds, were productive of the worst effects upon the health as well as the mind of young Warden; at the close of three years he had become so altered, that his nearest friends failed to recognise in the pale, emaciated young man of nineteen, the robust, fresh and handsome youth of a few short years before. To Lawton alone was this change justly attributed; he had bent the bow, and winged the arrow that had been sent with unerring aim to the young man's heart; be had ruined him, body and soul.

Alas! how pitiable a sight the poor youth presented, sinking day by day—we might almost say hour by hour—to that "bourne from whence no traveller returns," and not one friend nigh to warn him of the shoals against which his vessel was in imminent danger of everlasting shipwreck. No kind hand was stretched out to sustain his tottering footsteps—no gentle words were whispered in his ear to bid him hope and trust in the promise of a future and brighter state of existence. Dark and benighted, with no thought or hope beyond this world, his frail bark was about to put to sea, without chart or compass; the waters were all unknown, and yet he had secured no pilot, who might have guided his vessel to a safe and happy haven.

Young Warden's health had been gradually giving way for some months, yet he heeded not the hectic flush—the short, dry cough, and the numberless other symptoms that gave to him friendly warning of the approach of disease, till it so gained upon him that all attempts to repel its advances were utterly useless, then and not till then, did it occur to himself and his companion that they should seek medical advice, (as it is too often sought, when all remedies are unavailing.) Change of air, and more especially a sea voyage, were strenuously recommended as the most likely means to regain the lost treasure, health. In compliance with which advice, young Warden and his cousin took a trip to Madeira, stayed there some time, living in the same, free, dissipated manner they had done in London, and finally returned and took up their abode at Paris. Here, as we have previously remarked, they became acquainted with Moreton, who, with his mother, was likewise staying in that city. The kind feelings that he instantly entertained for the unhappy youth would doubtless have been productive of much benefit towards him, had not Lawton obtained so powerful an influence over his cousin, that induced him to follow his counsels in preference to all others. Lawton likewise regarded the assiduous attentions of Moreton with a jealous eye, the more especially as he observed that in a measure they were pleasing to the invalid. To separate him then from this, his only true friend, now became his greatest aim; in furtherance of which, he contrived to bring Christopher acquainted with a young girl, who was assistant to a milliner, and who was possessed of extreme loveliness. As he contemplated, the young man instantly became deeply in love with her, and greatly through his agency and intervention Marie (who fully returned the passion she had inspired in the breast of Christopher), was induced to yield to his wishes, whose love, evanescent in the extreme, soon began to weary of one whose confiding love and tenderness rendered her worthy of becoming his wife.

The reader is aware how strongly Moreton pleaded in her favour, and the result of his enterprise was exactly what Lawton desired; finding all his efforts unavailing, Ernest Moreton quitted the youth with disgust. He had, in his opinion, been guilty of a crime that rendered him unworthy of his friendship, and for the future he resolved to withdraw from his company; at the same time he determined, if possible, to find out where Lawton had placed Marie, in order that he might remove her from his control. He greatly distrusted Lawton, and trembled for the fate of the poor girl, who was so entirely in his power, for she was utterly friendless, and moneyless; and with true generosity of spirit, he resolved to make her cause his own, but vain were all his attempts to discover where he had placed her, and in reply to his expressed wish to be admitted to an interview with Marie, Lawton conveyed to him her assurance that she was perfectly happy and wished not for his interference. After this, Moreton felt that he could do no more.

In the meantime, the young man remained perfectly satisfied with his cousin's statement regarding the girl, whom he had won with protestations of eternal and honourable affection, never troubling himself to bestow even a transitory thought upon her comfort or happiness. Now that he had wearied of her charms, his own failing health demanded, he considered, all his care and attention; still, though he felt himself growing weaker and weaker, and each day marked the rapid progress of his disease, he never for a moment thought of death. No one had dared even to hint to him the probable result, and though now the chief part of his time was passed upon his couch, yet strange to say, he laughed, drank, and gamed, and nothing on earth was further from his thoughts than death.

"Well, how do you feel now, my boy," said Lawton, one evening, after he had assisted him in dressing, and placed him on a couch, which (that he might be amused with passing objects,) was drawn close to a window.

"Oh! I feel very well," returned the youth, "with the exception of this cursed weakness; it is devilish hard for a young fellow like me to be laid by here, when I ought to be enjoying life. I get very thin, don't I?" he added, after an interval of silence, as he glanced at his wasted hands.

"Oh, that's nothing," replied Lawton; "when you once more get out, you will soon fetch that up."

"Ah! when I do," said the young man with a sigh, "I hope to God it won't be long; I think now a run in the green fields, that I loved so much when a boy, would not be at all amiss. What say you, Lawton?"

"I think it would by no means be advisable for you to quit Paris, till you are a little stronger, which I have no doubt a few weeks will accomplish; and then there is Marie, her accouchement is now drawing near, and it is necessary that I should inquire into her welfare."

"Quite right," returned the other, "your judgment is always the best; by-the-by, you have spared me a great deal of trouble by taking that affair off my hands. I should have been sorry if the girl hard come to harm."

"You cannot do better than leave her entirely to my management, and I'll take care that she does not trouble you again. I shall be obliged, perhaps, to draw upon your bankers somewhat largely, but that, I know, you do not mind."

"Fill up the checks to any amount that you may require, our interests are as one. I know it must be cursed dull for you to be shut up here with me day after day, but when I can get strong we'll make up for lost time, my boy."

"That we will," returned the other, laughing, "and now for a bottle of your favourite wine."

The youth assented, the wine was brought and drunk. Bottle succeeded bottle, and the evening was spent in mirth and hilarity.

CHAPTER XIV.

Ah, Zelica! there was a time when bliss
Shone o'er thy heart from every look of his;
When but to see him, hear him, breath the air
In which he dwelt, was thy soul's fondest prayer;
When round him hung such a perpetual spell—
Whate'er he did, none ever did so well—
Too happy days; when if he touched a flower
Or gem of thine, 'twas sacred from that hour;
When thou didst study him, till every tone
And gesture and dear look became thy own,
Thy voice like his—the changes of his face
In thine reflected with still lovelier grace.

WITH a palpitating heart that throbbed between hope and fear, Catherine Montravers proceeded towards the abode of her fondly treasured sister. "I shall see her again, behold her happiness, and in contemplating her bliss, forget for a while our sorrows; my sweet and innocent sister I cannot believe that you are doomed to disappointment;" these were the thoughts that passed through the mind of Catherine, as she approached the spot that would at once realise either her hopes or her fears.

She had not apprised her sister of her arrival in London, wishing suddenly to present herself, and thus enjoy the pleased surprise she knew her visit would occasion. Yet, when she arrived at the abode of her sister, she paused an instant on the threshold. A sense of suffocation for a moment oppressed her, as the thought, fraught with sadness, crossed her mind, "If I should find her ill!" then striving to overcome her emotion, she knocked timidly at the door. The instant it was opened she inquired for her sister. There was a hesitation in the servant's manner that alarmed her already excited feelings, which the approach of Mrs. Villiers, who showed signs of having been weeping, greatly increased. Sinking on the nearest chair, for she had no longer power to support herself, Catherine, in a voice bursting with deep emotion, bade her impart to her the worst instantly.

" Ah, tell me, I beseech you, dear madam," exclaimed Catherine, " what has happened to Helen. Is she ill? I beg of you keep me not a moment longer in suspense."

" Compose yourself," returned the lady, kindly, " it is not so bad as you imagine. Helen, I trust, is quite well, but—"

" But what?" urged Catherine, tremulously. " Pray, pray, tell me all."

" Your sister clandestinely left this house, either late last night, or early this morning," replied Mrs. Villiers, " and as yet we have been unable to obtain any clue that is likely to lead to her discovery, the effect of which, you will feel assured, has been to plunge us all into the deepest distress."

" And your son," faltered Catherine, who evinced far more composure than might have been expected at this painful intelligence.

" Edward?" replied the lady, looking at her in suspicion.

" Yes, madam, your son; Helen loves him, she has herself told me as much, consequently I cannot but connect him with this unexpected conduct on the part of my sister."

Mrs. Villiers hastened to assure her that her son could not in any possible way be connected with the flight of Helen, inasmuch as he did not, and never had, intentionally encouraged her affection, but was at this very time the received lover of the Lady Grace Clavering. Still Catherine remained unconvinced. Helen was so tenderly attached to him that it was utterly impossible that she could have fled with another, and that she had willingly been induced to quit the friends to whom she was so justly dear was evident from the fact that her wardrobe had likewise been carefully removed.

" Madam," said Catherine, after she had patiently listened to the foregoing particulars, " where is your son? I must see him, and if possible, induce him to disclose to me the retreat of my sister."

Mrs. Villiers replied that he was at present from home, and reiterated her conviction that he was himself in total ignorance of Helen's movements.

" We shall see," returned Catherine; " at what hour do you expect him?"

" He is only gone," replied Mrs. Villiers, " to call upon the Lady Grace, and will undoubtedly return in an hour, at the longest."

" Since, my dear madam, you are so thoroughly convinced of your son's innocence, you will not of course, object to assist me in a little stratagem that will undoubtedly prove whether I am right or wrong in my conjecture."

Mrs. Villiers was all eagerness to assist in anything that was likely to prove her son's innocence, and begged that Catherine would at once impart to her the proposed stratagem.

" It is very simple," replied Catherine, " if you will have the kindness to furnish me with pen and ink, I will write a few lines to your son purporting to come from Helen—our writing is so much alike that he will not be able to detect the deception. Those lines you shall present to him on his return, and carefully mark the effect produced, and it will be an easy matter to confirm your own ideas on this subject, and as for the rest, leave everything to me. I require no further assistance."

Mrs. Villiers, assenting to this arrangement, placed her desk before Catherine, who, taking a pen, wrote as follows:—

" MY DEAREST EDWARD—All is discovered, and I find myself compelled instantly to quit the retreat your kindness had secured for me. As you love me, avoid that spot. I cannot enter into particulars now; neither dare I inclose my present address for fear this should fall into other hands than your own, but meet me this evening at nightfall, and all shall be explained. In haste, Ever yours, HELEN."

" P. S.—There is a retired lane close to your own residence; look for me there."

When Catherine concluded this epistle, she read it to Mrs. Villiers, and then having sealed and addressed it, gave it to her care, to deliver to her son, on his arrival home.

" Though I cannot," said that lady, " for an instant suppose that he is at all cognisant of your sister's proceeding, yet if he should determine to keep this appointment, you—"

" I shall meet him," said Catherine, " in a dress similar to that usually worn by Helen. Our height and figure are not so unlike, but that, aided by the darkness, I can contrive, for a time to pass for her, and now, my dear madam, I must, for the present, bid you farewell. You will of course make no mention of my visit to your son, let him remain in total ignorance of all; I shall await his coming this evening, at the place I have appointed; if he does not arrive, I shall call upon you again."

Thus all arranged, Catherine took her leave, and, having the entire day at her own disposal, repaired to a small cottage situated at the outskirts of London. Her heart was full of care and sorrowful anxiety; yet, as she opened the gate that led into the little garden that fronted the cottage, a smile of intense joy for a moment irradiated her countenance, and she ran with outstretched arms to meet a stout country girl, who was nursing a beautiful and blooming boy of about eight months. Taking this sweet infant from his nurse, Catherine pressed it almost convulsively to her bosom, while she showered kisses upon his downy cheek, and, bearing it into the interior of the abode, she continued for some time wholly absorbed, gazing with rapture on its infantile grace; its cheeks, its forehead, its hands, were again and again pressed rapturously to her lips, and each time apparently with renewed transport. Suddenly her brow darkened—the soft joy with which, the moment before, it had been radiant, gave place to a sterner expression—and, restoring the child to the arms of the girl, who had been gazing upon her with unfeigned surprise, she exclaimed, half aloud,—

"Now, now, my sister, I am thine again. I have been selfish enough to forget for a moment the wrongs to which you are subjected; but (turning to the girl, and averting her eyes) take the child away—I will not look upon him again till I have done my best, sweet Helen, to redress thy injuries; no more will I kiss his cheek till I have folded thee to my bosom, my own loved sister."

The mistress of the cottage, who had been apprised of Catherine's arrival by the girl, who had taken the child from the room, in obedience to her command, now entered, and began with officious civility to place refreshments before her guest, of which Catherine slightly partook, and then requested to be shown into a private apartment, where she could pass the remainder of the day undisturbed.

"You would, of course, like to have the child with you," said the woman, in a tone of inquiry.

"Oh no," returned Catherine, hastily, "keep him from my sight, I have much to think upon, and his presence would, undoubtedly, disturb my reflections."

"Oh, certainly, ma'am, just as you please. I hope you are perfectly satisfied with his appearance, I have endeavoured to act by him exactly as if he was my own, and his being, as you say, an orphan, it is but right."

"Yes, yes," interrupted Catherine, who was wearied by the woman's loquacity; "I am perfectly satisfied; he has, indeed, improved greatly, the short time he has been under your care."

"Why, to be sure, ma'am, people about here do say they never saw a child so wonderfully improved, and of course, it is a great charge for any one to undertake, let alone the expense, which is far from inconsiderable."

"I had forgotten," replied Catherine, "that I am indebted to you; let me know the amount, and I shall be happy to settle it."

"Oh dear me, I hope you did not think I was any way anxious about the trifle that was due; it will be perfectly agreeable to me, if we settle about that the next time you favour me with a visit."

"But as it is quite uncertain when I may have an opportunity of doing so again, I would rather——"

"Certainly, ma'am, if you would rather," said the woman, catching at the word, "it is, as I said before, all the same as regards myself; but as you wish it, I will bring you the little bill." And she bustled from the room, determined, as Catherine seemed so willing to pay, to swell the account as much as possible, and quickly returned bearing with her the important document, which Catherine instantly discharged, without the slightest remark, which drew a volume of thanks and curtsies from the woman.

"And now," said Catherine, "as I may not see you again for some time, I may as well leave you a trifle, that will enable you to provide all that is requisite in my absence, and mind that your care of the child does not in the least diminish."

Having thus arranged with, and dismissed her troublesome companion, Catherine was enabled to turn her thoughts exclusively to the meeting she anticipated would take place between herself and Villiers, in the evening; to learn from him, if possible, what had become of her sister, was of course the sole end and aim she hoped to accomplish, in appointing an interview with him. And though she had spoken so confidently to Mrs. Villiers of obtaining from her son the knowledge she so much desired, now that she was enabled calmly to think it over, she began much to doubt whether the young man was really implicated in the flight of Helen; in that case, she feared her sister was lost to her for ever. If he she suspected were in truth innocent, she was without the slightest clue to her recovery. And as she had herself witnessed the affectionate attentions of young Villiers to the fair lady Grace, to whom he was shortly about to be united for life, it appeared somewhat monstrous to suppose that he could be concerned in the unlooked for departure of Helen. And yet Catherine was so thoroughly convinced of the warm attachment her sister entertained for the young man, that she could not suppose it possible she had been induced to elope with another; the affair either way appeared involved in mystery, and though she hoped the evening would afford her some explanation, she at the same time feared it might only make it more inexplicable.

Trembling, therefore, with anxiety, as regarded the result, Catherine attired herself in a dress closely resembling that usually worn by her sister, and enveloping her figure in a loose cloak, she started for the appointed rendezvous.

Arriving at the spot she had indicated, she found that impatience had caused her to miscalculate the time it would consume to bring her there, and consequently she was full half an hour before her time; it was yet broad day-light, and the street thronged with pedestrians.

Oh, that long, long half hour; poor Catherine felt as though it would never pass; the street she had named in her letter, as the place of meeting, though in a close vicinity to London, yet was generally well nigh deserted after nightfall, inasmuch as it contained no public thoroughfare, but merely branched out into some fields; and people persuaded themselves it was a pretty country walk, and strongly favoured it, in the early part of the evening.

As Catherine sauntered at a slow pace up and down, she amused herself by remarking the different passengers.

An antiquated old gentleman was evidently taking his evening walk, pausing ever and anon to stare at those he chanced to meet through a gold eye-glass which he wore suspended round his neck, and through constant practice had acquired the ability of keeping it fixed to his eye without aid from his fingers.

A pretty black-eyed nursery-maid, perfectly conscious of her own attractions, was dividing attentions to her youthful charge with a respectable mechanic, who, in his fustian jacket, and basket of tools over his shoulder, she had come to meet as he returned home from his day's toil.

Presently a young ladies' school came slowly winding their way at a funeral pace, two and two, the governess, a sharp-faced old maid, bringing up the rear, frowning darkly at a young body who ventured to cast a sympathising glance towards a poor woman who, with a child on either arm, was humbly soliciting charity. Catherine noticed this, and the look of utter despondency that sat upon the face of the poor woman as they passed her without the slightest donation.

Many, doubtless, would have been willing to have given a trifle from their little hoards, but the look of withering contempt, cast upon her by their superior, froze up in their young hearts the sweet stream of charity that flows from so pure and holy a fount, and so invigorates and increases the growth of the best feelings of our nature, that it should ever be encouraged in the breast of the young.

Such thoughts as these filled the breast of Catherine as she stepped up to the suppliant, and unsolicited tendered a gift, in which she far more consulted the poverty of the receiver than the low state of her own finances, and the many claims she had already upon her own hard but small earnings. Tears filled her eyes as she received the repeated blessings of the poor woman, and witnessed hope once more sparkle in her eye as she hurried away to procure food for her starving babes.

That "it is far more precious to give than to receive" all must have felt that have ever been the means of putting, by some slight gift, new hope and happiness into another's breast. We envy not the feelings of those who can coldly pass a suppliant by, and urge in excuse the fear of imposition. Better, far better, is it to bestow a trifle upon twenty undeserving characters than to let one suffering heart appeal to our sympathies in vain. This we have never failed to press upon the minds of all those who would hold back under the selfish dread of being imposed upon.

As the time drew nigh when Catherine expected the arrival of Edward Villiers, her agitation was so excessive, that she trembled in every limb; still he came not. The shadows of evening each moment deepened; the street was nearly deserted, and now only echoed back the tread of some wayfarer, whose quickened footsteps showed his anxiety to reach his destination.

And now uprose the moon, fine and bright, shedding a soft radiance on all around, yet dark clouds gathered over its disk, and speedily obscured its brightness, leaving, from the contrast, all things in a deeper intensity of shade.

"And life," thought Catherine, "is like this fading hour, its beauty dying as we gaze. In early youth, how bright and beautiful are all one's hopes; yet how frequently do clouds obscure its glory, and leave our hearts dark and desolate."

Still he, for whom she thus patiently waited, came not, and, wearied both in body and mind, Catherine had almost resolved to quit the spot, when the figure of a man, on the opposite side of the street, arrested her intention, dropping the veil over her face and counterfeiting, as near as possible, the gait of her sister, she prepared to approach him, though far from certain it was him she expected. As they drew near each other, she observed that he cast an anxious and frenzied glance around him, and for the first time catching sight of herself, he hastened his steps, the next moment he was by her side, and the words,—

"My own dear Catherine," fell upon her ears, at the same instant he grasped her hand within his own, "God of Heaven," she uttered, with a faint scream, and, but for his supporting arm had sank fainting to the ground, for it was the touch and voice of her betrayer.

CHAPTER XV.

There's a beauty for ever unchangeably bright,
Like the long sunny lapse of a summer day's light.
Shining on, shining on, by no shadow made tender,
Till love falls asleep in its sameness of splendour.
This was not the beauty, oh, nothing like this,
That to young Nourmahal gave such magic of bliss.
But that loveliness ever in motion, which plays
Like the light upon autumn's soft shadowy days.

MARIE, whose greatest crime lay in the depths of her unalterable affection for the youthful Christopher, was conducted by Lawton to an obscure lodging house in a dull and dirty street in the neighbourhood of Paris. The house was of more than a questionable character, and kept by a wretched looking woman, whose love for money would, undoubtedly, make her a ready agent in the commission of crime.

The poor girl upon being introduced to this creature naturally shrank from her with a feeling of loathing and disgust.

Madame Chevasse (as such Lawton addressed her,) appeared tottering on the very verge of the grave; wrinkled and hideous in the extreme, there was yet a lowering brightness in her sharp, black eye, which gave token of deep cunning, and there was still a slight colour on her shrivelled cheek that strongly resembled what is frequently to be seen on a withered apple; her thick masses of grey hair seemed as though they had been uncombed for years; her brow was low and contracted, and her small twinkling eyes were shaded by large black, bushy eyebrows, the hair of which was so coarse that it stuck out like wire from the loose skin that hung all about her. It would appear that she had once been stout, but had shrunk to a complete skeleton; her hands and arms (for she wore short sleeves,) were large and long; her voice shrill and piercing; but with all these disadvantages, Madame Chevasse had not entirely neglected her personal appearance. Perched on the top of her grey hair was a small round-eared cap, of the finest lace, which was ornamented with knots of rose coloured ribbon, a petticoat of muslin, rather short, was worn beneath a gown of rich and rustling brocade, which a small hoop caused to set out stiff all round her; pink silk stockings and high-heeled shoes, in which were placed an enormous pair of gilt buckles, completed her attire.

"Madame Chevasse," said Lawton, "to your kind care I commit this young girl, and mind you provide everything necessary for her comfort. Your reward will be liberal."

"Surely, monsieur, I doubt it not," replied the old woman; "you are generous," and at the thought of the anticipated reward, she clasped her bony hands as though she already clutched the gold.

"You had better then," replied Lawton, significantly, "conduct her to her apartment;" and then turning to the young girl, "remember, Marie, you are on no account to quit this house without my knowledge."

"Oh, do not leave me here," said the poor girl; "indeed I cannot stay."

"And why not here," returned Lawton, angrily, "but there is no compulsion; you are, of course, at liberty to go where you please. You voluntarily expressed your willingness to place yourself under my care; I promised my cousin to provide a home and a suitable attendant for you; I have done so, but it appears that it does not meet your approbation; you are therefore at perfect liberty at depart."

"I feel an unaccountable dread hanging over me—I feel as if I could not breathe within these walls; it may seem folly, but I beseech of you to take me elsewhere, and you shall see how willingly I will do all that you wish."

"I am sorry, Marie," replied Lawton, coldly, "that I cannot offer you a choice of abodes.

This is the only lodging-house with the owner of which I am acquainted.   In bringing you here, I consulted only your comfort and happiness.   If it does not please you, as I said before, you must seek one for yourself."

" I think, mademoiselle," said the old woman, in a tone of voice that she meant to be kind, and to reassure Marie, but which had a decided by contrary effect, " that you are somewhat prejudiced in the strange dislike you appear to entertain for my establishment.   Allow me to ask if you have heard anything in its disfavour?"

" Oh dear no," replied Marie, who dreaded arousing the anger of the old woman.

" I thought not," returned the other, " for I can assure you I have had quite ladies under my care, and ever gave them perfect satisfaction," laying great stress upon the adjective.

" Well, Marie," said Lawton, who had folded his arms, and affected to be waiting patiently her determination, " what course do you propose to pursue?   I have told you how anxious Christopher is for the welfare of his expected child, and the great probability, if it survives, of his marrying yourself, and legally becoming its father; and that is the only reason for his wishing me to place you under the superintendance of a person for whose faith I could vouch, and who would assuredly do justice to you both.   If you determine to seek an asylum for yourself, urging the frivolous excuse that my choice did not please you, it will, undoubtedly, arouse suspicions in his mind as to the truth of your statement regarding an expected infant.   It is such an easy matter to procure a child that you may pass for your own, and, moreover, such deception has been so frequently practised, that ——"

" Stop, stop," said the girl, whose simplicity made her an easy victim to the artfulness of Lawton's speech.   " You know this lady?" she added, after an instant's hesitation.

" Oh, certainly, ma'mselle," interposed the woman, with a satirical smile; " you surely do not suppose, after what Mr. Lawton has said about marriage, that he would place you under the care of a person of whom he knew nothing; but," turning to Lawton, " really the young lady seems so strangely averse to myself, that I would rather decline having anything to do with her."

The heart of Marie began to rejoice at these words, but it was instantly quelled by Lawton, who replied, with a sinister curl of his lip,—

" If the young lady consents, you will take her, madame."

" She manifests so very strange a dislike towards me, that ——"

" You'll take her, madame," interrupted Lawton, with a shrug of the shoulders.   " Think of the reward."

" Ah! you said, I think, the reward should be liberal;" and the eyes of the old woman rolled greedily; " and, if I accept the care of ma'mselle under the present peculiar circumstances, it ought to be liberal."

" It shall," replied Lawton, laconically.

" Then, ma'mselle, you consent to remain with me.   I am sure you will be very happy—indeed, it will be your own fault if you are not."

Still the young girl hesitated, and, much as she disliked Lawton, drew closer to his side, as the old woman approached a step or two nearer the spot where she stood.

" Marie," said Lawton, " I perceive you do not feel satisfied; and, as it is far from my wish to persuade you against your own inclination, I will return, and inform Christopher that you prefer choosing your own residence.   Madame, therefore, I wish you good day, and trust you will pardon this unnecessary intrusion."

" Certainly, monsieur; if this young lady cannot make herself happy with me, I would much rather not undertake the charge of her."

" But will Christopher be as willing to do justice to myself and his child, and to provide for our wants, in a more cheerful and healthy neighbourhood?"

" I am sure, ma'mselle, you are the first person that has ever found fault with this neighbourhood.   I have lived here for upwards of thirty years, and never had as much as a day's illness the whole time."

" The place is healthy enough, madame, but Marie does not like it, and we are only wasting your time by remaining here.   Come, Marie, you had better go at once."

" But you have not answered my question as to whether Christopher will provide for me elsewhere."

" Scarcely so," replied Lawton; " he delegated to me the task of finding you suitable lodgings, which I have done, and you ——"

" Stay," interrupted the girl, and her voice faltered, " I have no choice—I must consent to abide here."

" There is no compulsion, ma'mselle," said the woman.

" None at all," re-echoed Lawton; " but if you decide to remain, you must distinctly understand, Marie, that you cannot quit this house till your health is thoroughly established."

"I have said I will consent, but for Christopher's sake alone. Tell him this, and perhaps it may be the means of inducing him to regard me more tenderly. If," she continued, "I live to quit this roof, I shall hasten that instant to his side."

"If you live to quit this house, ma'mselle!" said the woman, with apparent indignation. "I see no reason why you should not do so; I never yet undertook the care of a person who did not recover, and who did not likewise leave this house, thanking me for the kind attention I had bestowed upon her during her residence with me."

"And so will Marie," said Lawton; "it is only for want of knowing you better that she at

present entertains a slight prejudice against you; but, when you are more intimately acquainted, it will speedily vanish, take my word for it."

"I hope so, monsieur," replied the old woman in a doubtful tone—"I hope so, indeed."

"As you have resolved to remain here, Marie, you had better allow Madame Chevasse to conduct you to your apartments, where I hope you will find everything arranged to your satisfaction; and if the neighbourhood is not altogether so lively as you might desire, your stay being only for a limited period will, I hope, induce you to bear it cheerfully."

No. 7.

"I will endeavour to do so," replied the girl. "Convey, I beseech of you, to Christopher my fondest love; tell him that he will never for an instant be absent from my thoughts, and ——"

She could say no more, but, burying her face in her handkerchief to conceal her rising emotion, she followed Madame Chevasse from the room. As they did so, Lawton seated himself, having first exchanged a glance with the old woman, to the effect that he would await her return.

The house was large, roomy, and old-fashioned, but was sadly out of repair, and evidently fast sinking to decay. The stairs, up which Madame Chevasse and Marie proceeded, creaked under their feet; the walls were festooned with cobwebs, and everything looked dark and dirty. At length they reached the top of the staircase, and a number of rooms appeared to branch off in all directions; and the doors, all of which were close shut, were numbered, after the fashion of an inn. A narrow landing led right and left. Madame Chevasse turned to the right, and opened a door numbered twenty, and which Marie naturally supposed to be the room she was destined to occupy; great was her surprise, therefore, at perceiving an exceedingly narrow spiral staircase, up which her conductor proceeded to ascend. The girl hesitated a moment, and then, feeling she had gone too far to retreat, prepared to follow. The loud and constant creaking of the stairs jarred painfully on her ears, rendered still more so from the fact that they were in entire darkness, and the stairs, which they still kept ascending, seemed but to gather, as they wound, yet greater density of shade. Their progress was, after a few minutes, stopped by a door, and Madame Chevasse drew a key from her pocket, and applied it to the lock, in which it turned, with a rusty disagreeable sound, and Madame Chevasse entered, closely followed by Marie, who was oppressed with a vague sense of fear, which was somewhat relieved by the appearance of the room being more cheerful than she expected.

It was very large, and the floor thickly carpeted, so that it gave back not the slightest sound to their tread; the furniture was but simple, comprising merely a few chairs, a dressing-table and glass, and an old-fashioned bedstead. Two windows lighted this apartment, which were closely shaded by crimson curtains. At the farther end of this room there was a door, which Madame Chevasse opened, and bade Marie enter. She did so, and found herself in a room considerably smaller than the one she had left. A round table stood in the centre, on which were scattered some books; a small work-box, of exquisite workmanship, and richly inlaid, was likewise placed on the table. Marie noticed, too, that most of the books were elegantly bound, and the modern appearance of them contrasted strangely with the old-fashioned rooms and furniture in which they had found a resting place.

"Well, ma'mselle," said the old woman, as Marie returned to the outer room, "I hope these apartments please you."

Marie replied in a faint affirmative.

"Here are books, you see," resumed Madame Chevasse, "if you are fond of reading; and I shall be happy to give you as much of my company as you may desire."

"I have not as yet made any preparation for my expected infant," said Marie, trying to assume a cheerful tone, "and shall therefore be glad to employ myself with my needle if you will have the goodness to furnish me with the necessary materials."

"You are at liberty to amuse yourself in any manner you think fit, ma'mselle," returned the other. "If you do not object to being left alone, for a short time, there are a few matters that require my presence below, but rest assured I will soon return." Saying which, Madame Chevasse turned from the room, closing the door behind her.

Marie listened in profound silence till the last faint echo of her retreating steps had died away, and then, with a feeling of deep despondency, she walked towards the windows; but they commanded no better prospect than a vast range of chimnies, and the roofs of other buildings; she next opened the door of the room, and groped her way down the spiral staircase, determined to take advantage of the absence of Madame Chevasse, to discover, if possible, who inhabited the number of rooms she had passed below.

"There may be some persons," thought Marie, "whose company I may find more agreeable than that old woman, for whom I already entertain a settled dislike." But, alas! when she reached the bottom of the stairs, she found, to her deep regret, that the door at the bottom was strongly secured, so that it resisted all her efforts to open it.

"Alas!" exclaimed Marie, as she again entered the room, and threw herself upon one of the chairs, "I am a prisoner, and God only knows whether I may ever quit this place."

A feeling of utter distraction at the thought came over her, and in a few moments she buried her face in her hands, and wept aloud.

Marie, we have said, was lovely, and her beauty was of that soft and changing kind, which varied with every thought and feeling of her breast. Hers was not that cold, regulated beauty, which gives the possessor the appearance of having been chiselled out of marble, but of that warm, expressive character which never wearies the eye with the sameness of its loveliness. And now, when she again lifted her face from her clasped hands, to gaze once more round the room, hope again shone in her beaming countenance, and the dark of her eye at once took a darker, a heavenlier dye;

> "And her short passing sorrow
> But seemed to awaken
> New beauty, like flowers that are
> Sweetest when shaken;"

and pleasing herself with the thought of the joy she should experience when, with her as yet unborn babe, she should quit that gloomy house, and hasten to the side of him whom she so fondly loved, to present to him their child, the sight of which, she hoped, would induce him to make her his wife, and perchance love her more, she dried her tears, and resolved to make the best of the circumstances in which she was placed.

CHAPTER XVI.

> "'Twas his own voice—she could not err—
>   Throughout the breathing world's extent
> There was but one such voice for her,
>   So kind, so soft, so eloquent;
> Oh! sooner shall the rose of May
>   Mistake her own sweet nightingale,
> And to some meaner minstrel lay,
>   Open her bosom's glowing veil,
> Than love shall ever doubt a tone,
> A breath of the beloved one."

POOR Catherine was so utterly overpowered by her feelings, that for the time she seemed to have lost the faculty of speech, and she could only gaze upon the intruder, as if doubtful of the evidence of her own senses; so wholly unlooked for, was this unpropitious meeting; but the voice of the earl recalled her at once to a sense of their respective situations; his tones breathed forth the same soft melodious strain that had so often entranced her listening ear, but, for one brief moment only, they possessed the same power to charm her. Now the magic spell that he had wove in such sweet enchantment over her young affections was broken; the veil that had concealed all his duplicity was rent asunder, and she knew him now, not as her fond and tender lover, but as the deceiver and ruthless destroyer of her first pure dream of love.

Oh! had she died ere she awoke to a sense of his cruelty, she had indeed been blessed.

> "Alas! and could no other arm be found
> Than the one which once embraced her,
> To inflict a careless wound."

"My own Catherine," murmured the earl, as she endeavoured to free herself from his grasp "I love you with the same devotedness as ever. Oh! what have I not endured, by your coldness and disdain."

"This is language to which I cannot listen," said Catherine indignantly; "could my eyes convey one half the feelings of my breast, their glance would wither and destroy you."

There was something in the noble bearing of Catherine, and the cold proud flashing of her dark eye, plainly visible even amidst the shades of evening, that caused the earl involuntarily to drop her hand and draw a step or two back.

"You are wealthy," continued Catherine, in a tone of excitement, "and that is sufficient as the world goes, (though with shame be it said) to place you above the punishment you so well merit. I am poor, and must submit without a murmur to the cruel wrongs you have inflicted upon me. Who would give the lightest attention to ought that was urged against the honour and unsullied escutcheon of the rich Earl of Clavering, by the humble and dependent Catherine Montravers."

She ceased, but every word she had uttered found a quick and truthful echo in the young man's breast; his eye quailed before her indignant glance, and for the first time he began to regard his conduct towards her (as in truth it was) as base and selfish.

"Catherine," he began, in a low, and gentle tone, "had I loved you less, I had not given you occasion thus to reproach me. I loved, I do love you as——"

"As men can only love," she interrupted bitterly; "with a cold unfeeling selfish passion, that heeds not the sufferings and persecution to which it exposes the unfortunate object who may serve for a time to please the eye and captivate the heart; to offer such love for acceptance to woman's heart is an utter profanation of its sacredness."

" You judge me too harshly. Catherine,—you do, indeed; not as you describe it, is my love for you."

" I have done," said Catherine, " it is worse than useless for me to waste the time that is so precious to me, bandying words with you. I would shun your very presence, for of you I have nothing to expect, or to request; there is another with whom I have an account to settle."

" Oh," she exclaimed, starting with surprise, as she observed a dark figure just visible in the distance, " by Heaven here he comes, and I must compose my ruffled spirit, and meet him with kind and tender words. Now, sir," she added, turning towards the earl, " if you feel any interest for your sister's future happiness, be a silent witness to all that passes between me and Mr. Edward Villiers."

" Villiers, the betrothed husband of Grace," exclaimed the earl, in surprise. " You come not here purposely to meet him this evening."

" Indeed, sir, I did," replied Catherine, " for I have a sister as well as yourself, whose interest is as dear, aye, perchance dearer, to my heart than the lady Grace is to your own; but Mr. Villiers must not find me engaged in converse with another : remain here while I go forward to meet him, and fear not that I will afford you an ample opportunity of hearing all that passes between us."

Saying which she walked quietly on.

" By St. George," exclaimed the earl, " this grows interesting," as he observed the unmistakeable figure of Edward Villiers approach Catherine, and taking her hand in his own, carry it warmly to his lips. " The conceited puppy," he muttered, " and to pretend to be in love with Grace,—bah !—I can understand it, titles find great favour in the ears of persons who have never been accustomed to mix with rank and station; Edward Villiers married to the Lady Grace Clavering, sounds uncommonly fine, I have no doubt, in the atmosphere of the east."

At this moment Edward approached, with Catherine leaning on his arm, and the earl instantly assumed a listening attitude.

" My sweet Helen," he heard him say, " ever since the receipt of your letter I have been harrassed with the most distressing anxiety on your behalf. I thought the apartments I had provided for you at Hampstead were too far removed to be so soon and so easily discovered. You were perfectly right to communicate with me instantly. I had fully proposed to join you this evening, and had calculated upon the happiness of spending a few days with you alone. I was fully prepared with an excuse for being absent from town, and this morning took leave of the Lady Grace ; but this little affair shall not my dear girl, disappoint me of my promised happiness, although the hour is late, it will yet be easy to procure other apartments."

Catherine in a low voice expressed a wish to be furnished with the address of the apartments at Hampstead, alleging that she wished to send for a box, that in the hurry of departure had been overlooked, and that her stay there had been so short, that—

" I remember," interrupted her companion, " that you had not an opportunity of learning the exact spot, it being dark at the time of our arrival ; but I think I wrote the address upon a card for my own convenience, feeling assured that I should have occasion to write to you."

As he spoke, the young man drew a card from his pocket, and presented it to Catherine, who grasped it with the most intense eagerness, and then made some allusion to Edward's marriage with Grace.

" Let not that cause you a moment's uneasiness," replied the other, " my heart and affections will ever be all your own ; my marriage to the Lady Grace Clavering——"

" Will never take place," exclaimed the earl, rushing from his place of concealment, and confronting the two, with a lurid eye, and lowering brow.

" Ah !" exclaimed the young man, completely bewildered by the suddenness of the other's appearance. " I am betrayed ; this is a planned thing, Helen !" turning to Catherine, who had relinquished his arm, and now stood a little in advance of himself ; she turned round as he spoke, and throwing aside her veil, displayed to his astonished gaze, not the small pretty features of Helen, but the high, commanding, yet handsome face of her sister, whose raven ringlets, now pushed back from her flushed brow, and the cold yet triumphant glance of her black eye, spoke volumes.

With an impatient movement, the young man dashed his hand across his eyes, as if doubtful whether he saw aright; but there she stood, and near her the brother of his affianced bride. It was no deception, all was dread, stern reality; and with the conviction of this, came alas, the agonising thought, that he must relinquish for ever all hope of ever gaining the so coveted hand of Grace; he must resign it, now that it was all but won. And, alas! the thought fraught with soul-felt anguish, that he had himself alone to blame for all, that he was the victim only of his own sin, made his very brain dizzy, and he felt tottering on the verge of madness.

There was a momentous and painful silence of a few moments, which the earl was the first to break.

"I thank you, Catherine," he said, "for having thus opened my eyes to the real character of the man whom I was about to receive as the husband of my sister. Good God!" he added, with more warmth, "Providence must surely have guided my steps here to-night."

"Do not for a moment suppose that Providence troubles itself so much with your affairs," said Catherine, smiling sarcastically.

And it really did seem very much like Satan reproving sin, to hear a man who had been guilty of exactly the same crime himself, thus bitterly apostrophising another.

"My errand is accomplished," added Catherine, after an instant's silence. "I have discovered the retreat of my sister, and shall hasten immediately to her side, poor girl; she greatly needs a sister's love and sympathy."

"Stay," said Villiers, recovering in a slight degree his composure, as Catherine expressed her inclination to depart. "Give me back the card; you obtained it through falsehood and duplicity, and have therefore no right to keep it, so give it me back."

"Never," said Catherine, firmly, "no matter how I obtained it. Stand off," she exclaimed, it from her by force. "It would be dangerous to touch me now. I heeded not the injuries I have myself received," glancing at the earl, "but, Helen, thy wrongs are amply avenged." in a tone that arrested his footsteps, as he approached with the apparent determination of taking

And with a smile of triumph, she turned away.

"Ay, she is indeed avenged," said Villiers, "for God in heaven knows that I never loved any but Grace."

"Name her not," said the earl, "henceforth you are strangers to each other; yet, flatter not yourself that your conduct will be allowed to go unpunished; expect to hear from me to-morrow."

"You will find me perfectly willing to respond to your call, if you do not think differently of this affair when your blood has had time to cool, but resign my pretensions to the hand of Lady Grace, unless she herself (which I cannot believe) expressed a desire for me to do so, I never will."

"Your insolence by no means surprises me," continued the earl; "but my sister's happiness shall never be sacrificed at the shrine of your inordinate ambition; but words are useless; blood alone can wipe out the dishonour you have put upon my sister, and till we meet to settle this affair as such affairs only can be settled, I wish you good day."

And filled with anger and disdain at the conduct of Villiers, the earl wended his way towards a fashionable club-house in St. James's. And strange as it may appear, it is nevertheless the fact, that in venting the spleen the affront Villiers had put upon his sister occasioned, it never occurred to him that his own conduct towards Edith and Catherine was equally as culpable; truly some persons have acquired a knack of stifling conscience, till at length its still, small voice ceases to make itself heard.

CHAPTER XVII.

"With linked hands, for unrepelled
Had Helen taken Rosalind's;
Like the autumn wind, when it unbinds
The tangled locks of the nightshade's hair,
Which is twined in the sultry summer air
Round the walls of an outworn sepulchre,
Did the voice of Helen, sad and sweet,
And the sound of her heart that ever beat,
As with sighs, and words she breathed on her,
Unbind the knots of her friend's despair,
Till her thoughts were free to float and flow,
And from her labouring bosom now,
Like the bursting of a prisoned flame,
The voice of a long-pent sorrow came."

WITH the card she had received from Villiers, still firmly grasped in her hand, as a treasure that she dreaded to lose, Catharine hastened her steps towards a spot where she knew she should be able to procure a vehicle that would convey her to Hampstead; self for the time was entirely forgotten, every thought and desire was given to her sister.

The evening was considerably advanced, and the hour that she had promised to return to Mrs. Porter's was already gone by, but this never once entered the mind of Catherine, so entirely was she engrossed with the absent Helen. Long and tedious was the journey, that would otherwise have been short and pleasant, and when after the lapse of an hour, she alighted at Hampstead, from the conveyance that had brought her thus far, she found considerable difficulty (from being an entire stranger to the neighbourhood,) in finding her way to that part where her sister resided.

After some time had thus been consumed, Catherine succeeded in reaching the spot she so much desired; she glanced cautiously in at the window of the little cottage to which the card she still retained in her hand had directed her, before she ventured to make her coming known to the inmates; the curtain was drawn, but not so closely as to prevent Catherine obtaining a glance within. The room was small, but neatly and prettily furnished; a snow white cloth was spread over a small round table that stood in the centre of the room, on which was placed refreshment; two chairs were likewise drawn towards the table, as if in readiness for the evening meal, but the room was vacant.

As Catherine thus stood peeping in between the half-closed curtain, the room-door opened and a young girl entered, her back was turned towards her, yet from her figure she felt at once convinced it was her sister; she seated herself, and seemed endeavouring to beguile the time with a book, which she held in her hand, yet frequently raised her eye from its pages to fix them on a time-piece that stood on a sideboard close by, and each time apparently with increased anxiety.

" Alas !" thought Catherine, "poor Helen, she loves him, and even now expects his coming; how can I break to her the painful intelligence that they must meet no more; how tell her that he is the promised husband of another. Unhappy girl, what arts he must have used to induce you to quit all that were near and dear to you, that you might fly with him."

Presently the young girl threw down her book, rose, and left the room. Catherine still retained her station at the window; she seemed rooted to the spot, and waited with extreme impatience the return of her sister, when she resolved to make her presence known.

In another instant the street door opened, and the girl she had seen in the parlour stepped out upon the threshold, and endeavoured to penetrate the surrounding gloom. Catherine could contain herself no longer, but springing forward, pronounced the name of " Helen;" the other started back with surprise, and then recovering herself, in a voice wholly unknown, inquired her errand.

" Alas !—alas !" said Catherine, ready to sink from exhaustion and disappointment, " you are not my sister !"

The young girl regarded Catherine with unsuppressed amazement, but, with ready sympathy for her apparent distress, begged her to compose herself, and acquaint her with the name of the person whom she desired to see.

With the necessity for renewed exertion, Catherine's natural strength of mind returned, and apologising for the unseasonable intrusion, she briefly acquainted her hearer with the fact of her having just arrived from London on a visit to her sister, on business which admitted of no delay; and from the card (which she presented to the girl) she conceived that to be the house in which her sister resided; and from her height and figure being similar, she had unwittingly taken her for the sister she so earnestly longed to see.

The young girl glanced momentarily at the card, and then smilingly informed Catherine that the mistake was easily explained; the place she sought, though some little distance from thence bore a name but slightly differing in sound, so that to a person unacquainted (as Catherine was with the two places, the mistake was by no means surprising.

The heart of Catherine grew lighter at this intelligence, and with thanks for the other's kindness, begged to be directed to the abode of her sister.

" The road is across fields," replied the stranger, " which renders it very dull to traverse at so late an hour, especially alone. I would strongly advise you to tarry till the morning; a few hours would make but little difference."

" Pardon me," returned Catherine, " my anxiety to see my sister admits of no longer delay than will suffice to bring me to her. If you will have the goodness therefore to point out the nearest road, you will confer an additional obligation."

" It is unfortunate," replied the other, " that my brother is from home; but I am momentarily expecting his arrival, and I am assured that he would be happy to accompany you."

With many and warm expressions of thanks Catherine declined the kind offer, for she shrank from the very thought of being accompanied by an entire stranger; and receiving full and plain instructions from the stranger as to the route it was right for her to pursue, with renewed hop she started again in pursuit of her sister.

An hour's fast walking along dull and dreary roads, or across still more dreary and deserted fields, brought Catherine within sight of her destination; and this time she resolved to seek admittance without a moment's delay. Buoyed up with the delightful anticipation of soon again beholding her beloved Helen, Catherine was unconscious of fatigue. Under other circumstances the natural timidity of her sex would have induced her to conceive it impossible to traverse the streets at that late hour alone, and entirely unattended; and being but slightly accustomed to walking, she would doubtless have been so overpowered by fatigue as to utterly incapacitate her from accomplishing the journey. And yet now, as we have said, she was conscious of no weariness nor exhaustion, either of body or mind. It is truly astonishing how much a woman can endure—with what patience and fortitude she can triumph over what might appear insurmountable difficulties, in order to accomplish some noble or darling object.

A man may weary in the pursuit of what he even most ardently desires—may fold his hands and sit down in despair, as he views the thorns and briers that start up between himself and the object of his dearest wishes—may be beguiled from his pursuit by other thoughts and other hopes; his eager hand, outstretched to grasp the rose, may perchance be arrested by the gaudy colours of the tulip, and he may forget its soft perfume, and coldly pass it by.

It is well possible for a man to do all this, but a woman never; forgetful of her sex's weakness and delicacy, or remembering only to triumph over it all, she never wearies or relaxes her exertion while her object is unattained; nought can for an instant even beguile her thoughts, much less her steps from the accomplishment of her hopes. Amid all difficulties, trials, and bewilderments, there is but one way left her—on; when her end is attained, she may sink from exhaustion, but while she is in pursuit, self and all feelings appertaining to self are entirely forgotten.

Thus it was with Catherine. When she knocked timidly at the door, and falteringly inquired for her sister, and learnt that she was indeed beneath that roof, that she had at length reached the goal she so ardently desired, she instantly became sensible of her over extreme lassitude, consequent upon the fatigue she had undergone, mentally as well as bodily; her voice failed, and it was with difficulty, she desired that Helen should immediately be apprised of her visit. And when the messenger returned, and requested her to walk into the little parlour, where her sister would be happy to see her, she felt scarcely capable of doing so.

Instantly that she entered, Helen, who was very pale, and her eyes red with weeping, closed the door, and then, turning to her sister, threw her arms tenderly round her neck, as she exclaimed, "Catherine, love, pardon me, had I followed the dictates of my heart, the moment I heard your name I should have run to embrace you, but you will forgive me dear, this seeming coldness."

Catherine folded her affectionately to her bosom, as she replied in a tone that sounded slightly like reproach in her sister's ears,—

"Alas, Helen! after so long and painful an absence, is it thus we meet? how different to what my fond imagination pictured."

"Catherine," returned Helen, in an affectionate yet firm voice, "I have sinned deeply, almost unpardonably, in quitting the kind friends with whom you placed me, without even informing you, my own dear sister, of my intention; but I know your kind heart, you will forgive me, dear," and she pressed a kiss upon her cheek.

"Dear Helen," replied Catherine, bitterly, as a sense of her own sins pressed heavily upon her heart. "However deeply you may have sinned, it is not for me to blame."

There was a short pause; the sisters were still clasped in each other's arms, but painful thoughts filled the heart of each. Helen was the first to speak.

"Catherine," she said in a low but earnest voice, "I know not how, nor by what means you contrived to discover my retreat; wait a minute, love," she added, seeing Catherine was about to speak, "I was saying, I know not how you discovered my abode, but I cannot do otherwise than connect your sudden appearance here with the absence of him whom I fully expected thi evening."

"You are right," said Catherine, as Helen paused for her reply, "for the moment I was made acquainted with your flight, I was assured that to Edward Villiers alone it was attributable, and by the use of justifiable deception gained your address from him."

"And he," said Helen, inquiringly.

"You must never see him again, love," replied Catherine, gently.

"Oh, my sister, you know not how dearly I love him."

"I know it all, but it is a painful truth, though necessity requires that you should hear it Helen, he neither loves nor cares for you."

"He loves me," replied Helen firmly, "dearer than ought else on earth; he has repeated assured me so."

Catherine shook her head as she answered,—

"All the love that he has to bestow, is given to the Lady Grace."

"You mistake," said her sister, quickly. "I heard that he was about to be married to Lady Grace Clavering, having engaged himself before he knew of my love for him, but now he has resolved all hazards to decline the intended match, in order that he may link his fate with mine; and surely, sister," she continued warmly, "this generosity on his part required a little sacrifice of mine, and therefore I consented to elope with him, though I knew it was wrong, but then I trusted, as his wife, even you, my dear sister, would pardon and forgive me."

"But, my love," replied Catherine, kindly, "he has not married you."

"Not yet," said Helen, eagerly; "he only conducted me here this morning, and left me instantly, promising to be with me again this evening, and arrange for our marriage to take place to-morrow."

A feeling of intense joy shot through the heart of Catherine at these words—a joy so pure and holy that it more than repaid all the anxiety and suffering she had endured on behalf of this treasured sister; yet, sweet and extatic as were her feelings, they for a moment choked her utterance; but, when she did speak, it was in a soft and musical voice, as, bending on her sister a look of tender love, she said,—

"Then you are still my own pure, innocent Helen."

"Alas, Catherine," she replied, in a tone of reproach, "is it possible that you for a moment doubted it? Oh, my sister, I could not thus rest in your almost maternal arms, were I otherwise than innocent. I could not thus unblushingly meet your reproving eye, were I guilty of aught; but, having quitted the kind friends with whom you placed me, oh, say, Catherine, say that you believe me innocent."

"I do, I do," said Catherine, holding her convulsively to her bosom, and, bending down to kiss her cheek, she sobbed and wept aloud. Helen could only strain her to her heart, and mingle tears with hers.

Oh, beautiful and holy is sisterly affection; sweet the ties that bind their hearts as one—their interests as inseparable; the memory of early, happy days, of one blest home, where gathered round the parent hearth, and shielded by a parent's love from every ill, they "discoursed sweet music," and painted future days of mutual bliss, in colours far too bright ever to be realised! Oh, such memories as these cling round the heart, and render sisterly affection pure and unsullied as the snow when 'tis driven—as the one bright well springing up amid the many dark streams of the heart, and making them more fresh and pure from its presence.

Nothing can alter or efface a sister's love—all others may, and frequently do, wither and decay, but a sister's affection is ever the same.

> "Sweetest ties that bind together
> Father, mother, sister, brother;
> Sad, indeed, that they should sever,
> Who, loving once, must love for ever."

Catherine had borne up bravely till this moment. She had shed no tear; though harassed with the most distressing doubts and anxieties—though worn down with her own sorrows, and beset with trials on every side—yet this could not wring even a solitary tear from her eye. The sweet source from which that precious relief flows, to moisten the parched feelings of the breast seemed dried up within her; but now they gushed forth, large and bright, while hope, sparkling in her eye, betokened them no longer to be tears of sorrow, but sacred only to the purest feelings of tender sisterly affection.

CHAPTER XVIII.

> "Oh, love, what is it, in this world of ours,
>   Which makes it fatal to be lov'd? Ah, why
> With cypress branches hast thou wreath'd thy bowers,
>   And made thy best interpreter a sigh?
> As those who dote on colours pluck the flowers,
>   And place them on their breast—but place to die—
> Thus the frail beings we would fondly cherish
> Are laid within our bosoms but to perish."

EDITH passed a sad and solitary morning; the certainty that her cousin had given his hand to her, while his heart and affections were bestowed upon another, forced the burning tears in torrents from her eyes. Alas! poor Edith was unformed for sorrow—totally unfitted to bear misfortune. Hitherto her life had been one continual sunshine of happiness; she had never known a wish that remained ungratified. Beloved and idolised by the little circle in which she moved, all of whom were anxious to shield her gentle bosom from even the semblance of care, she had unconsciously so leant on them for kindness and support, that she felt, in a measure, incapacited for acting without their advice and assistance. Never, indeed, had she done so; and, now that sorrow had touched her young heart to its very core, she naturally experienced a

strong and ardent desire to open the secret source of her grief to the light-hearted, yet warm and affectionate Grace. But no; that sweet and sure consolation was denied her—she would not, could not, impart to Grace what must reflect shame and unkindness on her brother.

And Grace, too, was so blest in the prospect of her own approaching marriage with him she so fondly loved, that it would be cruel to make her a participator of her anguish. So Edith bowed her head, and wept anew, as she felt that she must forget the blessing she so yearned after—sympathy, and must lock up all her sorrows in the secret recesses of her own mind.

As the dinner hour approached, Edith felt the necessity of endeavouring to calm her feelings, and removing the traces of sorrow from her countenance, strove to meet her husband with the sweet and happy smile that ever welcomed his return.

No. 8.

"He is unhappy," she murmured to herself; "and I alone the unwilling cause; more need, then, that I should strive, by love and tenderness, to banish his gloom."

Filled with such thoughts as these, Edith descended to the dining-room, but, to her surprise, found it vacant, and on inquiring of the servant, learned that the earl had not yet returned.

Edith walked towards the window, and gazed eagerly upon every passenger, each moment half fancying she caught a glimpse of his well-known figure. While thus employed, she was joined by Grace, who came tripping into the room with her usual light elastic step, and the sight of whose bright and happy countenance, somewhat reassured the trembling heart of Edith.

"I am afraid I have been the means of delaying dinner a few minutes," said Edith, drawing a chair towards the table.

"Come, Edith, we must, it appears, dispense with ceremony this morning."

"Had we not better wait a little longer?" replied Edith, gently. "Arthur——"

"Is not returned," interrupted Grace. "I know what you would say, my dear, but if the question is put to the ballot, I shall certainly throw all my influence against another moment's delay."

"I thought," said Edith, "he might think——"

"It is not, my dear, what he may think," replied Grace, laughing; "but what two ladies may be supposed to think, who are not only treated with the indignity of being left to dine alone, but are absolutely likewise kept in suspense as to his intention of returning."

"He promised to meet me at dinner," said Edith, still hesitating.

"I see," replied Grace, in the same lively strain, "that I shall be obliged to take your place for to-day; come, my dear, which shall I send, soup or fish?"

Edith had but little appetite, and as far as she was concerned, the dinner was sent away almost untasted. When the cloth was removed and the servant had withdrawn, Grace began to rally her sister on her evident depression of spirits, and for which, as far as she was aware, the sole cause lay in her husband's absence.

"Really, Edith," she began, "I am positively inclined to scold you."

"What for?" inquired Edith with a sigh.

"Why, my dear, for the ostensible reason that you are silly enough to allow the unlooked-for absence of your husband to infect you with sad and gloomy thoughts. Now I feel assured that you are mentally engaged in running over the whole catalogue of accidents, ready to fix upon the most fearful as having befallen Arthur, and all forsooth because he is an hour or so beyond the time he promised to return."

Edith tried to smile at the lively remarks of her companion, as she replied that it was the first time he had ever broken his promise.

"Well," urged Grace, "granting that, you know there must be a first time. For my part, I am resolved never to keep dinner waiting a moment, my husband of course knows at what hour it is in readiness; and if he is not within at the time appointed, I shall of course conclude that he had made some other engagement, and dine without him."

"But suppose," cried Edith, "that he was unexpectedly detained, he would think it unkind when he returned to find that you had not thought it worth while to wait a short time."

"I do not think so," replied Grace; "on the contrary, he would be far more likely to be displeased with the reproachful appearance of cold dinner, vexed servants; and sad serious countenance of his wife, all of which have been waiting his arrival Heaven knows how long. If I were a man, such a set out would annoy me far more than the trifling circumstance of dinner having been taken in my absence."

And so far we are inclined to think Grace was perfectly correct in her opinion. Many wives from a feeling of mistaken kindness, often disarrange the entire household by delaying dinner, in the anticipation of the return of their absent lords, who, more often than not, are dining elsewhere, and are far from pleased on their return to be told how long their presence has been expected, and how spoilt the dinner was in consequence. And even if nothing is said, it looks like reproaching them, for, perchance, unavoidable absence, to see all waiting with anxious faces their arrival as the signal for dinner. It is far better as a general rule to have it served at the regular hour, let who will be absent.

As the evening sped on, Edith grew still more sad and thoughtful: and proportionately disinclined for conversation. It was passed over almost in silence, and Edith stole many and anxious glances at her watch.

Grace had been for some time yawning over a book, from which she strove in vain to extract amusement; she began to feel vexed at her brother's protracted stay from home, inasmuch as it caused uneasiness in the heart of Edith, and she inwardly determined that when she became the wife of Edward Villiers, dearly as she loved him, and much as she prized his company, to allow him the same liberty he enjoyed, now that he was single, to go and come when he pleased, and she expressed herself to this effect to Edith.

"Depend upon it, my dear," she remarked, "men greatly value liberty of action, and it appears to me right and proper they should possess it."

"Very likely," replied Edith, "yet methinks if I had a fond caged dove, I would not let it pine; and Grace, if your husband loved you, would you not regard it as but sorry proof if he quitted your society for others."

"Men are differently constituted," returned Grace, "and therefore I regard it as no want of love on their part to occasionally desire other society; therefore, when Edward informed me, this morning, of his wish to spend a few days previous to our marriage in the country, whither he was invited to join a friend in a shooting excursion, I did not, as many silly girls perhaps would have done, pout and look displeased; but warmly expressed a wish that he might enjoy himself, and hastened his departure; so that he has gone happy and pleased with my willing assent to his proposition."

"I hope," said Edith tremblingly, "that he loves you in sincerity and truth; how dreadful to discover, when too late to change, that some motive you cannot fathom induced him to offer you his hand, while another possessed his heart."

"I will not wrong him, by entertaining, for one moment even, so unkind a supposition," replied Grace warmly.

"Pardon me, dear Grace," murmured Edith, "for entreating you well to consider the subject; there are so many reasons that might act as inducements on his part to the match; for instance, your rank and station in society are so far above his own, that——"

"Edith," interrupted Grace, "I can forgive anything, no matter what, that is said by you, but none other should dare even to breathe a word in the strain you have just now spoken; if they did, they would soon bitterly repent it."

"You are not angry, Grace," said Edith kindly, and drawing her chair closer to her sister's.

"Not with you, Edith; it were impossible I could be angry or offended with you," and she laid strong emphasis on the personal pronoun, "though I cannot conceive what Mr. Villiers has done or said to excite so strange a prejudice in your mind against him."

"You mistake, Grace," said Edith quickly, "I believe him all my warmest wishes could desire, and not the slightest prejudice against him does exist in my breast. I only wished you to act warily in this matter, for fear he should love you less than you imagined."

"A very wise and proper caution," said the earl, speaking as he entered the room; they both started at the sound of his voice, not being aware of his return, and Edith ran to greet him, with tears of mingled joy and sorrow.

"What ails you, Edith?" inquired the earl, perceiving her emotion; "are you unwell?" Grace answered for her.

"Edith," she said, "has been rather uneasy at your protracted stay from home—a thing so unusual that it is scarcely surprising that it should have excited her fears in your behalf."

"If that is all," replied her brother, "I can scarcely think it otherwise than childish. What tears, my love!" he exclaimed, as the gentle-hearted Edith bowed her head at this slight reproof; "this is indeed silly, I have said nothing that need make you weep."

There was a coldness in her husband's tones that touched the heart of Edith, and it was with difficulty she repelled the rising tears, and when Grace retired for the night, and they were left alone, she perceived an unusual colour upon his brow, and felt hurt that he made not the slightest allusion as to where he had spent the day. Sad indeed were the thoughts that she carried with her to her pillow, and which entirely banished sleep; her husband, too, passed a restless night, and occasionally murmured incoherently in his sleep. Edith naturally connected his half-expressed thoughts with the letter she had discovered on his desk, and doubted not that his dreams were of the fair being who so engrossed his waking thoughts; when, therefore, she caught the name of Edward Villiers coupled with angry reproaches, she started with amazement, and began to fear some fresh calamity, threatening the happiness of Grace as well as her own.

CHAPTER XIX.

"Methought I was about to be a mother;
    Month after month went by, and still I dreamed
That we should soon be all to one another,
    I and my child; and still new pulses seemed
To beat beside my heart, and still I dreamed
    There was a babe within—and when the rain
Of winter through the rifted cavern streamed,
    Methought, after a lapse of lingering pain,
I saw that lovely shape, which near my heart had lain."

WHEN Madame Chevasse left Marie alone in the garret, for such in truth was the room to which she had conducted her, she joined Lawton in the parlour below.

"You have been a long while absent, madame," he said, rising as she entered. "I have waited here for the purpose of speaking a few words with you; that done, I am anxious to depart; for I'm cursed if I don't think the girl has had wit enough to judge the place as it really is, devilishly dull and unhealthy. Have you got a glass of brandy in the house, madame?"

"Oh, certainly, monsieur," replied that personage, opening a cupboard and producing a small decanter; "here is mine that I generally keep exclusively for my own use, and I think you will admit it is of the very finest quality."

"Ah, no doubt," returned Lawton, as he poured some into a glass; "here's to your good health, madame;" and he tossed off the contents.

"Well now, monsieur, perhaps you will have the goodness to tell me your object in bringing the young girl, Marie, to me."

"Oh, to business," replied Lawton, as he refilled his glass; "you see, madame, you have already given me proof that you are trustworthy, at least that money can make you so."

Madame sagaciously nodded her head, and Lawton again proceeded:—

"My wealthy cousin, Christopher Warden, cannot possibly live much longer, he is now in the last stage of consumption, he has already made his will (though by no means apprehensive of his own decease), and bequeathed his entire property to myself." Here Lawton paused, to impress the importance of this communication on the mind of his hearer, but, though the old woman's eye sparkled, she merely nodded her head, and motioned him to go on.

"I have so contrived it," continued Lawton, "that Christopher has not made the smallest legacy, even, to another, nor have I the slightest apprehension that he will alter his will, unless it should be in favour of this girl whom I have brought to you. Marie is very artful, and if her child survives its birth, it is very possible she may induce him ultimately to provide for it and herself, in which case, I of course must be the sufferer."

"Of course," reiterated the old woman, "I see all that very clearly."

"Well then," returned Lawton,—"by-the-by, though," he added, glancing suspiciously round the room, "there's no danger, I hope, of our being overheard."

"None whatever," returned the old woman, "you may speak freely."

"Then," said Lawton, bending his head closer to her ear, "that child must not live!"

"Must not?" repeated the other in feigned surprise.

"Ay, you understand," reiterated Lawton; "the child must not live; remember, the reward is to be liberal!"

"And what is to become of the girl?"

"You must keep her here, under the pretext that she is not strong enough to leave."

"For how long?" inquired the old woman.

"Till after my cousin's death," replied Lawton.

"That may be a long while," said the other; "consumption is the most deceptive of all diseases, so that it is impossible, as in other cases, to calculate the time when it will probably prove fatal, though the end may be certain."

"Whether the time is long or short, Marie must on no account have her liberty, till after his death," replied Lawton, firmly.

"I am afraid I shall find her a troublesome patient—she has too much spirit to please me."

"There are means of quelling it," returned Lawton, "to which you are no stranger. You have undertaken such charges before."

"This is a peculiar one," replied the other, "for the girl is interested in the life of the child, and will therefore be most anxious that it should survive, while, generally speaking, patients are only too glad if the child chances to be still-born."

"Well, well," said Lawton, who saw clearly that all these objections were merely raised to enhance the price she was desirous of putting on her services, " if the child dies, and Marie is retained under your care, on the death of my cousin, you will find yourself one thousand pounds the richer."

" Make it two, and I'll engage that neither the girl, nor her child shall trouble either yourself or cousin."

" Two thousand pounds is a large sum," said Lawton, hesitatingly.

"Monsieur must bear in mind," replied the other, " that I am about to undertake a very unpleasant and hazardous charge ; indeed, the money I have named is scarcely equivalent to the risk if anything should be discovered."

" It will be entirely your own fault," returned Lawton. " However, to save more words, I am willing to agree to your terms."

The old woman instantly produced writing materials, and asked Lawton to make a little memorandum of their mutual agreement.

" I scarcely see the utility of it," said Lawton.

" It is just possible," replied the other, " that you might forget the sum."

" Ah," returned Lawton, laughing, " you are afraid I might offer you a smaller remuneration than the one I have agreed to. You might, under the circumstances, trust me ; but never mind —give me the pen."

And he wrote as follows,—

" I hereby promise to pay to Madame Chevasse the sum of two thousand pounds on the death of my cousin, Christopher Warden, for certain considerations agreed to between ourselves.

"JOHN LAWTON."

" There," he said, pushing the paper towards her, " I have put more trust in your faith than you were disposed to do in mine ; but mind, the certain considerations are strictly complied with or the two thousand pounds will not be forthcoming."

" I perfectly understand, monsieur," returned the other, " and am fully prepared to do your bidding. You are well assured though," she added in a tone of inquiry, " that your cousin cannot——"

" By any possible means, last much longer," said Lawton, anticipating what she was about to say.

" The sooner everything is settled, then, the better."

" Decidedly," replied Lawton, " and now, madame, I'll do myself the honour of wishing you good morning."

While this villany was being planned below, the unfortunate Marie, as we observed in a chapter or two back, was employed in meditating on the probability of her ever being allowed to quit what may now be truly termed her prison-house, for she was herself aware that she was a prisoner to all intents and purposes. And the kind offer she had received from Moreton rose reproachfully before her mind's eye, and deeply she regretted that she had not availed herself of it. How far preferable to have confided herself to his protection, than to be there left sad and solitary, under the care of such a woman as Madame Chevasse ; and she shuddered at the recollection of the sinister expression of Lawton's eye, when he first introduced her to her present abode ; but hope, that sweet though oft illusive beam, had shed a ray of light across the dark and dreary sadness that enveloped her. And gladly was it treasured and encouraged in her agonising and trusting heart ; and, for woman's love is ever true, she consoled herself with the thought of a speedy and blest reunion with the man she so devotedly loved.

Pleasing herself with such anticipations as these, and with which were entwined fond hopes of her unborn child, when Madame Chevasse returned, she found her more cheerful and resigned than she anticipated.

A month passed slowly by ; Marie had busied herself during the whole of that period in preparation for her expected infant, and now with delight she hailed the near approach of its birth. None but a mother can tell the soft, sweet sensations that fill the breast of a mother, as she looks forward to the joy of pressing her first-born to her bosom. All sorrow and anxiety as regards herself is swallowed up in the depths of her maternal tenderness, as she trembles lest the flickering spark of life that dwells in her infant's delicate frame may be extinguished, ere she can fold it to her bosom, and feel its soft breath fan her delighted cheek.

Thus Marie heeded not the approaching danger that must shortly assail her own life, nor gave even a passing thought as to whether the experience of Madame Chevasse would suffice to carry her safely through it ; but for the life of her child she trembled sometimes even with a vague feeling of fear that it would be doomed to perish ; and wept to think how hard it would be that the sweet babe should never know

"The sense of light, and the warm air,
And her own fond and tender care."

In vain Madame Chevasse bade her be of good courage, and trust that all would end well; a sense of sorrow weighed down her usually buoyant spirits—the dreariness of her chamber, and her long-continued confinement therein, without fresh air and necessary exercise, most probably oppressed her spirits, and weakened her health.

In order to banish sorrowful ideas from her mind, Marie would frequently endeavour to find amusement from the books that were scattered about the room, and which had undoubtedly been left there by other individuals similarly circumstanced as herself; and often would she wonder if they, like her, had experienced the same sadness of heart during their temporary stay.

To her repeated inquiries concerning Christopher, the old woman invariably assured her that he was fast recovering his usual health, and was very anxious regarding herself.

"Alas! how can that be?" said Marie, when the old woman was endeavouring to impress it upon her mind. "If he really loved me, and felt that anxiety for my welfare you wish me to believe, he would at least have written me a few lines before now, but I begin to fear that——"

"Fear what, ma'mselle," interrupted the old woman angrily. "You give yourself fine airs forsooth. You ought to be very thankful that a gentleman, so far above you, should trouble himself so much with your welfare; he has placed you under my care, and pays liberally for the comforts and accommodation with which you are provided; what more can you want?"

"Forgive me," said Marie, vexed with herself for having aroused the anger of the old woman. "I am very sad and low-spirited, and that, undoubtedly, makes me unjust."

"Well," said the other, somewhat mollified, "I dare say you did not mean any harm, but I have brought you some medicine, that, I think, will be beneficial for you; and she poured something of a darkish colour from a bottle that she held in her hand into a wine-glass, and presented it to Marie."

The young girl, fearful of offending her by her refusal, raised it to her lips, and with a shudder drank the contents.

"That will have the effect of composing you," said the old woman, with a smile, "and if you will amuse yourself for a short time with a book, I will presently return."

Marie endeavoured to do so, and seating herself near the window, reached a book from the table; but she had scarcely been alone ten minutes before she became sensible of an extreme dizziness in her head, that caused everything apparently to dance before her eyes. In a state of great alarm she arose with the intention of calling assistance, but she reeled like a drunken man; at the same moment a sense of death-like sickness came over her. She went back upon her bed, and clasping her hands, exclaimed,—

"Good God! I am dying, alone—all, all alone—how horrible."

The thought for the time deprived her of all power of action; but in a few moments nerved by desperation, she contrived to struggle towards the water-jug, and succeeded, not without great difficulty, in dashing a quantity of water over her head and face; this afforded her temporary relief, but the symptoms speedily returned with redoubled violence.

"Oh, God!" she exclaimed, in the intensity of her anguish, "what have I done to deserve so terrible a death? My sight fails me. I am dying—and my child—oh! I am doomed never to behold it."

A cold, icy sweat bedewed her forehead; she felt it to be the damp of death; she strove to cream, but the words died away in hollow murmurs on her lips; it was an awful moment; the reflection of her own pallid and ghastly face in an opposite mirror caused her to shiver with terror. And she was alone. Oh, how bitter the reflection—probably left alone to die. How welcome now were even the presence of Madame Chevasse.

Yet even in this moment of unutterable agony and terror, how vivid came back every scene of her early life:

"The garden where a child she played;
Or wearied sought the cooling shade."

Her tender parents long since departed, and even their look of love, and words of fond affection, came back in this sad hour, in such rapid succession, as to completely bewilder her o'er-fraught brain.

Suddenly a sound, a welcome sound, aroused her, as it were, from the torpor of death—it was the key turning in its rusty lock. And now she hears, though as one who hears it not, the footstep of Madame Chevasse, deliberately ascending the stairs. She strove to exert herself to call to her, to hasten her steps, but speech had failed her; and her senses seemed once more steeped in oblivion.

After the lapse of a short time, she became sensible of a half dreamy consciousness of acute suffering, and Madame Chevasse officiously attending by her couch. And then, oh, surely it could not be a dream—she hears the faint cry of a new-born child, and extends her arms to clasp it to her heart; the effort was more than her exhausted frame could bear, and she sunk back in a fainting fit.

When the truly unfortunate Marie again unclosed her eyes, the first object she beheld was the face of Madame Chevasse who was bending over her, half in surprise and half in alarm when Marie fixed her eyes upon her with a deep and penetrating gaze, but instantly recovering her composure, she inquired how she felt.

"Very weak and ill," replied Marie in a faint voice; "but where is my child?"

"Your child, ma'mselle?" returned the other.

"Yes, my child, it is alive, I heard its voice; give it me instantly."

"You are labouring under some strange mistake," replied the woman, counterfeiting the greatest amazement. "I left you (if you remember) for a short time, and on my return, I was greatly astonished at discovering you in an apparently dying state, since which time, I have not quitted your side for a moment; but with the aid of restoratives, that chanced to be at hand, I have so far succeeded in recovering you to your senses."

"Alas! and is it possible then," said Marie, "that the birth of my child is but a dream?"

"Nothing more," returned the old woman, "but compose yourself, ma'mselle; your mind, I fear, is still wandering."

"I fear it is," replied Marie, passing her hand across her flushed and feverish brow, and she sighed heavily.

"If you promise to remain perfectly quiet, ma'mselle," said the woman, "I will run down stairs, and fetch you a composing draught."

"No, thank you," returned Marie, shuddering, as recollection forcibly presented to her mind the horrible effects of the draught Madame Chevasse had so lately administered, "I do not require medicine; rest and sleep will be far more beneficial."

"As you please, ma'mselle, only I consider myself in a manner answerable for your recovery, and should your obstinacy be attended with an unfavourable result, Mr. Warden may blame me for the consequences of your wilfulness."

"You need not make yourself uneasy on that score," replied Marie, in a tone of bitterness; "if I die, no one will think it worth while to trouble themselves about the cause; but," she added, with renewed hope, "I am young and strong, and shall yet recover; it were too soon to die at the early age of seventeen. A short life," she continued, sobbing, "but, oh! how full of sorrows, Oh! were it not for the thought of another world, God knows how gladly I would lay down life's weary load. Oh! were the grave a place of rest, where grief could never win a tear, or sorrow never reach, I should only be too glad to die—I should indeed; but it is a dark untrodden road, and I shudder, as I view the entrance, so gloomy, so damp and cold!"

After the silence of a few moments, the unfortunate girl spoke again, and this time with more confidence.

"I am better," she said, "much better, and shall soon be quite well."

"Of course you will," replied the old woman, who was anxious to soothe and quiet her; "if you would only strive to sleep, you would, I am sure, wake up quite another thing."

"You are right," returned Marie, "but do not leave me; such terrible thoughts of death creep over me in spite of myself, and I feel as though I was on the point of being hurried into eternity."

"Nothing but nervousness," said the other; "yet make yourself easy, I will not leave you," and she drew a chair to the bedside. In a few minutes her deep regular breathing betokened the unhappy girl had obtained a temporary oblivion of her sorrows, though, now and then, a convulsive heaving of her bosom told all was not peace within. Madame Chevasse bent over the bed, and gazed with a strange and fearful expression on the sleeper's face, muttering as she did so,—

"She gives me more trouble than I expected: I thought that dose would have been sufficient. I must make the next stronger, though I am at a loss how to contrive to make her swallow it, I will, however, prepare it against she awakes." And she crept cautiously from the room.

CHAPTER XX.

" Yet, though subdued, the unnerving thrill,
Its warmth, its weakness, linger still,
So touching, in each look and tone,
That the fond, fearing, hoping maid,
Half counted on the flight she prayed,
Half thought her lover's soul was grown
As soft, as yielding as her own,
And smil'd, and bless'd him while he said,—
' Yes—if there be some happier sphere,
Where fadeless truth like ours is dear,—
If there be any land of rest
For those who love, and ne'er forget,
Oh! comfort thee—for safe and blest
We'll meet in that calm region yet.'"

EDWARD VILLIERS returned home, on the evening of his rencontre with Catherine, in no enviable frame of mind. The dread of losing Grace, to whom he was so fondly and tenderly attached, totally banished all thoughts of the ill-used Helen.

He now saw his conduct in the contemptible light with which in truth it deserved to be regarded ; he had allowed an absurd vanity to influence him to such an extent, that it perilled the happiness, not of himself alone, but that also of his betrothed bride.

"Alas," he exclaimed, my adored Grace, I cannot myself pardon or even extenuate my conduct ; how, then, can I hope or ask you to do so ?"

And in the bitterness of his feelings, he blamed Helen as the cause of all. Man, alas! is ever unjust to woman. This then, poor Helen, was thy (unmerited) reward, for thy fond enduring love, and trusting devotedness to the man of thy heart.

It required all the powers young Villiers was master of, to conceal from his dear home circle the deep-felt anguish that dwelt within his bosom. Mrs. Villiers had made no mention either to her daughters or her husband of the interview that had taken place between herself and Catherine, and though her son's reception of the letter supposed to be written by Helen had greatly aroused her fears that Catherine's suspicions were well founded, she confined it strictly to her own breast, and when on his return in the evening, with the quick eye of maternal tenderness, she perceived he was unhappy and dejected, she guessed the cause too accurately to grieve him by inquiries, though utterly at a loss to account for the motives that actuated him to such apparently inexplicable conduct; for the good lady could scarcely conceive it possible that her son was in love with two women at the same time. She therefore determined to watch him, and get him, if possible, to open his mind freely, without the necessity of asking him to do so.

Edward passed the night in racking thoughts, completely bewildered as to which course it would be the wisest for him to adopt under existing circumstances ; he at length determined at all hazards to ask an interview with Grace ; he was too well assured of her love to doubt for an instant that she would grant him one, even though her haughty brother should forbid her. To her he could humble himself, and sue for pardon, but of the earl, never—no if his doing so were necessary to win the hand of his beloved. Were they equal in birth and station, he might have relented, as far as to own his culpability, and desire it might be forgotten ; but ranking as an inferior, he deemed it would be foul dishonour to acknowledge that he had erred. His cheek burned with indignation, at the thought. No, the proud, disdainful earl should never brand him as a coward; he would meet him, and clear his honour of the slightest stain.

Thus reasoned Edward Villiers; and truly on such subjects men do reason most strangely. It is a curious notion that standing up to be shot at should cleanse their names from the aspersion that dishonourable actions might otherwise have cast upon them, and honour may well be interpreted as standing fire well; and satisfaction, as giving or receiving a deadly wound.

Grace, the reader is aware, retired to her couch with a lightsome heart, happily unconscious of all that had taken place between her brother and Edward. Accustomed to early rising from her infancy, she was the first to enter the breakfast-room on the ensuing morning, and scarcely had she seated herself, before the servant presented her with a small billet addressed to herself, and which she instantly recognised as the well-known hand-writing of her lover.

"How kind of him to write to me so soon after his departure," she murmured half aloud as she broke the seal and proceeded to make herself mistress of its contents, but the first line sufficed to chase the bloom from her cheek and filled her mind with doubt, and anxiety, it ran as follows :—

"My Dearest Grace,—Circumstances, over which I had no control, detained me in town last evening, when myself and your brother accidently met, and, I am grieved to say, a slight misunderstanding arose between us, concerning a young lady, who very lately resided under my parent's roof, but who suddenly and most unaccountably disappeared. A day or two since, accident made me acquainted with the place of her retreat, which I instantly felt it my duty to impart to her sister. And your brother has construed my doing so an affront to yourself, but I trust my dear Grace, shortly to convince him of the injustice of his conduct. In the interim I feel myself compelled to remain at a distance from you, though I have so much I wish to impart, that I even venture to solicit the favour of your calling on me early this morning.

"Ever faithfully yours, "EDWARD VILLIERS."

Grace hastily concealed this letter as her brother entered, and greeted him with her accustomed smile, but she observed that both himself and Edith wore a look of unusual anxiety.

During breakfast the earl mentioned his desire that his wife and sister would prepare for their immediate return to Ravensdale, where he himself intended to join them, in a few days.

Edith spoke not, but turned pale, and fixed a penetrating look upon her husband, as Grace enquired the reason for his sudden wish to quit London.

"It is but hastening our departure a few weeks," returned her brother, "you know Grace we had arranged to return to Ravensdale, in order to celebrate your expected nuptials."

"True!" said Grace, warmly, "but I also know that my marriage is not to take place till the early part of next month, and considered it definitely settled that we should remain in London till within a fortnight of that period."

No. 9.

"Circumstances have arisen, Grace," replied her brother, in a more softened tone, "that must for a time, postpone your marriage to Mr. Villiers, if indeed it is ever permitted to take place."

"You are joking, Arthur," said Grace trying to smile, "my dresses are prepared, and every arrangement completed; Edward has likewise received the sanction of my mother, and of yourself," she added after a moment's hesitation.

"Grace," replied her brother, "rumours have reached my ears seriously affecting the honour of the man to whom you were so shortly to be united."

"They are false," returned Grace, warmly.

"That remains to be proved," replied the earl, "and it is a duty I owe to yourself, to seek a full explanation of them."

"I would earnestly, and heartily desire it," said Grace, with increasing animation, "and am certain that Edward will be only too glad to afford you every facility for doing so. Yet not for my own satisfaction do I desire it, for I know full well that he is incapable of even a dishonourable thought, much less action; but for the sake of others, I am anxious that the foul breath of slander should not for an instant be allowed to rest upon his unsullied name."

"You speak confidently, Grace," said her brother.

"Not more so than I feel," she replied.

"Then if I can make it clear in your eyes, that he has insulted you with the offer of his hand, while his own lips averred to another, that she alone possessed his heart, will you give me your solemn promise never on any pretext to become his wife?"

"It is utterly impossible Edward could ever thus act. I believe, my brother, that you conceive you have reason for thinking so, but let him act ever so dishonourably, I could not tear his image from my breast. No, he would be still glorious, still to this fond heart, dear as its blood, no matter what guilt might encompass him."

"I thought, Grace," said her brother, somewhat contemptuously, "that you had more self-respect."

"To prove to you," she returned, without heeding his remark, "how confidant I am in the unblemished honour of Edward Villiers, I willingly tender you my unalterable assurance, that if you can convince me he has acted towards either of us with baseness and duplicity, this hand, and she stretched it forth, "shall never be given to him."

"I am satisfied," said the earl, "and under these considerations it is my desire that you and Edith should set off instantly for Ravensdale. I shall remain here and institute the most searching inquiries into the truth or falsehood of the reports that are circulated to the disadvantage of Mr. Villiers."

Edith had not once spoken during this conversation, but with a pale and anxious countenance had listened to all that passed between her husband and her sister, but now in a timid voice she ventured to inquire of the earl how long he intended to remain in London after their departure.

"It is impossible definitely to fix the day on which you may expect me," he replied, "but you may be sure my love, that I shall be anxious to join you as soon as possible."

Edith made no answer. But a few short hours before, his speech had found a ready echo, but "a change had come over the spirit of her dream," blighting her fond warm hopes, and withering her young affections. Edith was a being in whom love begot love, and now that she was convinced she was no longer all in all to her husband, the blossom of love that was expanding so sweetly and freshly began to droop for want of the nourishment which supported it, and bid fair to be nipped in the bud, for lack of the sweet refreshing dews that descended so softly each night and morn, and gemmed it with liquid lustre. It began to show signs of premature decay, and with it every hope and joy that had warmed and animated her breast; she therefore merely signified her intention of complying with her husband's wishes, and named the day following as the one for their departure.

In the course of the morning, Grace attired herself in a walking dress, and telling Edith that she had a few orders she wished personally to give to her milliner, started for her lover's residence; the distance was but short, and Grace, who was an excellent pedestrian, speedily accomplished it. She had scarcely time to knock at the door before it was opened, and Edward sprang to meet her. After the first warm embrace was given and received, the young man placed Grace in a chair, and warmly thanking her for this proof of affection, led the subject of conversation at once to what so intimately concerned themselves.

"Grace, my own darling Grace," he said, raising her hand rapturously to his lips, "I have been compelled to seek the undeserved favour of this visit, in order to justify my own conduct Your brother, dearest, has threatened to disunite us for ever."

"He cannot do it," said Grace, firmly; "but tell me at once, Edward, the full particulars of your interview with him last evening."

"I will, love. Now, listen—you doubtless remember my having informed you, almost on our first acquaintance, of your brother's attachment to a young lady, whom we met with in Paris?"

"I remember it perfectly," replied Grace. "Go on."

"Well, love, that young lady has recently returned to England."

"Ah!" replied Grace, starting. "I trusted they were separated for ever. I, myself, wrote to her at the address I received from you, informing her of my brother's marriage to Edith, and ventured to express my earnest hope, that she would see the necessity of discontinuing all intimacy with him for the future; but," she added, "I am interrupting you."

"This young lady's mother was twice married," resumed Villiers, "and dying, some years ago, she left a younger child, by name Helen Thornton, who inherited a small property under her father's will, to the care of Catherine, the elder; but through her persuasions my parents consented to take charge of her, and for many years she was an inmate of our house, and regarded by all as a sister. You will not, I hope, Grace, accuse me of vanity when I inform you that this young girl unfortunately conceived an attachment for myself, that my ardent affection for you prevented me reciprocating, and ultimately, as I told you dearest, in my note, Helen clandestinely left this house. Under the peculiar circumstances of the case, I was naturally very desirous to discover her retreat, and after considerable difficulty succeeded in doing so.

"In the meantime I received a note from her sister, appointing a meeting for last evening, which appointment I kept, pleasing myself with the anticipation of relieving the anxiety under which she laboured. Alas! how cruelly was I disappointed—she came, accompanied by your brother, to whom she immediately denounced me as the betrayer of her sister. In vain I endeavoured to explain; the earl refused to listen to even a word, of what I endeavoured to urge in exculpation of myself, bade me never more look upon you as my betrothed bride, and left me, dearest, in utter despair."

"Alas!" exclaimed Grace, "I see—I understand it all—that unhappy girl will be the cause of utter misery both to myself and Edith."

"It is, indeed, a strange fatality," replied the young man, "that the two sisters should thus threaten your mutual happiness; and yet I know not how to avert the calamity."

"Edward," said Grace, kindly and firmly, "I am, myself, so confident of your honour and integrity, that I shall ever turn a deaf ear to all that may be urged against you; but it may suit my brother to do otherwise; he may endeavour, and alas, it is by no means impossible, but that he may succeed, in separating us for ever."

"He may, he may," replied her lover, clasping his hands before his eyes. "What madness does the thought conjure up."

"Then listen to me," returned Grace. "It rests with ourselves, Edward, to avert so direful a calamity; we are now together. My brother has no suspicion of my being here. I shall not be missed for several hours, let us then, dear Edward, cast all foolish scruples from our minds, and profit by this golden opportunity."

"My adored Grace!" replied the young man, gazing on her with the fondest affection, 'what is it that you would propose?"

"That we should never more separate; it will be only hastening our marriage a few weeks, and by doing so it will put it out of my brother's power to part us. If I quit you now, dear Edward, I tremble with the apprehension that we may never again meet. To-morrow, by my brother's order, myself and Edith return to Ravensdale."

"So suddenly!" replied her lover, starting with surprise. "Ah, Grace, we may well tremble for the result. And yet, it is so hard to resign you."

"What need is there that we should again separate?" replied Grace, warmly. "Our friends have all given their consent to our marriage, and my brother has no right to insist upon my leaving London; had he known it he would not have permitted even this parting interview, and the unreasonableness of his conduct will be a sufficient excuse for ours."

Edward clasped the fair pleader in his arms, while tears that he could no longer repel, bedewed her face, as he pressed upon it the warm kisses of affection; and Grace, as she timidly returned them, half counted on the flight she prayed; but though Edward's heart beat in anxious yearnings to comply with the request of the fond, warm-hearted girl, yet he felt, under existing circumstances, he could not with honour do it; he clearly saw that the earl's motive, in sending his wife and sister to Ravensdale, was to remove them from his vicinity, and his own stay was doubtless intended to be devoted to settling his dispute with himself; therefore, he could not, as he ardently desired, consummate his marriage with Grace, till after he had met the earl; but bitter as were his own feelings, as these thoughts passed through his mind, he endeavoured to speak calmly and cheerfully, so as to reassure the trembling Grace. And as he kissed off the pearly tears that sprang unheeded to her eyes, at the thought of separation, he whispered her they should again meet, safe and blest.

"We first met, dearest, at Ravensdale, and that spot is sacred to me, above all others, for that very reason; let us hope, then, love, that I shall speedily join you there."

Grace smiled as she expressed her willingness to be guided entirely by his wishes.

"And now, love," said Edward, tenderly kissing her, "you must promise me n to allow any painful forebodings to cast a shadow on your spirit."

Grace gave her assurance that she would not, and having first introduced her to his mother, and sisters, all of whom were delighted with her easy, unaffected manners, and proud of the kind greeting she bestowed on each one of them separately, Edward accompanied her on her road home.

Grace bade her lover adieu with an aching heart, but still without any fear that the aspersions on his character would not be soon cleared away; but Edward wrung her hand, while a sense of suffocation impeded his utterance, for he knew not what might occur to prevent his ever seeing or speaking to her again.

CHAPTER XXI.

> "I sat through the sweet sunny day,
> By my window bowered round with leaves,
> And down my cheeks the quick tears ran
> Like trickling rain-drops from the eaves ,
> When warm spring showers are passing o'er.
> Oh! Helen, none can ever tell.
> The joy it was to weep once more !
> And happy I would dream, 'twere sweet
> To feed it from my faded breast,
> Or mark my own heart's restless beat
> Rock it to its untroubled rest,
> And search the depths of its fair eyes
> For long departed memories.'

"My own sweet sister," sobbed Catherine, "forgive me, for having wronged you by an unkind and unjust suspicion. Say Helen love, that you will forgive me !"

"Dear Catherine, it is I that must ask, entreat forgiveness of you; have I not acted towards you with cruelty and deception ; nay, I feel as though it were impossible you can regard me so tenderly as hitherto ; your conduct has ever been so free from even the semblance of impropriety, that I fear my imprudence will have the effect of lowering me in your eyes."

A deep burning crimson glow mounted to the cheek of Catherine, as her sister breathed these words. Helen had unconsciously touched a chord in her breast that awoke a sense of her own injuries, bitter and soul-destroying ; her eye for a moment shot fire, and the next drooped in self-abasement to the ground.

"Helen," she said, in a low husky tone, that startled her sister, while her whole frame shook convulsively, her lip quivered as with deep emotion, and her cheek burnt like fire.

"Catherine," exclaimed Helen, "you alarm me; what have I said to call forth this emotion ; if I have grieved you, sister, pardon me, indeed I meant it not."

"No, my Helen, you have not offended me, though your words awoke a thousand stings of self-accusation, and bitter remorse. How can I find words in which to convey to your spotless mind the lost, degraded state of your unhappy sister."

Helen was thunderstruck at these words ; what, her proud, high-minded, virtuous sister thus to speak ! she surely could not hear aright, and without the power of replying, she gazed upon her with an expression of utter amazement and confusion.

"Helen, you despise me," said Catherine, "but not more than I despise myself."

"My sweet, sweet sister!" exclaimed Helen, bursting into tears, " were it possible that you could have sinned, you would have double claims upon my love and tenderness; but I cannot believe it."

"Alas! Helen," she replied, kissing off her tears, " I knew that you would scarce believe it. You whom I know once thought

> ' That nought beneath God's sky,
> Could tempt or change me—and so once thought I.'

And my sister, I had firmly resolved,

'Never to let you know, how deep the brow
    You kissed at parting, is dishonoured now;
But when I heard you call me good and pure,
    Oh, 'twas too much, too dreadful to endure.'

"And Helen, love, I resolved to tell you all. Oh, there will be balm and consolation to pour my sorrows into your gentle, virtuous breast. You weep, dearest, and so I do the same; and oh! it is joy to weep once more; it is months—many months, since last these eyes were wet. I began to fear Helen, I should never weep again."

Seated side by side, fondly entwined in each other's arms, Helen listened while her sister poured out her long pent sorrow, and the indignant blood forced its way to her cheek as she learnt the cruel oppression that had wrung the heart and crushed the hopes of her sister.

"Oh! Catherine," she murmured, "how dreadful must have been your sufferings, a child too. Oh! Catherine, when shall I behold him, sweet innocent; we will for the future make one home, thou my sister, thy child, and me."

Catherine bowed her head upon her sister's bosom, and wept out her joy and sorrow there.

"You do not despise me then, dearest," were all the words that found utterance.

"My sister, my dear, dear sister, you do not, you cannot think so."

"No Helen, I do not," she replied, pressing a fervent kiss upon her brow. "I am happier now, far happier than I have been for a long, long time; but it grows late love, let us retire for the night, and to-morrow we will converse more freely."

When the sisters met at breakfast, which was prepared for them in a small but pretty little parlour, the morning sun shone in through the open window, so fresh and bright, that spite of their many cares and anxieties, it gladdened their hearts, and they blest its sweet reviving rays. And drawing the table to the window, they looked out upon the green fields and inhaled the soft pure air which fanned their fevered brows, and invigorated their minds with its delightful freshness.

Breakfast is ever a pleasant, cheerful meal with ourselves, associated in our minds (as doubtless in most others) with all that has cheered our hearts or gladdened our minds.

We rise refreshed, and invigorated with sleep, and all things starting into renewed life, assume at early morn a brighter aspect; the birds carol their brightest songs, the flowers put forth their fairest tints and throw their sweetest perfume on the morning air, the grass wet with the pearly dew looks greener than it did at eve, and all things tend to turn our hearts to joy. And are not our own thoughts more fresh and bright before the cares and trials of the day commence?

We never remember to have seen any but smiling faces around the breakfast table. Mirth and good humour possess an undisputed right to preside over that pleasant and agreeable meal; the petty cares and vexations of life which we frequently carry to our pillow, are never taken away again, they all vanish into air before a good night's rest.

Busy day with its multiplicity of cares chains down all our thoughts and hopes to earth, but dark and lonely is the eye that turns not in the morn to heaven.

Thus felt Catherine and Helen: they could now converse with less of sorrow on the past, and something like hope on the future. And Catherine felt that the time was suitable to impart to Helen all that she deemed it was right for her to know regarding Edward Villiers.

She therefore acquainted her with the full particulars of her own interview with him on the preceding evening, and in conclusion, she said, "you see my dear Helen, Edward entertains no honourable regard for you; he himself avowed, in language which was unmistakeable that he loved none but the lady Grace."

"Then why," replied Helen, in a tone of saddened surprise, "did he use all his persuasive powers to induce me to quit his mother's roof and protection."

"Why indeed, my Helen," returned her sister; "because, love, men are base, wicked, and deceitful. God be praised, you have escaped the snares that he spread to entangle you."

"I cannot think so ill of Edward," replied Helen gently, "I believe he loves me, but the rank and station of the lady Grace has—"

"Helen, love," said her sister, "had the Earl of Clavering offered you his hand, would the title have so delighted you that you would have been willing to forsake Edward, in order to accept it."

"Oh! never, never," replied Helen, eagerly.

"Then, we may reasonably conclude, that had Edward entertained that regard for you he professes, the rank and title of the lady Grace would have sunk into nothingness. No, Helen, he loves you as men too often love women, just enough to make him desirous of gaining your affections, which he has done, caring nothing whatever for you, beyond the satisfaction of his own selfish passion. It is a painful and humiliating truth, dear sister; still, it is not less the truth."

Helen slid her hand into her sister's, which she silently pressed, but made no reply.

Catherine seeing that she felt hurt, and apparently still discredited the falsehood of her lover, after a short silence, during which she was turning over in her own mind, the course of action it would be most advisable for her under the present circumstances to pursue, said :—

"Helen, my love, I have determined to give you an opportunity of convincing yourself beyond the possibility of a doubt, of the truth, or falshood of Edward; I can truly sympathise with your present feelings, for I have loved myself, with all a woman's truthful affection; I therefore propose my love, to leave you here, at least for a time."

"Must we then part, and but so lately met," whispered Helen.

"For the present, it is absolutely necessary, but not for long, Helen; we shall speedily meet again; in the mean time, I propose, as I just said, to leave you here while I return to Mrs. Porter's. If Edward loves you, he will endeavour, I should suppose, to communicate with you, if he does not, you are at liberty to write to him, and enquire the cause; I rely so confidently, my dear Helen, on your own prudence, that, I shall not seek to impose the slightest restraint upon you; act in this affair as your heart dictates, and I am convinced you will act wisely, only do not buoy yourself up with the hope of his proving what you so fondly desire.

Helen thanked her sister for her kind consideration, and declared herself prepared to meet disappointment.

"You must write to me, Helen, the moment you know anything decisive concerning Edward."

Helen cheerfully gave the required promise.

"And now, sister," continued Catherine, (drawing forth her little purse, and having taken therefrom a few shillings she pressed the remainder upon her sister,) "I will bid you farewell at once."

The parting kiss was given and received, and Catherine was speedily on her road to town; her own sorrows were now so entirely merged in those of her sister, that she scarcely gave them a thought, still, the words of Helen, "we will henceforth make one home, thou, thy child, and myself," awoke a sense of gladness in her heart. Could it be realised! Oh, were it possible, then there might be something of hope and joy even for her; earth would no more be quite so dreary a waste, or life so heavy a burden; it would be sweet to trace daily and hourly in her infant's sunny smile, days of departed bliss,

"And search the depths of its fair eyes,
For long departed memories."

To be able to rear it under her own protecting care, and cautiously weed out the evil principles it might inherit from its father, this would be a dear, delightful task, and haply she might be enabled to restore her loved sister to happiness and peace, and in the course of years see her blest in a happier choice. Oh, there was joy in this, she would think of it, and see if such were practicable.

Fired with these hopes, (which gave a lustre to her eyes, and an elasticity to her tread) she pursued her way.

On reaching the abode of Mrs. Porter, the servant informed her, that that lady desired her presence in the drawing-room; and Catherine instantly obeyed the summons.

"Well, upon my word, Miss Montravers, you seem determined entirely to set at nought my authority;" began Mrs. Porter, the moment she entered. "You really take a most unwarrantable advantage of my kindness; few if any ladies would have received you back after the fortnight's absence at Paris, and which indeed you never reasonably accounted for."

"The plea that I urged, madam, of extreme ill health, I had deemed was accepted as sufficient excuse," replied Catherine gently.

"Then am I to infer?" said the lady, drawing herself up with an air of extreme dignity "that you have been attacked with a like indisposition again; if my memory serves me, I believe you attributed it to a severe cold; but I must confess, that now you appear entirely free from such a distressing malady."

There was a tone of peculiar bitterness in her voice, that Catherine could ill brook but she curbed her proud spirit, and answered without the slightest show of resent ment,—

"No, madam, I do not wish to plead illness as the occasion of my absence last night."

"What excuse then will you urge?" returned the lady, in the same bitter satirical strain, "truly you have succeeded in arousing my curiosity."

I can satisfy it, madam," replied Catherine, "by stating the truth; on arriving at the place yesterday where I fully expected to have found my sister, I learnt that she had removed to Hampstead, and experienced some little difficulty in gaining her address, which delayed me so long that I found it impossible to return last night; and, as it is now scarcely three o'clock," continued Catherine, "I trust the delay will not occasion much difference to my pupils."

"Regularity, I consider," replied the lady, " is one of the first principles that should be inculcated in the minds of young persons, regularity in all things, but more especially scholastic duties. And, then, if I out of kindness allow you to have a day occasionally at your own disposal, I regard it as an act of excessive ill breeding for you to remain beyond the time I stipulated you should return ; but, for this once, I am disposed to pardon it, on consideration that it is never on any account repeated ; by-the-by, I am not altogether satisfied with Miss Porter's music ; I called her down to play a few pieces yesterday, and detected many defects, that I hope you will look for and correct."

"Yes, madam," said Catherine, moving towards the door, thankful at the prospect of escape.

"Stay," said the lady, as she observed her movement, " did you expect to hear from any one ?"

" In what manner," replied Catherine, rather puzzled to understand the other's question.

" I mean, did you expect any letters?"

" Oh dear no, madam," returned Catherine, with surprise.

" One has come, nevertheless, which you will find in the school-room," replied the haughty lady.

Catherine merely bowed, and hastening from the room, she wondered much who the correspondent could be. On entering the school-room and glancing for an instant at the mystical epistle, her doubts were solved instantly, for she recognised the hand-writing of the Earl of Clavering, and drawing the note from its envelope, with a flashing eye perused the contents, and then proceeded quietly to destroy it.

She discovered by the date that it was written previous to their unexpected meeting of the evening before ; indeed we may as well inform the reader that it was the very letter that had caused so much uneasiness in the breast of Edith.

As Catherine once more turned her attention to the duties of her avocation, wearied in body, from her last night's fatigue, and her mind anything but fitted to encounter the tiresome routine of the school room, she mentally exclaimed, " I will cast off these fetters that enchain my mind ; there are surely some means by which I can earn an honest livelihood, without thus bartering my independence." And cheered with this hope, she endeavoured to conquer the lassitude that oppressed her.

CHAPTER XXII.

" 'Twere vain to paint, to what his feelings grew,
It even were doubtful if their victim knew.
There is a war, a chaos of the mind,
When all the elements convuls'd—combined—
Lie dark, and jarring with perturbed force.
And gnashing with impenitent remorse,
Deeds, thoughts, and words, perhaps remembered not,
So keenly till that hour, but ne'er forgot ;
Things light or lovely, in their acted time,
But now, to stern reflection each a crime,
All—in a word—from which all eyes must start,
That open sepulchre—the naked heart."

WHEN Edward Villiers bade adieu to Grace, and watched her light form till it was no longer visible, he felt a dead chill creeping through his veins, a fearful foreboding that he had done with happiness.

How much would he now have given to undo the events of the last few days. Remorse, like a foul fiend, seized upon his heart, and to avoid its self-accusing voice, he entered a club, near which he chanced to be passing, and called for wine, of which he partook freely, but it could not drown the stings of conscience that preyed upon his mind. On the morrow he felt assured he should hear from the Earl of Clavering, and it was with feverish impatience he counted the hours that must necessarily intervene,

He resolved at all events to behold Grace once more, Yes, he would see her, though himself unseen, early the ensuing morning ; she had told him, herself and Edith would start for Ravensdale ; he steadfastly determined, then, to station himself near the spot ; he should thus be enabled to catch, at least, a glimpse of her he loved ; he might even be fortunate enough to be seen by Grace, and greeted with one of her bright beaming, happy smiles—smiles that were so peculiarly her own,

> That where it most sparkled, time had to discover,
> In lip, cheek, or eye, for she brightened all over.

It was those sweet smiles that had first enchanted his heart, and one such even now would nerve him with fresh fortitude.

Pleasing himself with this anticipation, he returned home at a late hour in the evening, in order to avoid the anxious inquiries of his mother and sister, and retired at once to rest; but the sorrows of his mind banished sleep from his pillow, and he arose in the morning with an aching head, as well as an aching heart; and having hastily partaken of breakfast, and succeeded in quelling, for a time, his mother's anxious fears, he proceeded to the quarter of the town in which the Earl of Clavering resided; stationing himself opposite the house, he waited patiently for the departure of Grace.

As he thus stood wrapt in eager anticipation of beholding her once more, he observed that there appeared an unwonted bustle; servants passed and re-passed the windows often; presently the carriage was brought out, and the servants proceeded to place on it the trunks; in another moment Edith appeared leaning on the arm of the earl, who having placed her in the carriage, returned to the house, from which he led his sister Grace. Edward observed that she lacked her usual bloom, and seemed wrapt in painful thought. The earl having bade adieu to the two ladies, once more returned to the house; the door was closed behind him, and the carriage was just in motion, when Grace raised her head and beheld the face of her lover gazing tenderly on her, but never before had she seen him pale as now. She started; her cheek glowed crimson, and beckoning him to the side of the carriage, she stretched out her lily palm, and laid it on his hand.

"You are ill, Edward," she exclaimed, as she did so; "your hand burns with fever; tell me what has happened."

"Nothing, dear Grace," he replied, "I am slightly indisposed, but it is scarcely worth mentioning. You will pardon me this intrusion," he added, "but I was so anxious to behold you once more. I could not resist the opportunity of doing so."

"Once more, dear Edward? how strange those words sound," said Grace, sadly.

"I meant, love, once more before you leave London, just to say farewell."

Edith here whispered Grace that she was fearful Arthur might observe them in conversation with Villiers.

"And if he does," replied Grace spiritedly, "I am not ashamed to be seen speaking to the man who is soon about to become my husband."

"Believe me," said Edward, bowing politely to the countess, "I have too much respect for he earl to be desirous of risking his displeasure. I hope speedily to convince him of the injustice e is now practising towards us both, dear Grace."

"When may I expect to see or hear from you?" said Grace, bending an anxious glance upon her lover."

"In a few days at the furthest," replied Edward, "you may depend upon doing so."

"They will be days of painful anxiety," returned Grace. "Alas, that this separation should be needful."

"I will not detain you longer," said the young man, pressing her hand tenderly in his own, and venturing for one brief moment to carry it to his lips; "farewell, dear Grace, till we meet again."

"Farewell, dear Edward," she returned, her eyes streaming with tears, strive, if possible, rather to convince than irritate Arthur, and all may yet be well."

She released his hand while she spoke, smiled a last adieu, and in another minute she was gone—gone for ever.

> "Yes, hapless pair, you've looked your last,
> Your hearts should both have broke in twain,
> Your fate is sealed, your doom is cast,
> You'll never meet on earth again."

Edward Villiers felt the truth of this as he wended his way towards his own home, once so blessed and peaceful, as it still might have been, had he been content with the love of one whom he so fondly treasured.

"How madly I have acted," was his inward exclamation. "Oh, Grace, I have made you wretched as well as myself, for the sake of gaining one for whom I have no regard, beyond the kind feeling our relative position naturally occasioned."

On his arrival home, his mother, with an anxious countenance, presented him with a letter, which had come for him in his absence. Breaking the seal, he read the following lines :—

"DEAREST EDWARD,—Is it possible that you have totally forgotten me, is a question I have asked myself a thousand times, during the last two days; and I cannot believe it is possible. And yet how otherwise am I to interpret your protracted silence?

"I have seen my sister, and learnt from her the full particulars of her interview with you, but she has now left me to act as my heart dictates.

"Dear Edward, I fully believed you spoke truth when you told me that you loved me, or I never had left your mother's tender care. My heart, even at the moment of doing so, accused me of cruelty and ingratitude towards the kind friends who had so long afforded me a shelter. Nothing but your repeated assurance, that our marriage would be more forwarded by my absence,

and that your happiness depended upon such an arrangement, would have induced me to act in the manner I have done.

"You will come or write to me soon? in full expectation of which, believe me, dear Edward,

"Affectionately yours, HELEN."

Edward avoided his mother's searching looks, as he read this epistle, and crumpling it into his pocket, hastened from the room, and descended to the counting house. His father was absent on business; this was well, as it afforded him an opportunity of replying to Helen's letter without fear of interruption, and seizing a pen, he scrawled a few lines.

No. 10.

WE beg to apologize to our numerous subscribers for unfortunately putting the same engraving in Nos. 9 and 10 of Ravensdale. With the accompanying number are issued two other pages in lieu of those which now stand 73, 74. By sending them to the binder with the other parts of the work, you will not

He was in the act of sealing this letter, when a gentleman in military uniform, an entire stranger, entered, and requested to know if his name were Villiers.

"It is," replied Edward, guessing instantly the nature of his errand.

"And that is mine," replied the stranger, politely handing him a card, on which the young man read "Captain Johnstone."

"Oh, indeed," said Edward, conceiving it was necessary for him to say something, and yet scarcely knowing what to say.

"Yes," replied the other, "and when I inform you that I call here this morning on behalf of my friend the Earl of Clavering, you will at once comprehend the nature of my a——busi-ness," he added emphasising the last word.

"There is no difficulty whatever about that," returned Edward, "the earl it appears has taken affront at something in my conduct towards——

"His charming sister, the beautiful Lady Grace," interrupted the other.

"I think you rather misapprehend the case," began Edward.

"By no means," returned the the stranger, "the earl explained the circumstances connected with it, fully and clearly to me this morning."

"Indeed! then, perhaps you will have the goodness to enlighten me; for I must confess I am somewhat in the dark."

"Nothing easier. It appears that you have offered an unpardonable affront to the Lady Grace."

"Is that the lady's opinion, or merely that of her brother."

"That it is utterly impossible for me to determine."

"But I desire to have it determined, sir, for if the Lady Grace considers I have at any time behaved with the slightest disrespect ever towards her, I am ready, nay eager to offer any atonement she may desire."

"I came not here to canvass this subject, but merely to bring a message from my friend," coldly replied the other.

"Deliver it then at once," returned Edward.

"In such cases as the present, it is customary to refer the party bringing a challenge to a person whom you would like to act as your second," said the stranger, with increased coldness.

"Oh," said Edward, "then I have at last obtained a clue to the nature of your——business—I believe that is the word," he added somewhat sarcastically.

"As you please," returned the other; "but the earl is anxiously waiting my return."

"I am sorry, indeed, to put him to so severe an inconvenience," replied Edward; "You may tell him from me, that I utterly deny having offered any affront to his sister. I love and revere her too much to be capable of doing so."

"She is, indeed, a charming girl," replied the other; "I admire her much.',

"You had better speak of her, then, in more respectful tones. Perhaps, sir, you are not aware that in a few weeks the Lady Grace will become my wife."

"Oh, I heard a rumour to that effect; but, depend upon it, it's all u——p now."

"You will do well, sir," said Edward, striving to keep down his rising passion, "to confine yourself entirely to the business that brought you here this morning."

"Very good," returned the other, in the cold contemptuous tone that seemed natural to him. "I am waiting to receive your answer, and then I'm off."

"My answer to what?" said Edward.

"To the message I have brought from the Earl of Clavering."

"Well, sir, when you think fit to deliver that message, you shall have my answer immediately."

"The earl wishes you to refer me to a third party, with whom I can make arrangements concerning a duel that he is desirous should come off between you two, the earlier the better."

"As I am not prepared to name such a person at present," said Edward, "if you will have the goodness to favour me with your address, it will answer the same purpose."

The captain named a fashionable club, and pressing upon the mind of Edward the necessity of his instantly seeking a suitable person, bowed himself out.

"Well, it is all clear now," thought Edward, as soon as he was alone, "there is nothing mistakeable about it; and the sooner I can select a person who may be willing to befriend me in this matter, of course it will be the better."

Yet who to apply to was the difficulty at this juncture. He bethought himself of an army acquaintance. Perhaps the sight of Captain Johnstone's regimentals refreshed his memory on his point, but be that as it may, he instantly resolved to lose no time in soliciting his assistance for although their acquaintance was of a very slight nature, he knew sufficient of the other's character to induce the belief that he would readily undertake the office he wished to assign him.

Young Villiers, consequently, without more delay, repaired to the lodgings of this gentleman, and sending up his card was instantly admitted.

Lieutenant Marston was in the full enjoyment of a bachelor's breakfast, when Edward Villiers was announced, and appeared to be dividing his attention pretty equally between the buttered toast, eggs, ham, chocolate, &c, and the morning papers, which, with the different monthly journals, were scattered about the table.

"Ah, Villiers!" he exclaimed, looking up from his paper, as the other entered: "be seated—no ceremony, my boy—make yourself quite at home." And the lieutenant prepared to refill his plate.

"I am afraid I am intruding at an unseasonable hour," began Edward.

"Not at all, my boy," interrupted the other, "only make yourself comfortable. Allow me to offer you a slice of this ham; I can recommend it as possessing the true Westphalian flavour."

"No, I thank you," returned Edward, "do not allow me to be any interruption to you; but for myself, I have already breakfasted."

"Ah, indeed. Well, I thought you intended me the honour of dropping in to partake of my bachelor's fare. No bad thing, eh?"

"Not at all; if I am to take this as a specimen," replied Edward, smiling; "but then you know the old adage says,

"'What's a table richly spread
Without a lady at its head?'"

"Oh, the deuce take that," replied the other. "My word for it, those lines emanated from the pen of a sour benedict, who wanted to make people believe how happy and blest he was, and so forth."

"It may be so," returned Edward, "and yet there is a want of sociability in a bachelor's life, that makes it anything but covetable in my eyes."

"My good fellow, look at me; see me here, monarch of all I survey. My right there is none to dispute; I go out happy and contented; I stay as long as the humour pleases me; when I return, I am in no dread of being lectured for my absence, neither have I any occasion to fear the frowns and pouts of my wife; books are my constant companions; if I want company they afford it me, and always with instruction and amusement. Moreover, the ladies, God bless them, are ever glad to receive me. I am welcomed with the sweetest smiles into all their little coteries, partake of all their plans for amusement and diversion, and in short, I enjoy all the pleasures of a married life without any of its ills."

"I cannot argue with you," replied Edward, "which you will readily believe, when I inform you that I hope myself, in a very short time, to become a benedict."

"This, then, is the secret of your early visit to me this morning. You have called personally to invite me to the wedding,—very kind of you, my boy, and though I am myself in no humour to follow your example, I shall make it a point to attend. I have no objection whatever to assist at the weddings of persons who have a fancy that way. Let me see, when did you say the interesting ceremony (as they call it) was to come off."

"You are too fast," replied Edward, "indeed you are quite out of your latitude. I do require your services, but not in the way you imagine."

"Ah, well, it matters not, I am entirely at your service," returned the good humoured lieutenant, "only let me know in what capacity I can oblige you."

"You are very kind," replied Edward, "and as you appear to have finished your breakfast, I will at once proceed to open the case."

And in as few words as possible, Edward informed him of the manner in which his services were required.

"What a duel! God bless my soul," exclaimed the lieutenant, all alacrity, "why, my good fellow did you not tell your errand the moment you came?"

"Then you are willing to oblige me," replied Edward.

"Willing, why, my good fellow, you surely could not for a moment doubt my willingness," returned the lieutenant, seizing the hand of Edward, which he wrung cordially in token of his good faith.

"No," replied Edward, "I did not doubt your willingness, I felt convinced if any one of my acquaintance would stand by me in such an unpleasant affair, it would be yourself, and I see that I have not judged erroneously."

"Well, let us waste no more time," returned the other, drawing forth his watch; "it is now on the stroke of twelve. I had better call upon this Captain Johnstone immediately."

"If you please," replied Edward, "and if convenient I will remain here, till you return."

"Perfectly, my dear fellow, make yourself as comfortable as possible. As you have break-fasted some time, I think you cannot do better than amuse yourself by partaking of lunch; order whatever you think proper, there's some prime old ale in the cellar."

"You are very kind," replied Edward, "but I must confess that anxiety for the result of my anticipated meeting with the Earl of Clavering leaves me but little inclination for eating."

"Pshaw, stuff," replied the other, "treat it (as it really is) as a mere matter of business, and you will find that it has no longer power to annoy you."

"Well," returned Edward, smiling as he took up a book, "I shall find amusement in your absence without having recourse to sensual enjoyment."

"Then give me my instructions and I'll be off."

"I have none to give," returned Edward.

"None to give?" replied the astonished lieutenant.

"None whatever," reiterated Edward, "I must, my good fellow, throw myself entirely upon your kindness to manage everything for me in this affair, as I am so totally ignorant of the laws of duelling that should I attempt to interfere I am certain to make some blunders."

"In that case," returned the other, "I must do the best for you I can, you of course know how to handle fire arms."

"Never made use of any in my life," replied Edward.

"That's decidedly against you; but on my return I will endeavour as far as possible to re-medy this defect by giving you a few instructions; for myself, they come perfectly as natural to me as a knife and fork."

"I am greatly indebted to you," returned Edward, "and feel that I have good reason for congratulating myself on having secured your services."

"Not at all," returned the good-natured lieutenant, "it is a pleasure to assist a friend. And now, my good fellow, make yourself perfectly easy that I shall manage this little business to the full satisfaction of all concerned."

"I do not doubt it," returned Edward. "Good morning."

CHAPTER XXIII.

" How wonderful is death,
Death and his brother sleep.
One pale as yonder waning moon,
With lips of lurid blue;
The other rosy as the morn,
When throned on ocean's wave,
It blushes o'er the world;
Yet both so passing wonderful !"

CHRISTOPHER WARDEN was reclining on the soft, yielding cushions of a richly carved couch near which was drawn a table spread with viands that might have tempted the most fastidious appetite, but his half emptied plate was pushed aside, and his face wore a troubled and anxious expression, and he regarded his cousin, who was seated opposite, doing full justice to the delica-cies that surrounded him, with an air of irritation, which was perceptible likewise in the tone of his voice, as he inquired how much longer he intended to go on eating.

"I am sorry," replied Lawton, "that your own appetite is so indifferent, but it seems a pity to send so many good things away untasted."

"Eat what you please," returned the other, "only for God's sake don't be all night about it." And covering his eyes with his hand, he relapsed into silence.

After a short interval, Lawton rose and rang the bell, and as he did so the youth again looked up and inquired if his meal was ended.

"It is," replied Lawton, "and now I am at liberty to talk to you."

"The devil you are," returned the youth; "I think you have talked enough for one day. Poor Marie !"

"Hush! not a word now," whispered Lawton, as the man entered to remove the dinner; "more of this when we are alone."

The servant here placed a card before Christopher, saying that the gentleman who gave it him would be glad to see him, if convenient.

"Oh, yes; show him up, by all means," replied the youth, without, as was his usual practice, first appealing to his cousin.

As the man departed to do his bidding, Lawton inquired the name of the party who so unceremoniously honoured them with a call.

"It is Mr. Moreton," replied the youth, with a slight hesitation in his manner. "I have not seen him for a long while, and, as I am terribly ennuied to-day, I thought his company might enliven me a little."

Lawton frowned, but was prevented speaking his displeasure by the entrance of the object of his dislike, who at this moment was ushered in by the servant.

Moreton bowed very distantly and coldly to Lawton, and then, seating himself by the side of the youth, took his hand, and kindly inquired after his health.

"I learnt from the waiter," said Moreton, "of whom I have daily made inquiries regarding your health, that, so far from approaching convalescence, your disease appeared to gain upon you; and this, Christopher, induced me to seek an interview."

"I was afraid," replied the youth, "that I had seriously offended you, it is so long since you have been here."

"I must confess," returned Moreton, "that I was both vexed and displeased with you, for so resolutely refusing to listen to advice, that was intended only for your own good."

"I fully believe what you said, when we were last together, was meant in all kindness and good feeling, and as such I received it, though I could not profit by it."

"Why not, Christopher?" replied Moreton, kindly.

"Oh, hang it, the deuce knows why, I suppose," returned the youth, with a show of irritability.

"Because," said Lawton looking up from a paper, with which he had up to the present moment, feigned to be absorbed,—"because it is neither proper nor customary for a young man of wealth and good family to unite himself to a poor and obscurely born milliner's assistant.

Your pardon Mr. Moreton; but when my cousin's health permits him to think of marriage, he must seek a bride from the halls of the high, and noble born; such are alone worthy to mate with him; though a commoner his family stands second in respectability and worth to none."

"I am not supposing they do," returned Moreton, mildly; "our views I am aware, on this as on most subjects, are utterly at variance; still I cannot refrain from saying, that in my opinion the ruin of an innocent and virtuous girl, is a spot upon a man's honour, that nothing but doing justice to the unfortunate object of his love, can atone for, or wipe away."

"Christopher never refused her justice; he provided her a home, and every comfort that Marie might possibly require; less, he would not do; more, he could not do."

"You willfully misunderstand me;" replied Moreton; "but it is of little or no importance. I am sorry," he added, turning to the youth; "to observe that you look more indisposed than I was prepared to expect."

"The fact is," replied the youth, "that I cannot bear any allusion to be made in my presence to that unfortunate girl; would to God I had never seen her, she has caused me more misery than aught else on earth."

"That is rather a selfish regret," returned Moreton; "for if the connexion has been a cause of anxiety to yourself; how much bitterness and misery, think you, must it have resulted in to her? Poor girl!" continued Moreton; "she indeed must frequently wish she had never know you."

"Well," said the young man, "it is of no use making myself uncomfortable about it now,"

"None, whatever," said Lawton, shrugging his shoulders. "You have done all that was called for, Marie wanted for nothing."

"I may conclude then, that Marie is?"—— began Moreton.

"Dead," interrupted the youth; "I am sorry for her, but of course I could not possibly foresee,"——

"Dead!" interrupted Moreton, in his turn; "Good God! it cannot be!"

"You were not aware of it then," replied the young man, in a tone of surprise.

"Aware of it! no Christopher, indeed, I can scarcely believe it true. Who, may I ask, was your informant?"

"I was, Mr. Moreton; thoroughly grieved at the untoward event, and naturally fearing it might occasion a shock to my cousin's feelings in his delicate state of health, to be avoided if possible.

I yet conceived it a positive duty to inform him of Marie's accouchment, and subsequent death," said Lawton.

"The child," replied Moreton, surveying the other with a suspicious aspect.

"Was still-born," returned Lawton; "and hopes were at first entertained that Marie would recover, but though every attention was bestowed upon her, she gradually became worse, and ultimately expired within twelve hours after the birth of the infant."

"Then," said Moreton; "I have no hesitation in saying, that she came unfairly by her end."

"Unfairly by her end!" exclaimed the youth, starting from the couch; "Good Heavens! what would you say?"

"That your cousin shall be made to answer for her death. He, doubtless, considered her an easy victim, a friendless orphan; but he will find to his sorrow that there is an arm ready to revenge her injuries, and cause them to bitterly recoil upon his own head. Farewell, Christopher, I can stay no longer now;" and without even casting a glance towards Lawton, he prepared to leave the room.

Lawton, who had again taken up the paper, now laid it on the table, and turning towards Moreton, said, carelessly,—

"Of course, Mr. Moreton, you will apologise for the ungentlemanly manner in which you have just expressed yourself?"

"I am not accustomed to offering apologies," replied Moreton, with a look of withering contempt.

"Oh, very well," returned the other; "unless you choose either to offer an apology, or to withdraw the insulting expressions you just made use of ——"

"If you deem it an insult to affirm that you have, in an underhand manner, caused the death of that truly unfortunate girl, so far from withdrawing that statement, I again repeat it, and shall still continue so to do."

"Just as you please," replied Lawton; "only remember I shall expect satisfaction for this ungentlemanly outrage."

"You shall have it to your heart's content, never fear," returned Moreton, sarcastically.

Lawton's lip curled as he repeated,—

"Fear and myself are utter strangers to each other; I leave such cowardly feelings to those who may like them better. Curse him!" he added, as Moreton, without offering a word more, left the room; "he had better take heed how he crosses my path again, the canting, hypocritical hound."

"Who do you mean?" said the youth, dropping back on to his downy pillows, with an appearance of extreme lassitude.

"Who should I mean," said Lawton, angrily, "but that sneaking, cowardly fool who has left us? He took care to make his escape, at the right time, too, in order to avoid a challenge. Bah! I hate such ——"

"There, that will do, Lawton," interrupted the youth; "can't you talk about something else?"

"Certainly, anything else you please; I am sorry that Moreton should have called, and thus disturbed the harmony of our evening."

"Curse it!" exclaimed the youth, turning uneasily on the couch; "I can't get that girl out of my head, and I am resolved, come what will, to see her once more."

"See her once more!" reiterated Lawton.

"Yes, see her once more. I speak plain enough, don't I?"

"As far as the words go, of course you do; yet I am puzzled to comprehend how you are to see the girl, when, as I told you before, she is dead."

"Well, but she is not buried."

"True, she is not buried; but, my dear Christopher, you surely do not intend ——"

"I do intend," interrupted the youth, peevishly, "to look upon Marie once more; and when I have thoroughly made up my mind to do anything, it is no use to attempt to dissuade me from my purpose. Curse it! I should think you knew that."

And Lawton did know it; and, though he would infinitely have preferred his cousin taking any other whim into his head than this, yet he conceived it advisable to concede to his wishes, with the least show of opposition he could possibly assume; he therefore merely said,—

"I am sure, my dear Christopher, that I have ever evinced the greatest desire to oblige you, yet I must confess that I regard this as a most unreasonable request."

"What the devil ——" began the youth.

"Stop, my dear Christopher," interrupted his cousin; "I was about to say that, although I regard this as a most unreasonable desire, yet I, nevertheless, shall not hesitate to oblige you."

"That's well," returned the invalid; "pour me out a glass of wine—I'm confoundedly out of sorts, Jack."

"My dear Christopher," returned the other, as he handed him the wine, "you don't go the way to recover—'pon my soul, you don't."

"Ah," replied the youth, tossing off the wine, "I wish to God that I could recover. What a dreadful prospect to be laid up as I am now for, perhaps, the whole of my life! And yet there are times when I feel so well, that I think there is nothing at all the matter with me; and then again I feel so horridly weak and queer, that I'm cursed if I know what to make of myself."

"I tell you what it is, Christopher," replied his cousin; "if you would only keep your mind quiet, and not let every little thing worry and vex you so, my life for it, you would soon get quite strong and well."

"Do you think so?" returned the unhappy youth, with a wistful glance at his cousin's face.

"Ay, I'm sure so; you must keep up your spirits. Come, what do you say to a hand of cards, just by way of passing the time, and preventing you getting dolorous again?"

"I'm not much in a humour for cards, but still, as you say, they may be the means of keeping off the ennui that so threatens to oppress me; but pour me out some more wine—after all, wine's my best friend."

"You forget your humble servant," replied Lawten; "and yet I think you would be sometimes dull without me."

"True, true, Jack," said the young man; "I am often unkind, and forgetful of your services, but ——"

"Say no more about it," replied his cousin; "here comes more wine, and the cards; so let us be merry while we can, and happy when we may."

CHAPTER XXIV.

"Oh, that I now were dead!
Or, that I once again were mad!
And yet, dear Rosalind, not so,
For I would live to share thy woe.
Sweet boy! did I forget thee too?
Alas, we know not what we do,
When we speak words!"

ONCE more left entirely alone, Helen's thoughts naturally recurred to her lover. Yes, spite of the tender warnings of her sister, she did hope—nay, she almost believed that he was true. Catherine, she judged, was prejudiced. Cruelly betrayed and deserted herself, by one upon whom she had placed implicit reliance, it was by no means surprising that she should entertain a mean opinion of the sex. "But oh," thought Helen, "I am convinced she has judged erroneously of Edward; though all others are false, I cannot think it of him."

And thus, unfortunately for themselves, women ever make a saving clause in the favour of the one they love. Be it ever so apparent in the eyes of others that he is unworthy of her deep trusting tenderness, she refuses to be convinced, wilfully blinding herself to his failings. To her at least, he is all her warmest desire would have him.

Helen bitterly felt the unmerited wrongs that were heaped upon her sister; still she could not, or, perhaps we should rather say, would not, for a moment think it possible that Edward would have acted in a similar manner towards her.

Pleasing herself, therefore, with the hope that he would assuredly redeem his promise, and return to make her his bride, Helen's delighted imagination portrayed, in glowing colours, the sweet pleasure of making a home for Catherine and her child.

"We must all dwell together; Edward, I am sure, will offer no opposition to my wishes on this subject," she fondly whispered to herself. "Dear, dear sister, we shall yet be happy."

But as the day gradually drew to a close, and she neither saw nor heard from her lover, doubts and misgivings began to chase away the hopes she had so confidently entertained in the morning; sad and chilly forebodings crept through her mind, and tears, that sweet relief to the aching heart, fell in warm showers from her eyes.

"Alas," she exclaimed, "if Catherine has judged him right—if, in truth, he loves me not, oh, never more will I place faith or confidence in man; but I will not form too hasty an opinion. He may come to-morrow; at all events, I will write to him, to know the worst at once—it would be far better than this intolerable suspense."

In accordance with this resolution, Helen rose early the following morning, and wrote to Edward the letter which is already before the reader.

After she had despatched it, some hours at least must intervene before she could receive a reply, and Helen hovering between hope and fear, could only fold her hands and weep.

How sad and painful the thought that a woman's fond and tender devotion is frequently, only too frequently turned to gall and wormwood, and made the instrument of destroying for ever her own peace and happiness.

It is customary to think but lightly of blighted affection and disappointed love, but persons who can thus consider it, know little of a woman's heart, or how formed it is by nature for deep enduring tenderness; when she loves, she loves for ever; clings to the object of her adoration through good and ill report; and if he but smile upon her, cares not if all others pass her coldly by. Not even unkindness and neglect can utterly estrange him from her love, or make him an alien to her heart; how acute, then, her sufferings—how bitter her sorrow, when he for whom she was willing to make any and every sacrifice; with whom she fondly looked forward to years of happiness, made sweetly blessed, by the hopes of spending them with him;—oh! if he turn against her and coldly give her back her love as a prize he no longer values, though once so fondly sought, no words can depict her anguish. She may smile again, as brightly as in days gone by; may mingle in the giddy throng, and dance and sing the laggard hours along, but though pride may thus induce her to hide from an unpitying and selfish world, the intensity of her feelings, even in her gayest moments, be sure there is a sadness hovering o'er her spirit. A dark shadow has passed over life's bright sunny landscape, which nothing can efface; it will linger there to her latest day; the memory of her first, best love, clings nearer than aught else on earth to a woman's heart. She may love again, and perform well and tenderly the arduous duties that appertain to a wife and mother, but the recollection of her early love never fades from her breast, 'tis fondly cherished there. Yes; amidst many, perchance, "trivial fond records," it is engraven "on the tablet of her memory," in letters which even that ruthless destroyer—Time cannot efface.

Helen, we were saying, could only fold her hands and weep, as fear or hope by turns agitated her gentle bosom. How long, how dreary, the hours seemed, as one by one they passed away, and he came not.

The shadows of evening began to draw the dark curtains of night over the face of all created things, and despair sat heavily on the heart of Helen, when she was aroused from her despondency by the ever welcome knock of the postman, her breath came thick and short, while a cold perspiration stood in large drops on her forehead, as a letter in the well-known writing of her lover was placed in her hands—hands that trembled so violently, she could scarce break the seal that secured the envelope.

"He has not quite forgotten me; this will doubtless satisfactorily explain all, and I have been unkind enough to entertain suspicion of his faith," were the thoughts that quick as lightning shot through her mind, as she unfolded the welcome epistle. Alas! the first line sufficed to wring her heart with bitter anguish, but she steadfastly perused the contents, though frequently obliged to stop to dash away her tears, that nearly blinded her; the letter was as follows:—

"DEAR HELEN,—I feel that I have acted with cruelty and deception towards you, in leading you to believe that I returned the passion I was unfortunate enough to inspire in your breast. I say unfortunate, because I could not, and did not feel, that affection for you, I am sensible you merited. I was, from the first moment I beheld her, heart and soul, devoted to the Lady Grace and must acknowledge that I am rightly punished, now that I am threatened with the loss of her, who alone is dear to my heart.

"I cannot, Helen, ask you to forgive me, inasmuch as I cannot forgive myelf the duplicity I practised towards you. Thank God you are still innocent, and I am spared the additional misery of knowing that I have injured you.

"Forget the past, or if that is impossible, remember it only as a painful dream. Obliterate me as much as possible from your memory, and I hope that no thought of me will possess the power to disturb your peace.

"That your affection may speedily be placed on a more deserving object—one who has a heart disengaged to bestow, in return for your love, is the earnest wish of him who now begs to subscribe himself your sincere friend and well-wisher,　　　　EDWARD VILLIERS."

Alas! poor Helen, then, he whom thou hast so fondly loved and treasured in thy young heart, as the very type of honour and sincerity, has been only amusing himself at thy expense; deluding thee with the semblance of a passion he never felt; cheating thee with words of love, while his heart was entirely estranged. Alas, alas! that any should be found capable of acting so base and cruel a part, and yet many there are who, for the mere selfish gratification of a most unpardonable vanity, practice this species of deception towards the young and unwary.

Helen, after the first burst of sorrow was over, felt deeply humbled and mortified.

"Oh, that I were dead!" were the first words in which her overcharged feelings found vent, but the next moment she became sensible of the unkindness of such a thought, and she exclaimed, "No, no, my dear sister I must live to share thy sorrows and thy dear child's. Alas! did I forget him too? henceforth I devote myself to the task of assuaging my sister's sufferings, and in blessing and protecting her darling boy."

Thus nobly resolving, Helen ceased to weep. She earnestly prayed that her lover might be blessed with her he had chosen in preference to herself. Edward hinted in his letter that he was threatened with the loss of Grace. She could scarcely conceive how this might be, unless Grace had become acquainted with his conduct towards her. In that case it was possible that she might now refuse him her hand; but she hoped that all impediments would be removed, and that they might both be happy and blessed in their union.

Helen, as we have said, was deeply humbled. Every spark of pride was extinguished in her bosom; and the blush of shame crept over her cheek as she felt, that had she disguised her real

No. 11.

feelings towards Edward, she had been spared her present mortification. And yet how unmanly how ungenerous of him to take advantage of her love, to crush her spirit, and wring her heart.

"I could never," thought poor Helen, "thus cruelly trample and triumph over the meanest object that loved and reverenced myself." And we would reply, "No Helen, you could not; but men are seldom blessed with the gentle, tender feelings that ever animates the heart of woman; self is generally the first object, and little they regard aught that interferes with or opposes it.'

"Adversity, like the toad, ugly and venomous, wears yet a precious jewel in its head," and this affliction had taught Helen a useful lesson; she became sensible that she had been guilty of great ingratitude to Mrs. Villiers, who had filled towards her the place of her dead parent, and that she had likewise been far too eager to receive the overtures of Edward, although she knew him at the time to be engaged to another, and last, though far from least, how unwisely she had acted in permitting herself to elope with him.

She saw it all now. If he meant to marry her what need of her quitting his mother's care—that mother, who was only too anxious to forward a marriage between them. As these thoughts passed through her mind, the tears again coursed each other down her cheeks; but this time they were shed for her own sins, not for the falsehood of her lover. And on her bended knees did she return her thanks to God, for having in the midst of danger preserved her still pure and innocent. She shuddered at the thought of what she might have been, but for the tender perseverance of Catherine, who had acted so resolutely in drawing from Edward the secret of her abode.

"Dear sister," she exclaimed, her eyes again filling with tears, "had any one thus befriended you, you too had been still innocent." And with the thought of her sister came also the recollection of the promise she had given to write to her as soon as she saw or heard from Edward.

And she instantly wrote a few lines, begging her to come to her as soon as possible. "We must henceforth live together, dear Catherine," she wrote in conclusion, "our wants are but few, and we can surely find some employment, that will be sufficient to procure the necessaries of life; more, neither of us desire; each other's society will supply the want of all else. My heart assures me, dear sister; that you will not refuse me this favour. Animated therefore, with the sweet hope that we shall soon meet, never to part again. I shall, my dear Catherine patiently await your arrival."

This done, Helen retired to rest, with a more peaceful bosom than she could have anticipated. The consciousness of her own errors had calmed the storm of sorrow that would otherwise have threatened to overflow her soul with anguish. And though she felt that, most probably, the whole of her after life would be tinged with melancholy, yet she resolutely repelled the starting tear, and hushed the rising murmur, determined, if possible, to forget him who neither loved nor cared for her.

CHAPTER XXV.

"Oh! speak not so,
But come to me and pour thy woe
Into this heart, full though it be,
Aye, overflowing with its own.
I thought that grief had severed me,
From all beside who weep and groan.
Its likeness upon earth to be,
Its express image; but thou art
More wretched. Sweet, we will not part
Henceforth, if death be not decisive;
If so, the dead feel no contrition."

CATHERINE was busily engaged with her pupils, though it must be confessed, her thoughts frequently wandered from her youthful charge, and fled back to her sister from whom she had not heard since her departure and anxiety began to fill her breast. Yet, she strove to confine her thoughts wholly to the school room; when, to her surprise, a servant entered and informed her, that a gentleman who wished to see her was waiting below.

"What name did he give?" inquired Catherine, doubtfully.

"He declined to give any," replied the servant; "but he wishes to see you immediately."

"It is a very inconvenient time," said Catherine; "and I do not think Mrs. Porter will like me to leave the school-room."

"Oh! yes," returned the servant; "she desired me to tell you that you were to come down."

"Then she has seen this person herself?" replied Catherine.

"Oh! yes, he inquired for her in the first instance."

Completely bewildered as to whom the party could be, or the nature of his business, as regarded herself, Catherine was yet by no means forgetful of her duties; and, having first given each of the children employment, and cautioned them to continue it during her absence, she descended to the parlour, feeling pretty well assured in her own mind that her visitor would turn out to be no other than Edward Villiers. Great was her surprise, then, on entering the room, to behold the Earl of Clavering. Vexed and angry at this unlooked-for intrusion, Catherine would have retreated, had he not instantly closed the door; and taking her hand, drew her into the middle of the room, saying, as he did so,—

"Catherine I wish to speak to you anxiously, you will not surely refuse to listen to me."

"Say on," she returned; disengaging her hand from his. "Only, let me entreat you to be brief."

"Oh! Catherine, this coldness is almost more than I can bear; though not more than I deserve. You that were once all tenderness and love, to be thus changed, and I alas! the cause."

"To the point, sir," replied Catherine, scornfully; "I have neither time nor inclination to listen to this tirade."

"You discredit me," replied the Earl: "I have deceived you once, and you fear to trust me again. But, I love you Catherine! I have loved you with a tenderness and constancy, that men seldom know. Had I consulted my own heart, none dear Catherine, but you, would ever have become my wife; neither was I actuated, as perhaps you may imagine by mercenary motives in giving my hand to my cousin, while you alone possessed my entire love and affection. The truth is dear Catherine, that from childhood, I was betrothed to Edith. I promised her dying mother that I would love and protect her child, and when we were of age make her my wife. I have fulfilled that promise as far as it was possible for me to do so, I strove to tear your image from my heart, to give to her the vacant place, but it was all in vain. I felt, I feel that love dwells with the free. You alone can make me happy, your smile will ever be to me a sweet solace; without you I am lost and wretched."

Catherine had listened patiently to the foregoing expressions of the earl without offering the slightest remark, or attempting to interrupt him; but now that he paused, she looked up with a scornful eye, as she said,—

"Well, sir, have you done? for my time is too precious to be wasted thus."

"Is, then, every spark of love for me extinguished in your breast?"

"Wholly and entirely," replied Catherine, "nor is it possible, under any consideration for it ever to be rekindled. I blush with shame to know that such ever existed. Will this satisfy you?"

"No, Catherine; love may sink by slow decay, but by sudden wrench, believe not hearts can thus be torn away. A duel is about shortly to take place between myself and Mr. Villiers; if I survive, will you, dear, dear Catherine, be to me again what you once were?"

"Never!" replied Catherine, indignantly.

"Stop a moment, Catherine, before you decide. I will remove you instantly, from this life of toil and anxiety, and place you in a situation of ease and comfort; no want, nor even wish, shall remain ungratified. I will secure to you a competence that even my death cannot deprive you of; your child (at these words Catherine started, and turned deadly pale) shall be amply provided for; your sister, likewise."

"And in return for all this vast amount of benefits, what will you expect?" replied Catharine, and her lip curled proudly.

"Nothing beyond your love and kindness. Be to me what you once were, and you secure to yourself and child (and he laid great stress upon the word 'child,') everything that makes life pleasant and desirable."

"Your offer is an insult, a deep and burning insult; but I am poor and friendless, and must, therefore, submit to it. But know, sir, that I renounce all your offers with the scorn and contempt they so well merit."

"This conduct, Catherine," said the earl, sternly, "forces me into the conviction that you never loved me, but only feigned a passion with the hope of becoming my wife."

"Think so, by all means, if it please you," returned Catherine. "I shall be at no pains to undeceive you," and she turned towards the door.

"Am I to understand, Catherine," replied the earl, "that you have fully decided to refuse my offer?"

"Most decidedly," said Catherine, and she placed her hand upon the lock, with the intention of leaving the room, but she was arrested by the voice of the earl.

"Catherine," he said, "think well before you decide upon a course of action that may result in the ruin of yourself and child. I will give you three days to consider my proposition."

"I am infinitely obliged to you," replied Catherine, satirically; "but at the same time, beg to inform you that, from this moment, I shall dismiss the matter entirely from my thoughts, therefore, your kindness is wholly lost upon me."

"Will you doom your child," said the earl, scornfully, "to a life of care and toil, when it is in your power to secure to him ease and independence?"

"Cheerfully will I do so," replied Catherine.

"You refuse to take time to consider my proposal?"

"If I did not," returned Catherine, "I should be an object of contempt even to myself!"

"Then," replied the earl, warmly, "it is my duty to provide for my child; its welfare is equally dear to me as to yourself."

Catherine laughed scornfully, and was on the point of making some angry retort, when she was interrupted by the entrance of Mrs. Porter, who swam into the room, at this juncture, with more even than her usual dignity.

"I am shocked, Miss Montravers," she began, darting a fiery glance at Catherine, "at the awful duplicity you have practised towards me. Such a compound of baseness and deceit is really dreadful to contemplate in one so young."

And the lady clasped her hands, and closed her eyes, as if the sight of the hapless Catherine was really too horrible for her to endure.

"I am at a loss, madam, to conceive to what you allude," replied Catherine, with a burning cheek. "I have endeavoured, at all times, faithfully to perform my duty towards my pupils; and——"

"This will not serve you," interrupted the indignant lady. "I have not listened to any part of the conversation that has taken place this morning, between yourself and the Earl of Clavering, but I could not shut my ears, and the consequence is, that—that——"

"That you heard what passed between us," said the earl. "In that case, my dear madam, you will be willing to allow that I am far more to blame than this young lady."

"It is very kind of your lordship to be so anxious to exculpate Miss Montravers," replied the lady, "but your lordship must admit that she is not a proper person to be entrusted with the care and education of young persons. I am sure I had no idea what sort of a person I was encouraging, she so completely imposed upon my credulity. Dear, dear, I never could have conceived her capable of such deceit; and that illness, too, at Paris, with which I so kindly sympathised, it appears was nothing but a feint."

To all this, Catherine made no reply; she hid her face in her clasped hands, but shame chained her tongue, and though her bosom heaved in painful throes, she remained perfectly silent; but the earl remarked, in reply to the lady, that, since she was cognisant of Catherine having borne a child, he could scarcely conceive how she could term her illness a feint.

"Your lordship must surely understand the sense in which I applied it. I meant, of course, as far as awakening my sympathy in her behalf, it was a feigned illness."

"I should suppose," replied the earl, "that under the peculiar nature of her illness, Miss Montravers would more greatly require kindness and sympathy; and to whom could she look for it, if not to her own sex?"

"I am sorry to be obliged to differ from your lordship," replied the lady, "but I cannot conceive that a woman who has outraged all propriety and decorum requires sympathy with the consequence of her error; and I know my own position and what is due to it too well to encourage such persons. Miss Montravers," she continued, glancing at her with virtuous indignation, "the sooner you quit this house the better."

"I will go at once, madam," replied Catherine, raising her head; "I had previously entertained thoughts of leaving, and shall therefore gladly do your bidding."

"Of course you cannot expect me to give you a recommendation to any other family."

Catherine merely replied, "Of course not," and left the room to prepare for her departure; her wardrobe was but scantily stocked, and therefore required but little preparation previous to removal her arrangements were soon completed, and this done, she was preparing to descend to acquaint her employer of her readiness to depart, when the servant presented her with a letter. It was from Helen, urging her instant return to her. Catherine pressed it tenderly to her lips, as she mentally exclaimed, "Yes, dear sister, our wants are but few, and those my hands shall supply, we are now all the world to each other, and our mutual love will supply the place of all others."

Filled with this sweet hope, Catherine presented herself before her unfeeling employer with a serener brow and calmer aspect; she was, nevertheless somewhat vexed to find that the earl had not (as she anticipated he would have done) left during her absence; she, however, heeded him not, but addressing Mrs. Porter, stated her readiness for instant departure.

"It is well," replied the haughty lady, "I shall not reproach you for the deception you have practised towards me, neither do I consider it worth while to seek to convince you of your error, inasmuch as you must be lost to all sense of decorum."

"My dear madam," interrupted the earl, angrily, "do pray spare us; we are conscious of having committed a most flagrant error in supposing you to be endowed with the tenderness and gentleness which forms so pleasing a characteristic in most of your sex."

"Do you intend to insult me?" replied the offended lady.

"On no account, madam," returned the earl, "nothing was farther from my thoughts; come Catherine."

"I am going, but not with you, sir," said Catherine; "I should well deserve the deepest obloquy and shame to be heaped upon my head, were such my intention; but it is not." Then, turning to Mrs. Porter, she added, "You overheard our conversation, madam, and will therefore do me the justice of believing that there is not another creature on earth I hold in such bitter scorn and contempt as the Earl of Clavering."

"You have already acted with such unparalleled duplicity, Miss Montravers," replied the lady, "that I cannot believe aught that you affirm; to be sure, there may be a motive for your thus refusing his lordship's offers."

"You say truly, madam, I am actuated by a motive—a deep and powerful motive; nor do I hesitate to declare it; it is, madam, a thorough hatred of vice. None can know what a bitter poisonous draught it is, like those who have (by specious and delusive promises) been induced to drink therefrom; I am one of those unfortunates. I did but raise the fatal cup to my lips, but the draught was too soul sickening, and I dashed it to the ground; nothing on earth would ever induce me to drain it to its dregs. No, I have steadfastly turned away my head, and refused to touch it more."

Catherine spoke these words with deep emphasis, and her glowing cheek and sparkling eye bore ample testimony to the truth of what she said. Sad indeed that the door of mercy should be too often closed against the return of the unfortunate. Oh, treat her kindly; let gentle words sink deep into her soul; oh, draw her with the tender cords of love back into the bright and flowering paths she has forsaken; speak peace to her troubled soul; open wide your arms to receive the wanderer back; never name her sin, or name it only as past and grifoven; oh, were there more of this, there would be much less of sin and sorrow in this sweet sunny land of ours.

Mrs. Porter was too indignant, and conceived herself, likewise, too deeply injured, to reply to Catherine's speech, otherwise than by a scornful toss of the head, and a stately good morning; having done this, she retired to another apartment, there to ease her excited feelings by bitter invectives against the unfortunate in general, and Catherine Montravers in particular.

"Once more," said the earl, addressing Catherine, when they were again alone, "let me entreat you, if not for your own, at least for your child's sake."

"Arthur," replied Catherine, "and it was the first time since their parting, that she thus addressed him, "I have told you that it is utterly useless for you to attempt ever to induce me to regard you otherwise than as an entire stranger; our paths in life are henceforth distinct and seperate. You are the husband of an amiable and deserving woman, and I should deem myself unworthy the name of one, could I for one moment encourage your advances. I see," she added, glancing towards the window, "that the coach I sent for has arrived; let this be the last time we ever meet, and I may, perhaps, learn to pity and forgive you. You have totally misunderstood my character, and—but it matters not."

"Am I then," said the earl, "to know myself a father, and yet to be allowed no interest in, or even to be permitted to see my child."

"Exactly," replied Catherine, "I desire to keep you entirely separate, and from me he shall never learn his true parentage; it will be better, far better, for him to remain in ignorance of the whole."

"But I am anxious to provide for him."

"Cease, cease," said Catherine, "you weary, but do not, and never will move me. I have no occasion to linger here a moment longer. Good morning," and Catherine left the house of Mrs. Porter with far more satisfaction than when she entered it.

The earl quietly followed her example, and took the road to his own home, out of temper with himself, Catherine, and indeed the whole world.

Possessed of almost every blessing that is coveted by the world; young, noble, and wealthy; united to a beautiful and deserving woman, whose greatest pleasure was to make him happy, surely the Earl of Clavering ought to have considered himself blessed above the ordinary lot of mortals, but no; 'perverse fate' as he termed it, (but we should rather say his own folly), had willed it otherwise, and though an object of envy to others, he was very far from being happy, or even contented himself. And many there are who, like the young nobleman, are looked upon as fortune's favourites, could we but penetrate into the secret recesses of their bosoms, we should find them as far removed from happiness as he. Every heart knows its own joys, and i's own bitterness; consequently we should pause before we covet the lot of another. Rather let us endeavour to be contented with the portion of joy that Providence assigns us, for as there is no unmixed happiness, so surely is there no bitter without its accompanying sweets.

Catherine proceeded on her journey with a lightened heart, though shame had clouded her cheek, and lent an additional lustre to her eye. Yet the glad consciousness that she had steadfastly resisted all temptation that would have lured her again to sin and sorrow, made her almost happy, and when she alighted at her sister's residence, and clasped her once more to her bosom, she wept such precious tears—tears that were blest and sanctified as the herald of a penitent heart, whose sins are all forgiven.

> " Think, think, what victory to win
> One radiant soul again from sin,
> One wandering star of virtue back,
> To its own native heavenward track."

So thought and felt Helen, as she kissed off her fast falling tears, and with kind and soothing words bade her be of good cheer.

" I have been selfish enough, sweet sister," she said, " to think of little but my own troubles since last we parted, but I feel now, Catherine, how much more reason you have to be miserable than myself."

" We will not talk of being miserable, dear Helen," replied Catherine, kindly; " let us rather think how happy we may be. I have come, love, to stay with you; henceforth we will not part."

" Oh, sweet happy words," returned Helen, "they cheer my drooping spirits, and endue me with fresh hope. You are fatigued now, dear Catherine, but to-morrow we will settle our plans for the future."

CHAPTER XXVI.

> " Save him, my God! she only cries,—
> Save him this night—and thine eyes
> Have ever welcomed with delight
> The sinner's tear, the sacrifice
> Of sinner's hearts—guard him this night,
> And here, before thy throne I swear,
> From my heart's inmost core to tear,
> Love, hope, remembrance, though they be
> Link'd with each quivering life-string there,
> And give it bleeding all to thee!"

WE left Edward Villiers somewhat anxiously waiting the return of his friend Lieutenant Marston, whose absence was extended beyond the time he had looked for, and it was utterly in vain that Edward strove to beguile the tediousness of the hours by endeavouring to fix his attention upon the journals, which evidently interested his friend; his mind was too much employed in brooding over his own anxieties, to find aught of interest in works of fiction.

He rose from his seat and paced the room with rapid strides, revolving as he did so, the probable result of the expected meeting between himself and the earl. Alas! even if he survived, he almost despaired of gaining the hand of Grace, so fondly sought, and he had deemed, so proudly won; the love of that fair, fond, gentle girl, he well knew was entirely his own, and immediately after the duel, he resolved to write to her signifying his desire to have their marriage take place without farther delay. "I am confident Grace will willingly assent to any proposal that I may deem it best to make," said Edward, half aloud, as he pondered over all that was past, and the probable issue of the future.

"Ah, what's that you say?" exclaimed the lieutenant, bustling into the room.

"Nothing of any importance," replied Edward, laughing; "by Jove, I'm glad you have returned."

"Why, I've been talking the matter over with this Captain Johnstone," returned the other, "and talking is uncommon dry work; by-the-by, have you lunched, Villiers."

Edward replied in the negative.

"Dear me, no!" returned the lieutenant, with unfeigned surprise, "then I had better order it at once. I must confess, I'm confounded thirsty, just in cue for a bottle or so of ale.' And he rang the bell lustily.

A servant instantly obeyed the summons, and having received the lieutenant's orders, disappeared, but quickly returned with a tray laid for two, which she placed before them, together with the much boasted ale, to which the lieutenant prepared to do ample justice, inviting Edward to follow his example.

After a plate of cold fowl and ham had been disposed of, together with sundry glasses of ale, Edward ventured to inquire of the lieutenant, what arrangements he had made with respect to Captain Johnsten.

"Everything is settled," returned the other, "and I hope it will prove to your satisfaction."

"As far as you are concerned, I am sure it will," replied Edward, "but go on."

"You are to meet the earl to-morrow morning, at six o'clock, in some fields at Hampstead."

"So soon," replied Edward, turning pale, but he added, "it is all the better, it will sooner be over."

"Exactly, my dear fellow, these affairs ought always to be settled off hand, at once, and I invariably set my face against all delay."

"You are, no doubt, perfectly right, and for myself, I shall be heartily glad when it is over."

"You feel a little nervous of course: it is perfectly natural, a man always does the first time of going out, but it is astonishing how all that wears off, when you get a little used to it."

"I make no doubt of it," replied Edward, "and after all, a man can only die but once and as far as we are individually concerned, it is of very slight importance whether it come, a few years sooner or later."

"For myself," replied the other, "I could much easier be reconciled to a sudden and unexpected end, than to lie for weeks on a bed of sickness, deprived of all the enjoyments of life, and a trouble and burden likewise to others."

"And yet death is a sad and solemn thing," returned Edward.

"Rather so," replied his friend, "there is something offensive to the pride of manhood in the thought of becoming food for worms, and—but bah! I don't like to talk about such things; here, Edward, I'll pledge you in a bumper. Let me see," resumed the lieutenant, after a short silence, "I promised to give you a little instruction as regards the handling of pistols, and first of all, as you bear no malice and have no desire seriously to injure the earl, let me advise you to aim low."

"I certainly have not the slightest desire to injure my opponent," replied Edward, "but I verily believe, that he will do his utmost to injure me; if I escape, there will be no thanks due to the Earl of Clavering, you may depend."

"Ah, say you so," replied the other, "then listen to me; at a given signal you are both to fire, your aim must be, to be if possible a second before him, and so disable him, as to prevent him doing you any serious injury."

"Yes, that would be well of course, if I could so manage it, but I doubt my ability," replied Edward.

"Nonsense, stuff, with a little of my instruction you will find no difficulty; I'll take you to a shooting gallery this afternoon, where you will have an opportunity of practising."

"I suppose you have acted as principal as well as second," returned Edward.

"Twice; the first time I was as you may be, a little, a very little nervous, but the next time I was prime as a cock, regarded it as a mere matter of business, spent the previous evening among a party of choice spirits, contributed my portion for the amusement of the whole, slept soundly, walked out, settled the affair to the satisfaction of all concerned, and returned home with an excellent appetite for breakfast; that's the way to do things, my boy."

" Then you received no injury ?" inquired Edward.

" A trifle, scarcely worth mentioning, just sufficient to bleed me a little, and I was getting plethoric."

" And your opponent ?" said Edward.

" He likewise escaped with a trifling wound."

" I trust that I may be as fortunate to-morrow," replied Edward, " and though I cannot say that I am afraid to meet death as a man, yet I have many reasons for wishing to prolong my life, at least for a few more years."

" Ah, to be sure, and I have no doubt but you will come off whole and sound."

From this conversation Edward felt far more reassured, and began to entertain sanguine hopes for the result, and proceeded with something of his wonted alacrity to make the necessary arrangements for the expected meeting.

And first he wrote to his mother, informing her of his intention to remain for a few days a short distance from London, taking especial care to allow no word to creep in that could tend in any way to excite her maternal fears on his behalf.

Grace he was anxious to keep in total ignorance of the duel, at least till after it had taken place, and as he had but so lately parted from her he thought it best not to write till the following day, " When if I survive," he mentally exclaimed, " I will instantly take measures to secure her hand. Dear sweet Grace, it were hard to lose thee when so nearly won." Of Helen, whom he had so deeply injured, he never for a moment thought, nor did it once occur to him as possible that she was at that very instant weeping over his unkindness, and yet still praying for his happiness and welfare.

The day wore leisurely on, and towards evening Edward, accompanied by Lieutenant Marston, visited one of the shooting galleries, and received his initiatory lesson in the use of those deadly weapons, and after a little practice Edward found it much easier to hit a mark than he anticipated, and he determined as far as possible to follow his friend's advice, and make the right arm of his opponent his own aim, and by firing if practicable, a second or so sooner, prevent the earl doing him any very serious injury. We say as he had determined upon this, and hoped to be able to accomplish it, his spirits rose to almost their usual elevation, though he felt extremely annoyed by learning in the course of the evening from the lieutenant who had called, upon Captain Johnstone to definitively arrange the affair, that a mistake had arisen between them, as to the day appointed for the duel, it being not the morrow, but the day following.

" It is extremely annoying," said Edward, when his friend communicated this intelligence " how did the mistake arise ?"

" I scarcely know," replied the other, " but it is as you say annoying, inasmuch as we had hoped to have the affair settled earlier."

" Well, it is of no use lamenting," returned Edward, " it will make but the difference of one day, which will soon pass."

His friend assented, and ordering wine and cigars, they set down to enjoy the evening as they best might.

Lieutenant Marston was a warm-hearted, lively companion, rather perhaps overmuch given to the enjoyment of the good things of this world. Yet utterly free from selfishness in any and every shape, he liked to be happy himself, but not less did he like to see others so. And though in many respects gay and thoughtless, he was nevertheless open, manly, and generous. None ever appealed to him for sympathy or kindness in vain; he was equally ready to befriend all who needed his services, no matter what mode or station in life they might hold, and was never swayed by a thought even of mercenary motives. So that with some few faults, the young lieutenant was universally beloved, and as he was possessed of a goodly store of anecdotes, all of which were replete with wit and mirth, he contrived to beguile Edward of all sadness, and the evening was spent in pleasant and cheerful converse.

The following day too was far from being so tedious as might have been expected; indeed it passed away before Edward had time to wish it gone; it was of course, chiefly devoted to preparations for, and anticipations of the forthcoming duel.

" You must not, my dear fellow," said the good humoured lieutenant, " allow any melancholy reflections to disturb your sleep; a good sound night's rest is absolutely necessary, above all things else, to a man who requires all his energy and courage about him.

" I believe you are right," replied Edward, " and yet I feel as though it were impossible for me to sleep to-night;" and he rose from his seat, and approached the window which he opened and walked out into the balcony. The night was fine and beautiful,—

" On one side in the dark blue sky,
Lonely and radiant was the eye
Of Jove himself; while on the other
'Mid stars that came out one by one,
The young morn like a Roman mother,
Among her living jewels shone."

Edward looked upwards at the myriads of bright stars that spangled the heavens, then down at the sleeping earth, and as he did so, thoughts long forgotten came rushing back to fill his

mind with awe. He had never questioned the Christian creed, but rather taken it as the vulgar do, nor ever doubted the things men say, or deemed for a moment; were other than they seemed but now his mind appeared to expand as he looked abroad upon the wondrous works of God which though oft seen had never before thus affected him.

"How brightly the stars shine to-night," he remarked to his friend, who had joined him on the balcony.

" Not brighter, I think, than usual," returned the lieutenant.

" Perhaps not," replied Edward, " and yet, as I gaze upon them, a sensation appears to creep through my mind, filling me at once with awe and wonder, as I reflect that perchance each one of them is a world, and contains beings animated with like passions as ourselves."

"May be," returned the other, "but I have never been given to astronomy."

No. 12.

"Nor I," replied Edward; "and yet, as we must pass them on our road to Heaven, I'll contrive to get a look at them as I go by."

"Rather a strange subject for a jest," returned his friend, laughing.

"Jesting!" said Edward, with a serious expression of countenance, and in a tone of surprise; "I assure you nothing was farther from my thoughts. I was never more serious in my life than when I stated my intention of taking a peep at those bright worlds which so much excite my wonder now."

The lieutenant regarded him with a perplexed air, and then, gently drawing him into the room, closed the window, and strenuously urged him to retire to rest without delay.

Edward complied, more out of deference to the wishes of his friend, than with the expectation of obtaining that sweet boon to the weary—refreshing sleep, almost the only enjoyment that is not purchaseable.

Yet, notwithstanding his own anticipations, he no sooner laid his head on the pillow than he fell into a deep slumber, from which he did not awake till he was aroused by the voice of the lieutenant.

"Come, Edward," he exclaimed, laughingly; "it is time we were off, unless you intend to remain here, and allow me to fight in your place. Hang it," he continued; "I've half a mind to cut off, and leave you to seek what pleasure you can in the arms of Morpheus."

"Ah," said Edward, getting up in bed, and rubbing his eyes, "let me see—this is the morning appointed for the meeting of myself and the earl. What a confounded fool I must have been to lie sleeping here!"

"You had better proceed, then, to don your clothes," replied the other; "all is in readiness, but we have no time to spare; even using all haste, I am afraid we shall not reach the spot by the time appointed."

"Why, in Heaven's name, then, did you not awake me sooner?"

"Because, my good fellow," replied the lieutenant, "I was loath to disturb your apparently delightful slumber, and arouse you from pleasant dreams to the unpleasant realities of life."

While his friend was thus speaking, Edward had jumped out of bed, and commenced a hasty and somewhat unceremonious toilet, which having completed, with a little aid from his friend, he stated himself to be in readiness for starting.

"Wait a moment," replied the other, "it is absolutely necessary that we should take a little refreshment."

"But will the time admit of our so doing?" said Edward.

"It must," replied his friend; "it is utterly impossible for us to take so long a morning ride fasting."

"Be it as you please," returned Edward; "but for myself, I am impatient to be gone, and shall have a much better appetite for breakfast on my return than I at present possess."

But Lieutenant Marston was too accustomed to duelling to allow it for a moment to interfere with his appetite, and ate and drank till Edward was fairly out of all patience.

"Come," he said, at length, "I am sorry to be obliged to interrupt your breakfast, but will it signify if you finish it on our return?"

"I am quite ready, my good fellow," replied the other, "and shall likewise be ready for a second edition of breakfast after we have settled this trifling affair of yours."

"Then in 'Heaven's name, let us go; I should be sorry," he added satirically, "to keep the earl waiting."

"Very good," replied the lieutenant, rising from his seat, and reaching his hat, and turning to Edward. "Now then."

Edward was, of course, all alacrity, and in a few minutes they were seated in the coach that was engaged to convey them to their destination, and which was proceeding at a tolerably rapid pace.

"You must remember," said the lieutenant, "my instructions, and, above all, be cool—perfectly cool."

"I will endeavour to be so," replied Edward, smiling; "but you must bear in mind that I am a perfect novice at this sort of thing, and therefore cannot be expected to have that entire command of my feelings which might reasonably be hoped for from an experienced hand like yourself."

The lieutenant assented, and the remainder of their drive was passed in silence, for Edward was by no means inclined for conversation; an indescribable feeling of nervousness oppressed him—in vain he endeavoured to cast it off; and, though he attributed it to the right cause—the approaching duel, yet he felt vexed with himself for allowing it so powerfully to affect him. He strove to turn his thoughts to Grace, to picture the joy he should experience when he again beheld her—when he should clasp her in his arms, never more to part. But no; a dark and sad foreboding flitted, spectre-like, across his troubled mind, and warned him to bid adieu to earthly things.

He was roused from these mournful anticipations by the stopping of the carrriage, and in an instant more, the steps were let down, and his friend having jumped out, he prepared to follow his example.

"Have we far to walk?" he inquired, as they proceeded, at a brisk pace, down a retired lane,

"No, a few minutes will suffice to bring us to the scene of action," returned the other; "but, confound it, how pale you look! Come, this will never do, you know."

Edward made a desperate effort to rouse himself, and began to talk very fast about indifferent matters.

"Here we are," exclaimed the lieutenant, "and by Jove they have got the start of us."

At this moment Captain Johnstone advanced to meet them, and Edward withdrew a little on one side. The preliminaries were soon settled, and the seconds prepared to place the two opposite to each other.

The morning was dull and hazy, the sun was obscured by thick masses o clouds that rolled heavily along—it was one of those lowery mornings that frequently turn out bright, warm, and beautiful days. The closeness of the atmosphere was really oppressive—not a breath of air seemed stirring; the very heavens appeared to frown upon the deed of blood that was so soon to be enacted on that quiet spot.

Edward had not once caught even a glimpse of the earl till he confronted him face to face, and the distance was such that he could not obtain a clear view of his features. Yes, there they stood, each grasping the fatal weapon, waiting only the signal to raise them against each other

It was truly an awful pause; the very air was still—the light breeze fanned not their fevered brows —it paused to see them thus wantonly strive to break their Maker's law, "Thou shalt not kill."

Edward's very brow seemed on fire; he felt as though he were the victim of a horrid dream and the pistol shook in his hand like a reed.

Suddenly the signal that was agreed upon as the moment of firing struck upon his ear. In an instant he was calm; all nervousness was dispelled, as it were, by magic, and he raised the pistol, and levelled it at his opponent. As he did so, he perceived that the earl was evidently taking a deliberate aim at himself. Both fired, as nearly as possible, at the same instant; Edward's ball grazed the skin of his opponent's arm, and then fell harmlessly to the ground. Not so the earl's; it entered the left side of Edward, and passed out under his right shoulder.

"Ah, this is a bad job," exclaimed Lieutenant Marston, who was the first to raise Edward from the ground. "How do you feel?" he continued, bending anxiously over him.

"It will be my death," returned Edward; "I knew how it would be before I came." As he gave utterance to these words, his voice faltered, and he fainted from loss of blood. When he next opened his eyes, he found himself in bed, in a small, but clean and comfortable apartment. His friend was still by his side, and—could it be? Yes, Helen—the ill-used Helen smoothing his pillow, cooling his heated forehead, moistening his parched mouth, and, in short, performing, as woman only can, the kind and tender office of nurse.

CHAPTER XXVII.

" Hath, then, the gloomy power,
    Whose reign is in the tainted sepulchre,
    Seized on her sinless soul?
    Must, then, that peerless form,
    Which love and admiration cannot view
    Without a beating heart—those azure veins,
    Which steal like streams along a field of snow—
    That lovely outline, which is fair
    As breathing marble, perish?"

" Then you are still in the same mind," said Lawton, addressing his cousin Christopher

"Yes," replied the youth, "I am determined to see Marie once more. It will do me good to go out; I have been confined too long to the house."

"It would undoubtedly do you good to go out, Christopher, if you were strong enough to bear the exertion," said his cousin; "but I much question whether you are."

"I am resolved, at all events, to make the experiment," returned the youth.

"That being the case," replied Lawton, "I had better order a carriage."

"Do so, by all means," said the youth, "we had better go early."

The evening was warm and pleasant, and the sweet refreshing air really seemed to revive and invigorate the invalid; for many weary months he had been confined to the house, tossing backwards and forwards on his downy couch, languishing for health and vigour, and it was delightful in the extreme to be enabled to breathe once more the pure air.

"I have been a confounded fool, Lawton," said the youth, after they had proceeded a short distance, "to remain shut up for so long a time. Do you know," he added, smiling, "I am resolved to get well."

"A capital resolution," replied Lawton, with a shrug of his shoulders.

"Yes, is it not; why I verily believe that it is greatly in a man's power to live or die. Now, I want to get well, and I'm determined to do so. You see I have made a beginning."

"I do see," replied Lawton, "and I give you joy of it."

After a quiet drive through some of the principal streets of Paris, Christopher remarked that the carriage turned into the mean and obscure part of the city, and at length stopped at the entrance of a dull and dirty looking street.

"Are you agreeable, Christopher," said his cousin, "to walk a short distance, as it is scarcely worth while to take the carriage down here."

"Oh, yes; I think I can manage with your assistance."

"Then let me help you to alight," replied Lawton, and in a few moments they were walking arm in arm towards the residence of Madame Chevasse, at whose house they at length stopped, Lawton knocking gently at the door.

It was immediately opened by the lady herself, who evinced some surprise at seeing Lawton thus accompanied, but he hastened to reassure her by saying,—

"This gentleman, madame, is my cousin, Mr. Warden; you are aware of the attachment that existed between himself and Marie, and will not therefore be surprised, when I inform you of his desire to see her once more."

"Oh, dear; oh! pray walk in," replied the old woman, with officious politeness, ushering them into the room where she had received Lawton, when he introduced the ill-fated Marie.

"I am very sorry that she died," said Christopher; "I hope she received proper attention."

"Oh, dear," said the old woman, with an air of offended dignity, "you surely do not suppose that I was negligent. Ma'mselle had the very best of attendance, and she died thanking me for my kindness, and——"

"Yes, yes," said Lawton, "I do not for a moment doubt it, but you must excuse Mr. Warden, madame; he does not know you as well as myself; and his attachment to Marie excites fears that otherwise would never have existed."

"Certainly," replied the other, "I am willing to make every allowance; at the same time it is painful to my feelings to be accused of negligence."

"This is an uncommon dull sort of place," said Christopher, gazing at the dull and dreary prospect the windows afforded, and then at the dirty and forlorn appearance the room presented. "I don't at all envy those who are obliged to live here; indeed, the sooner we get out of it the better."

"You will oblige us, then, madame, by allowing us to see Marie.'

"Certainly," replied the woman, "this way, if you please;" and she proceeded up the staircase, followed by Christopher and his cousin; she halted on the landing, and opening one of the doors, bade them enter. As they did so, Christopher perceived that the room was of small dimensions, a carpet covered the floor, but in other respects it was totally destitute of furniture.

The coffin, supported on tressels, occupied the centre of the room, and the old woman cautiously advanced and removed the lid. Lawton stood a little behind, but Christopher approached and gazed for an instant intently on the face of the dead. He expected to have seen her pale, and changed, but not for a moment did he dream of seeing so sad and fearful a spectacle as met his eyes—so changed, so utterly and entirely changed, that he never could have recognised in the sunken and distorted features he now looked upon, the once beautiful and health-beaming countenance of Marie. He started back in horror, exclaiming as he did so,—

"How frightfully she is altered; come away, Lawton, for God's sake. I shall never get her out of my head; what a cursed fool I was to come!"

Lawton exchanged a glance with Madame Chevasse to the effect, that he fully concurred in the last part of his cousin's remark, but he offered no obstacle to their instant departure. When they were once more seated in the carriage, Lawton hugged himself with the belief that they had escaped unheeded; for neither of them observed Moreton, who, chancing to see them abroad, and with the quickness of perception for which he was remarkable, instantly suspected their errand, and followed stealthily in their footsteps, taking care to avoid recognition; but Lawton knew nothing of this, and was therefore well pleased with the success of their mission.

"Well, how do you feel now?" he began, as soon as the carriage was in motion.

"Why, curse it all," replied the youth, "did you not tell me how altered the girl was?"

"I beg your pardon, I am sure, my dear Christopher, but you really must excuse me, insomuch as I knew it not myself."

"Well," replied the young man, with an oath, "I have made a complete ass of myself, just as I was beginning to mend; it has thrown me back to that degree, I feel as though it were impossible for me to move."

"You would not be advised," replied Lawton.

"I know it, there is no one to blame but myself;" and he threw himself back in the carriage, completely exhausted both in body and mind.

On arriving at their hotel, the servant was obliged to lift the poor youth out and carry nim up stairs to bed, so utterly powerless had he become. His energy was entirely exhausted; and he passed a sad and restless night. The face of his dead victim constantly haunted his imagination; he saw it palpably and clearly even in the midst of the surrounding darkness: the sunken eyes, the distorted visage, the compressed lips, all were there. He shuddered, and he covered his head under the bed-clothes, but he could not shut out the horrid sight. A cold sweat bedewed his temples, and he trembled in every limb; he could bear it no longer; he seized the bell-rope, which fortunately was within his reach, and pulled it violently. Lawton obeyed the summons.

"For God's sake, don't leave me," exclaimed the youth, "Marie keeps staring at me so awfully, that I fear it will drive me mad."

"Compose yourself, Christopher," said Lawton, putting down the candle he held in his hand, and approaching the bed, "it's nothing in the world but imagination."

"You may call it what you please," replied the youth, still trembling, "but—ah! there she is again."

"Where—where, Christopher?" returned Lawton, "let me, if possible convince you of the folly of your present fears.'

"There, at the foot of the bed," said the youth, pointing in the direction, with ashy cheeks and trembling fingers. "See, she is peeping between the curtains."

Lawton instantly placed himself on the spot to which his cousin pointed, saying as he did so,—

"This surely must convince you of the fallacy of your supposition. You cannot see her now."

"Oh, yes," replied Christopher, still shuddering; "I can see her just peeping over your shoulder.'

Lawton moved quickly away, and at the same time an almost imperceptible chill appeared to creep over him, but he answered without any other show of uneasiness,—

"It is nothing in the world but your own foolish imagination, Christopher; were it otherwise she would of course be equally visible to myself."

"Well, stay with me, and I may perhaps be able to sleep."

Alas! poor Christopher; his mind was too full of horrors to permit him to sleep—it resolutely refused "to weigh his eyelids down, or steep his senses in forgetfulness."

"See—see," he constantly exclaimed, as he grasped Lawton by the hand, "how she frowns at us—how closely she bends over me—I cannot bear her presence. Ah! now I feel her hot, sulphurous breath burning on my cheek. It chokes—it poisons me! Away! away! Lawton— Lawton, take her away—drag her off me. I faint—I die! Will no one help me—air—I want air—open the window."

In vain Lawton tried to pacify him. Hardened as he was by nature, the sufferings of the unhappy youth touched even him—he summoned the servants, and sent for his medical attendant, who pronounced him to be in a high state of fever and delirium.

"Can anything be done for him?" inquired Lawton.

"Little or nothing," was the reply. "You must endeavour to keep his mind as quiet as possible. I will send him a composing draught that I hope may have the effect of rendering him more tranquil; that is all that can be done, but it would be proper to provide a regular nurse."

In accordance with this advice, Lawton despatched a servant to fetch Madame Chevasse, who instantly obeyed the summons, delighted at the prospect of speedily obtaining (by Christopher's death), the price of her guilty services; but Heaven is just, and suffers not the wicked to escape unpunished.

The moment Madame Chevasse entered the side chamber, the suffering youth, who had apparently fallen into a doze, opened his eyes, and uttered a dreadful scream; and when she approached the bed, and soothingly addressed him, he trembled violently, and manifested the greatest horror of her presence, and stretching forth his hand he grasped the arm of Lawton, and drawing him towards the bed, whispered,—

"Send her away, for God's sake, send that woman away; her presence is more terrible than even that of Marie."

"She is come to nurse you, Christopher and assist me in restoring you to health."

"I cannot bear her here, her and Marie too; one is too dreadful almost to be borne, but to have them both will kill me."

"Compose yourself Christopher, and I will send her away. Madame Chevasse," he added. turning towards her, "my cousin would prefer your remaining in the next room, and if we require your services, we can call you. She is gone now, Christopher," he continued, as soon as the door closed behind her. Will you promise me to try and sleep?"

"Yes, yes, if you will remain by my side; do not on any account leave me, even for a moment."

Lawton seated himself by the side of the bed, saying,—

"I will not quit this spot for a single instant, till I see you totally recovered."

"I thank you, I feel a little better now; if I could but shut Marie from my sight I should recover soon."

The chamber was hushed, and the patient lay still for awhile; his breathing was short and laboured, but presently it became more lengthened and easy, till at last he sank into a deep and as it appeared refreshing sleep.

CHAPTER XXVIII.

" 'Tis woman alone with a firmer heart,
    Can see the graces of life depart ;
    Can leve the more, and soothe and bless,
    Man in his utter wretchedness'.'

CATHERINE and Helen arose in the morning with happy hearts and strengthened love. Seated side by side, lingering over an already protracted breakfast; how sweetly did the two sisters open their whole hearts and souls to each other; they conversed freely and fully, discussing their plans and prospects for the future.

As Catherine had been for years accustomed to tuition, it appeared to both sisters that the most reasonable course for them to adopt in the hope of obtaining a livelihood would be to open an establishment for the reception of a limited number of pupils.

"If," said Catherine doubtingly, " we could insure success, I should feel no reluctance my dear Helen, to devote your little property to such a purpose."

"Dear Catherine" replied Helen, "I see no reason that we should not succeed and the sum that I inherit by my father's will cannot possibly be applied to a better undertaking, , let us then dear sister cast all doubts and fears from our mind."

"I believe love, said her sister, that we cannot do better; and yet I must confess I feel a great reluctance to use your—"

"Stop dear Catherine," interrupted Helen, "I cannot allow any meum or tuum to exist between us, all mine is thine, we will therefore draw upon our little hoard, sufficient to meet our present necessities."

"Dear kind sister," said Catherine, affected at the gracefulness of Helen's speech. "I will be guided entirely by your counsel."

Helen was about to reply, but was prevented by a loud knock at the door, which was immediately followed by an unwonted bustle, the two sisters ran to seek the cause, and were startled by the unlooked for appearance of two gentlemen, who were carrying a third, who bore signs of having encountered some fearful accident. into the cottage.

"You must excuse this intrusion, ladies; but my friend having sustained a serious injury, I make bold, this being the nearest habitation, to enlist your sympathies on his behalf."

"By all means," replied Catherine to the party who thus addressed them, stepping a little in advance of her sister; "you had better convey him to bed, and send for a surgeon instantly;" and she led the way towards the room occupied by herself and Helen.

The case was too urgent to admit of much ceremony, and the strangers gladly availed themselves of the kind offer.

"He seems in a very dangerous state," said Catherine, as the injured person groaned heavily, when his attendants had placed him on the bed.

"I fear he is mortally wounded," replied the person who had first addressed them.

"How dreadful!" said Helen, trembling; "may I ask how he received this injury?"

"Certainly. He has been engaged, as I thought you would have inferred, in an affair of honour."

"A duel," exclaimed Helen, "how very, very sad;" and as she spoke, she approached the bed; and with an expression of deep commiseration gazed upon the wounded man. As she did so, her face stiffened into an expression of intense anguish, mingled with astonishment; she clasped her hands, and with a countenance pale as are the dead, turned her eyes upon her sister. She spoke not, she moved not, but that fixed look was all her speech. Catherine was dreadfully alarmed. What could possibly affect her sister thus? To dart to her side, to cast a searching look at the object that had thus powerfully moved her, was the work of an instant, and sufficed to explain it all. There, pale, bleeding, insensible, and apparently dying, struck down to the very verge of the grave, lay the once gay, animated, and animating Edward Villiers, the object of her sister's fondest love and all absorbing tenderness.

Poor Helen, this unexpected sight was enough to rend thy very heart-strings asunder, to crush thy gentle spirit, and incapacitate thee wholly for exertion; but no. The most timid, and gentle are frequently, in times of necessity, the most active and courageous. Well might the poet say,—

"Oh! woman, in our hours of ease,
Uncertain, coy, and hard to please,
When pain and sorrow rend the brow,
A ministering angel thou."

In less than a minute, Helen was again herself, all her energy had returned with redoubled power, she felt herself capable of any, and every exertion. Stationed by the bed-side of her lover her only thought and hope was, to tend, by unremitting care and tenderness, to his recovery, or if that were impossible, to smooth his passage to the tomb, to assuage his sufferings, to mitigate his sorrows, and make death less sad and drear; this is an office that none but a woman can perform,—it is her alone that can watch over the sick and dying with unabating care, and in the words we quoted at the commencement of this chapter,—

"Love the more, and soothe and bless
Man, in his utter wretchedness."

When the surgeon arrived and prepared to examine the wound, Helen who was entirely free from any womanish terror at the sight of blood, was ready and anxious to assist him; what hand so light, so soft, so gentle, as a woman's; the doctor seemed conscious of this, and gladly availed himself of her services. The dressing of the wound appeared to be attended with great pain, for Edward groaned loudly during its operation, and manifested signs of returning consciousness, for he gave utterance, though not without difficulty, to several disjointed sentences.

"You are acquainted with him?" said the surgeon, in a tone of inquiry, to Helen.

"Intimately," she replied.

"Then speak to him by name," rejoined the other; "it may be the means of arousing him to sensibility."

She bent down, and gently breathed the name of Edward, he started at the sound of her voice, and opening his eyes, gazed upon her for an instant with an expression of intense joy, blended with tenderness; the next he turned away his head in evident disappointment.

"Speak to him again," whispered the surgeon.

"Edward," said Helen, again tenderly stooping over him.

Once more he started, and regarded her with a searching glance; and then closing his eyes, murmured,—

"I thought it was the voice of Grace."

The blood for a moment suffused the face of Helen with the deepest crimson, but it as quickly subsided, leaving her of an ashy paleness; as she laid her hand on his, and speaking in a firm and tender voice, said,—

"Dear Edward, if you desire to see the Lady Grace, I will this instant send for her."

"No, no," he replied, "it cannot be."

"It very easily can—and shall, if you wish it," said Helen.

He shook his head as though the subject annoyed him; and Helen thought it, for the present best to desist.

The surgeon having prescribed perfect quiet, and administered some medicine to the patient, prepared to take his leave, promising to renew his visit very shortly; Helen followed him from the room, and anxiously inquired his opinion of Edward.

"He is without doubt, dangerously, but I hope not mortally wounded," he replied; "but I shall be able to judge better when I have seen him again; at present I am induced to think h e will recover."

With a lightened heart, Helen returned to the room occupied by Edward, he had during he tempoary absence fallen into a soft and tranquil slumber, from which, after the lapse of an hou he awoke refreshed, though still complaining of great pain.

He was evidently surprised to see the face of Helen bending over him, and looked from her to Lieutenant Marston, as though he were scarcely conscious of what had occurred.

"I am ill," he said, "very ill," in answer to their tender inquiries; "but what has happened, how came I here?"

"Do you forget," replied the lieutenant, "having been engaged in a duel with the Earl o Clavering."

An expression of deep sorrow passed over the face of Edward, as he answered,—

"No, I do not forget it, but——"

"Hush," replied the other, "if you wish to get well, you must keep perfectly quiet; after you received your wound, Captain Johnstone and myself conveyed you to this cottage, it being the nearest habitation.'

"But, Helen, how came you to know that."

"I did not know it, dear Edward," interrupted Helen, "till you were brought here; but pray do not agitate yourself."

Edward sighed deeply, and remained silent for some minutes, then addressing Lieutenant Marston he said,—

"Let me ask you one question,—how has my opponent fared?"

"The earl has fortunately escaped unhurt," replied the other, "and now I shall absolutely refuse to answer any more questions."

Edward turned uneasily on his side, and appeared, from the smothered groans that constantly escaped him to be suffering intensely both in body and mind.

When the surgeon again arrived, and proceeded to examine into the state of the patient, Helen remarked that he looked anxious and serious, and finally he proposed that they should instantly send to London for further advice.

"You do not entertain so favourable an opinion, as when you last saw him," said Helen, in faltering accents to the surgeon when she had withdrawn into an adjoining room.

"I am sorry, my dear young lady, to inform you, that several symptoms have manifested themselves, which are certainly against his recovery; but I do not consider the case quite hopeless."

Helen could not reply, tears choked her utterance, but she speedily recovered her fortitude and again resumed her place in the sick room. Catherine, too, moved noiselessly about, directing and superintending every arrangement; everything that was requisite was done without the slightest bustle or confusion, and while the messenger despatched to London for a surgeon was absent, Catherine crept silently to the door of the sick chamber, and beckoned the lieutenant from the room.

In obedience to the summons, he followed her into another apartment, where refreshment was spread, and which was every way acceptable to the young man, who had partaken of nothing since he breakfasted with Edward in the morning.

"This is exceedingly kind and thoughtful of you," said the lieutenant as he seated himself at the table; "when I so unceremoniously intruded upon you this morning, I had no idea of finding such comfortable quarters."

"Make yourself perfectly at home, sir," replied Catherine, with true feminine dignity. "Mr Villiers has been, for years, an intimate friend of my sister, and that alone would induce us to use every effort that circumstances will permit to make your residence here agreeable; the painful nature of your visit will not allow us to do more."

The lieutenant bowed, there was something about Catherine's manners that repelled advance and though he admired her as a fine and handsome woman, he could not feel for her, that deep interest her more gentle sister awakened in his mind. Helen,—full of her sex's weakness, soft timid and moveable, yet rising superior to it all, conquering even the violence of her own mind, turning away to shed her tears alone, in order that she might alleviate the anguish and sufferings of another,—appeared to him little else than an angel; her blue eyes wet with tears, which hung trembling on their long fringed lids, now bent in mute sorrow on the face of the sick man now raised beaming with prayerful hope and confidence towards heaven, she looked in his eyes a ministering angel, sent in mercy to soothe and cheer. His heart, hitherto so obdurate to female charms, was touched; he felt for the first time woman's mission to be a blest and holy office, and that he had dimmed the brightness of her character by attributing to her less than she by nature merited.

When the young man again joined Helen, he found Edward awake, but suffering acutely from the effects of his wound; he seemed restless and full of anxiety, and inquired repeatedly, if the surgeon from London had arrived.

"You would like us to send to your mother?" said Helen, kindly, as she applied the cooling lotion to his burning forehead.

"Wait till you have heard the doctor's opinion," he replied, "as I should be sorry to alarm her unnecessarily."

After the lapse of a few hours, the messenger returned with the surgeon, who was instantly introduced to the patient, and proceeded methodically to examine the wound, and inquire into his
No. 13.

symptoms.   Helen with intense eagerness, watched his countenance in the hope of gaining therefrom a clue to his opinion, but his professional self-command prevented this, and Edward was the first to ask the question they were all so anxious to hear answered.

"Doctor," he said in a weak and trembling voice, "I trust you will be candid with me, I have no nervous fear of death; it is a debt we must all pay, and being obliged to do so, a few years sooner than we had looked for, is no very great hardship."

He ceased, and the surgeon hesitated for a moment and cleared his throat, after which he gave a preparatory cough, and then said,—

"Well, my dear sir, your situation is certainly a very critical one."

"In a word, shall I live or die," replied Edward, impatiently.

"That is wholly impossible for me to say, but certainly you are in great danger."

"You think, then, it is most probable I shall not recover."

"I do," replied the other, laconically.

The stillness that pervaded the chamber as the doctor pronounced the fatal words was only broken by the smothered sobs of Helen.

"Leave me alone," said Edward, in a subdued and husky voice; "I cannot bear to witness your grief, it will prevent my meeting death as a man.   Marston," he continued, "take her from the room," pointing to Helen, "and do not any of you interrupt me till I ring the bell."

The lieutenant instantly complied, and with gentle force withdrew Helen into an adjoining apartment.   Catherine received her into her maternal arms, and suffered her to weep out her sorrows uninterrupted upon her bosom.   The lieutenant could only gaze upon the two in silence, and occasionally dash away a tear that rose unwillingly to his eyes; strange visitants, they were the first he had shed since childhood.

Helen calmed the violence of her agitation, and fixed her eyes tremblingly on the timepiece; the minute hand had performed half its circuit round the dial, still the welcome sound of Edward's bell struck not upon her ear.

"Had we not better go to him," she timidly inquired; "he may be dying, and perhaps he is even now dead?"

"No," replied her sister, "let him be; he is no doubt endeavouring to make his peace with that God before whom he must so soon appear to render an account of his sins."

Catherine spoke these words in a tone of solemnity that struck truthfully upon the hearts of those who heard her.

An hour passed in profound silence, unbroken by even the slightest sound, when the bell of Edward's room summoned them back to him.   The two entered together; but Helen was the first to fly to his side, and inquire how he felt.

"Much the same," he replied, without any show of agitation, though his eyes gave signs of his having been weeping.   "I feel now," he added, evidently striving to speak calm, "that my time here is short.   Helen, I have acted unkindly, unjustly towards you—will you, can you forgive me?"

"Fully and freely, dear Edward," she replied, "as I hope to receive pardon of my Maker."

"Thank you, dear Helen—God bless and protect you.   I have but one wish or thought more, and that is for Grace.   Her I did not deceive, for I loved, and still love and cherish her, as dearer, far dearer, than my very life.   I should not have the slightest desire to rise from this bed in health and strength, but for her.   With all others I could part cheerfully—her name will be the last upon my lips ere I quit this mortal scene, in every prayer.   Tell her when I am gone, her name was mingled with mine, that for her dear sake I would gladly have lived, but God willed it otherwise, and I strove to say, His will be done."

At this moment he sank back in the bed, apparently quite exhausted, but in a very short time he gained strength to speak again.

"Marston," he said, addressing the lieutenant, "let not my death make you uncomfortable. You did the best for me you could—it was the chance of war—had I been as skilfull a marksman, the earl might now have been in my place and I in his."

"This unfortunate occurrence," replied the young man, grasping the hand Edward held out to him, "will have the effect of inducing me steadfastly to set my face against all duelling for the future; never again will I lend a hand towards hastening a fellow-creature into eternity; the very thought makes me sick at heart."

"You acted kindly, in befriending me at the time I was in want of a friend, and therefore no blame can possibly attach to yourself," replied Edward.   "I should like," he continued, "if possible to write a few lines to Grace, while I have sufficient strength."

Writing materials were immediately procured, and propped up in bed with pillows, and supported on either side, by Helen and Marston, he contrived with some difficulty to write a letter to Grace, whom, with all his faults, he yet so fondly loved.

When he had concluded, he gave it into the hands of Helen and addressed her as follows:—

"My dear Helen, I know that I can safely entrust this to your care; after my death, will you promise me to see that it reaches the hands of the Lady Grace?"

"I will," replied Helen, "fear not, dear Edward, but I will ensure its safe reception by Grace."

"Thank you," replied the young man; "and there is now but one thing more, and I shall have done with earth."

"Name it," said Marston, for Helen was too much overcome to reply.

"Both of you must promise to comfort, and console my mother; this will be a heavy blow to her."

"Would you not like to see her," suggested Catherine, who had just entered the room.

"No," replied Edward, "it would unsettle my thoughts. I had a presentiment (turning to Marston) that I should lose my life in this affair; I do not blame the earl, as perhaps had I been similarly circumstanced, I should have acted as he has done; he no doubt considered he was resenting an injury done to his sister, though God knows how dear she is to my heart."

"We are not altogether without hope of your ultimate recovery, dear Edward," said Helen, in a voice in which tenderness and sorrow strove for mastery.

He shook his head, as he answered,—

"It is useless to disguise the truth,—I shall never rise from this bed again; but I feel low and exhausted, and will try for awhile to sleep."

With what terrible anguish did Helen hang over his couch, smoothing his pillows, and wiping the sweat from his forehead; how dreadful to see him thus, in the prime and strength of manhood, bowed down to the grave; how much more dreadful the thought that this was the work of man.

Duelling, thank God, bids fair now, to be speedily and wholly suppressed, but, in the time of which we write, it was of common, almost daily occurrence; and the laws but very slightly restrained men's evil passions, so that when one killed another in a duel, he did not think it worth while, as now, to escape as quickly as possible from the country; he stood in no salutary fear of being arraigned at the bar of his country for wilful murder. Thus the Earl of Clavering immediately after the duel had taken place, set off for his country seat; it was the first time he had ever injured another, and though he considered that he had been guilty of no crime, a remorseful feeling gnawed at his heart. He dreaded to meet the inquiring looks of Grace and Edith, and therefore strove hard to wear an easy unconcerned appearance, but it was impossible while Edward lay in so dangerous a condition. He would have given much could he have ensured his recovery, it seemed so dreadful to have the death of a fellow creature pressing on his mind.

"Alas!" exclaimed the young, and wealthy lord, as he threw himself upon the soft luxuriant cushions of his own travelling carriage. "What a wretched unhappy creature I am; I seem as though I was formed not only to be miserable myself, but to be possessed of the unhappy faculty of making others so; Grace will henceforth hate and detest me, I shall see her bright and happy smiles give place to tears and anguish. Edith will weep because Grace does, and my mother will break her heart if Edith is unhappy. And I—" he stopped, the prospect was too painful for him to proceed; he hid his face in his hands, and gave himself up to the moody reflections which filled his breast.

"There is not one bright spot," he continued, "on which I can rest with anything like satisfaction. Catherine, even thee, whom I so doatingly love, and for whom I would have made any sacrifice, has turned against me; her love to all appearance has changed to loathing; and contempt she spurns and rejects me; my child too, will be early taught to despise my very name, to hate and shun me; Good God," he ejaculated, "what have I to live for?"

Filled with such bitter thoughts as these, he presented himself at Ravensdale; Edith ran to welcome his arrival; his mother too, with joy-beaming countenance, was eager to embrace him. Grace smiled brightly, and kindly inquired after his welfare; she seemed indeed more anxious than usual to please and gain his favour. And yet the young lord said, "What have I to live for?" Alas! how many would have envied his position, not certainly would any have done his feelings. Surely we do not err when we say the formation of our own happiness or misery lies greatly in our own power; how much of happiness and pleasure can some persons mould out of very indifferent materials; while others, possessed, lavishly, of the very substance out of which happiness is formed, through some unfortunate process, work it into wretchedness and misery. This was the case with the Earl of Clavering; by nature he had a heart formed for happiness and enjoyment; he was surrounded on all sides by pleasures that courted his acceptance, but his own hand had infused the bitter that poisoned his cup of joy; and as is the case with many others, he afterwards loudly complained, as though it were the work of another, and not himself.

Seated once more in the midst of his dear home circle, the young earl did, for the time contrive to forget some of the sorrows that oppressed him ; Grace was more gay even than usual, for she began to hope from her brother's silence on the subject, that Edward had been able to clear him. self of the sins imputed to him ; much she longed, before she gained courage, to put the question, but her brother's reply re-assured her.

"I am convinced, dear Grace," he replied, "that I have acted in this affair perhaps some. what too harshly, and if Edward again solicits my consent to your marriage with him, I shall not withhold it."

At these words, the face of Grace became radiant with intense joy ; she clasped her arms round her brother's neck, as she exclaimed,—

"Dear—dear Arthur, I knew it would be thus."

This was almost more than he could bear ; to conceal his feelings he was obliged to change the subject of discourse, and avert his eyes from the sweet and happy face of his sister.

Poor Grace ! what a blest and happy evening this was to thy young heart. With what sweet and delighted feelings didst thou rest thy head that evening on thy pillow—little dreaming that thy lover was stretched upon his dying bed, depending upon another for love and tenderness. Oh ! surely in mercy futurity is hid from our eyes—could we pierce through the folds of its dark veil the cup of joy would be frequently dashed from our lips at the moment we were about to drink—the sweetest, and purest of pleasures would be poisoned by the knowledge that dark clouds would hereafter break over our souls. Let us then thankfully enjoy the present—un-dimmed by anxious fears for the future, let us never anticipate sorrow ; sufficient for the day is the evil thereof ; grief that comes unexpected, ever troubles us the least.

CHAPTER XXIX.

"'Twas a long struggle—oft I thought
That in that whirl of waters caught—
I must have gone, too weak for strife,
    Down headlong at the cataract's will.
Sad fate for one with heart and life
    And all youth's sunshine round him still."

LONG and sound was the slumber in which we last left poor unfortunate Christopher. Lawton remained calmly seated by his sick cousin—his arms folded across his breast, and his head bent down as it were in deep thought.

Suddenly the slumberer awoke, and opening his eyes, gazed wistfully around ; as he did so, he shuddered, and muttering some incoherent sentences, covered his face with the bed-clothes and wept aloud.

"What ails you, Christopher?" said Lawton soothingly. The poor youth made no reply, but continued to give vent to his feelings in deep, and heart-rending sobs.

"Come, Christopher," continued his cousin, "do not give way so, you are better now—are you not ?" He only shook his head with an expression of utter despondency.

"This is not the way to recover," resumed Lawton ; "come, now, remember what you said to me yesterday. Why, you absolutely declared that it was greatly in a fellow's own power to live or die as he might choose. You wish to live, don't you ?"

The youth raised his head for a moment, and fixing his sunken eyes, which shone with an un-earthly brightness, full upon the face of Lawton, said in a tone, the earnestness of which thrilled the heart of his hearer.—

"I wish to live ? Oh, God ! what would I not part with to preserve my life a year ! A year, a month even were a boon." And sinking back exhausted with the exertion he had made, he lay for some time incapable of farther speech. Presently he relapsed into a state of unconscious-ness, and began to talk with his former wildness.

"A boat—a boat," he exclaimed "how dark and rough the waters look. See how high the waves rise, they will overflow me, and none to help. Oh, God ! Oh, God ! it is hard to die. How gracefully Marie skims over the waves—now rising almost to the clouds, and now sinking down, down to the very depths of the dark and turbid ocean—she beckons me to follow ; but—but I dare not go. I am sinking—she has caught my hand, and drags me down—how cold and icy is her grasp. Oh ! in mercy release me from her. Alas ! what pain it is to drown."

Thus continued to rave the unhappy youth, while a particle of strength remained,—conscious, even amidst the wanderings of his mind, of his own near approach to the dark and silent tomb—sad and drear to contemplate at all times; but oh! how much more so, when the unwilling soul stands trembling on the brink of eternity's river, fearing to launch away, surveying with horror each dark wave that wafts it farther from the shore, till at length the floods overflow, and sink it in everlasting despair.

Utterly prostrated in body and mind, Christopher lay for a while insensible to all around; his own mental sufferings, most certainly hastened what he so wished to avoid—death, that grim tyrant, before whom even kings must bow.

"Will he, think you, linger much longer?" inquired Lawton of the physician, who had been summoned to the sick-bed.

"He is sinking fast," was the whispered reply. "On no account speak to him, or suffer him to be disturbed, and I have no doubt he will go off without any return of consciousness."

In compliance with this instruction the most profound silence prevailed in the chamber of the dying youth. Madame Chevasse, who had resumed her place as nurse, crept occasionally on tip-toe through the thickly carpeted room, and glanced upon the face of Christopher, and each time returned with redoubled satisfaction to whisper to Lawton that he could not possibly last much longer.

Great was their surprise, therefore, when the young man, apparently without an effort, raised himself to an upright position in the bed, and in a calm clear voice, inquired for his cousin.

"I am here, Christopher," said Lawton, tremblingly approaching the bed. "Do you want for anything?"

"Jack, Jack," said the youth with deep emphasis, "I am dying."

Lawton made no reply, he had no word of kindness to cheer him on his dark unfathomable voyage, he had no kind thought, much less expression, to meet such an exigency as this; he could not bid him with an eye of faith, look beyond the narrow grave, and behold a fairer land than this. He was mute, and the poor youth must die without one word of comfort or even hope.

"Jack," continued Christopher, collecting all his energy to give effect to his dying words, "you must long have known that it was impossible for me to recover, and yet you never even hinted to me my probable fate; on the contrary, you encouraged me to the last, in the belief that I should get well. Had I known that I must die, I would have prepared myself for this dreadful and dreaded hour;" he ceased for a moment, and when he again spoke it was in a clear and distinct voice, "It is hard to die, how hard none but such as I may tell. What avails me now the wealth and consequent luxuries it flung around my path? I would part with all to become even the veriest wretch that has the chance of a few short years to amend his life, and prepare to meet that God before whose tribunal I must shortly stand; take warning, Jack, by my untimely fate. I believe you meant kindly towards me; you thought it better to keep me in ignorance of my doom;" and he could say no more, but sank back on his pillow, where he lay for some minutes panting and struggling for breath and life; once again his lips moved, and the emphatic words, "this is death," escaped him. A holy calm seemed to settle on his spirit, he smiled faintly and ejaculated, "Marie is changd, oh, how sweetly changed; she looks an angel of light and beauty, and smiling, beckons me to follow her. Hark!" he exclaimed, raising his finger in a listening attitude,—"she speaks, God be praised, she whispers me to, fear not, and reminds me of her last word, ' we shall be united only in the grave. I am ready; yes," and eternity heard the remainder of the sentence, for it was not uttered in time. With fixed eyes and outstretched arms, Christopher expired. Lawton felt greatly relieved when assured that his spirit had indeed taken its flight to worlds unknown. A weight seemed to rise from his mind, and yet a strange and heretofore unexperienced feeling hovered over him. What could it mean? it seemed a sort of foreboding that evil was at hand, though from what quarter to look for it he was utterly at a loss.

He resolved at all events to hasten the funeral of his cousin, settle with Madame Chevasse, and take his own departure to England as early as possible. As yet he fully believed that Moreton (of whom of all others he most suspected) had up to the present time obtained no clue to the death of Marie, and if he once contrived to quit Paris unremarked, he doubted not his ability to escape detection in London.

"Pshaw," he exclaimed, rousing himself from a fit of abstraction, "the time has now arrived for which have so long and so ardently panted. I am in possession (by my cousin's death.) of a large and Iindependent fortune, which I have earned, ay, honestly earned, by nursing and humouring a sick and petulant boy. And as for Marie, it was absolutely necessary to have her kept at a distance; that was all I bargained for, and if this Madame Chevasse to serve her own onds chose to make away with her altogether, or at least hasten her death, why that, of course, no affair of mine; she alone must be answerable for it."

"Monsieur forgets the little affair about the child," said Madame Chevasse, who had entered the room unperceived by Lawton, and overheard a portion, at least, of his soliloquy.

"No, no, madame," replied Lawton, in a tone that he intended to pacify her—for she manifested no slight symptoms of anger, and he dreaded to arouse her indignation. "I do not forget either that, or the promised reward; I had rather that Marie had lived, but it is no matter; let me see, the funeral of Christopher will take place in five days. At the closet of that period, I shall be happy to settle this little business with you, as I intend to leave Paris immediately."

"Certainly, monsieur," replied the old woman, "only let me beg you, for your own sake as well as mine, not to be talking so loudly for the future about things you wish to be kept quiet; servants have ears, and it is well that none but myself entered just now, or they might have heard more than you desire to have known." And with this gratuitous piece of advice, Madame Chevasse left Lawton to his own reflections.

For five long days Lawton sat alone within the darkened room where he and Christopher had so often held their midnight orgies, drinking and carousing till the bright rosy tints of morn would warn them to their chamber, to sleep off as far as possible the effect of their revels. He still drank deep, perhaps deeper even than heretofore, but the effect was different. The death bed of Christopher had left an unpleasant impression on his mind, that wine could not efface; so far from it, that when under its influence he was more perturbed, and in a greater state of fear and agitation, than at other times.

By indirect inquiries, he learned from the servants belonging to the hotel, that Moreton had without any previous intimation settled his bill, and accompanied by his mother, left the very day that Christopher breathed his last.

"This," thought Lawton, "looks well; he sees it is useless to contend with me; so far, so good. Ah, he has doubtless sneaked off in this hurried manner to avoid a challenge; well, I gave him credit for more courage, but I would rather have it thus. I was a fool to perplex myself about him; he is equally as anxious to shun my society as I can possibly be to shun his. A coward, Ernest Moreton, that can talk as big, and use on occasion such threatening menaces. A coward, bah!"

And Lawton shrugged his shoulders, and indulged in a chuckling laugh at the discovery he deemed he had made; indeed, so greatly did it relieve his mind that he sat down to dinner with a much better appetite than he had experienced since the death of his cousin.

The following day, with great pomp and state, Christopher was conveyed to his sad resting place, there to repose in the long sleep of death; he had played his part on the stage of life, was gone, and would shortly be forgotten.

> "How loved—how valued once, avails him not,
> To whom related, or by whom begot."

The evening of this day was devoted by Lawton to preparations for his own departure; the will of his unfortunate cousin was formally opened, and as was already anticipated, the whole of his large property found bequeathed, unconditionally, to Lawton, who expressed his determination of instantly starting for England, in order to take possession of his so lately acquired wealth.

Everything was in readiness—his passport was obtained—his bill at the hotel discharged—carriage and horses engaged for an early hour the ensuing morning—his wardrobe and valuables all packed; nothing, in short, remained to be done but to settle the claim of Madame Chevasse, and that Lawton was in the very act of doing. A pile of gold and bank-notes was spread on the table, before which the two were seated. Madame Chevasse had drawn the glittering heap towards herself, which she surveyed with greedy eyes; for an instant they sparkled with an expression of intense delight, the next she seemed dissatisfied, and stretched out her hand as in for more.

"How, now, madame?" exclaimed Lawton, surveying her with surprise; "I have paid you the full sum you bargained for; what else do you want?"

"True, monsieur," replied the woman, "you have paid me the sum you agreed to give, on condition that the child Marie was expected to be delivered of was not permitted to live, lest it might interfere with your desires, regarding your cousin's property."

"Well, well," said Lawton hastily.

"Well, monsieur, I was about to say, that so far I am paid, but you have given me nothing, not even so much as a single franc for my attendance upon your cousin."

"Be satisfied, madame, you are well paid," said Lawton, angrily.

"You think so, do you," said the woman, her anger getting the better of every other feeling;

"then I tell you what, monsieur, unless you choose to pay me a hundred francs for my care and attention to your cousin, you do not quit Paris so soon or so easily as you imagine."

"How, madame," said Lawton, in a violent burst of passion. "You dare to threaten me; have a care how you exasperate me, it may lead to the discovery of your crimes."

"Don't trouble yourself about mine," said the woman, ironically, "rather think of your own; what should hinder me going before the magistrate, and making oath that you bribed me to destroy the girl and her child."

"It is a lie," exclaimed Lawton.

At this moment a slight bustle was heard in the adjoining room; the next, the door that separated them was thrown open, and Moreton entered, followed by several *gens-darmes*.

"Your villany is discovered," said Moreton, sternly; "I swore to avenge the death of that unhappy girl, whose life was sacrificed through your means."

"I had nothing whatever to do with it," replied Lawton. "I merely stipulated that she should be kept out of the way, till after my cousin's death; how hers occurred, I know not; you must seek that information of this woman," pointing to Madame Chevasse, who had shrunk to the extreme end of the room, doubtless hoping that she might be overlooked.

"It matters not," said one of the men, who was evidently commissary of the police, stepping forward, and drawing a paper from his pocket; "I have orders to arrest you, John Lawton, and you, Leoline Chevasse, for the wilful murder of one Marie de Seviere, and likewise that of her infant child." Then turning to the others, he added, "Secure your prisoners."

CHAPTER XXX.

"Fond maid the snow of thy soul was such,
E'en reason sunk blighted beneath its touch;
Though health and bloom returned, the delicate chain
Of thought once tangled never cleared again.
Warm, lively, soft as in youth's happiest day,
The mind was still all there, but turned astray;
A wandering back upon whose pathway shone
All stars of heaven, except the guiding one;
Again she smiled, nay much, and brightly smiled,
But 'twas a lustre, strange, unreal, wild."

THE earl had been at Ravensdale two days—days to him fraught with gloom and despondency; he absented himself as much as possible from his fond and anxious relatives, and with his gun would wander forth with the ostensible intention of shooting, but with the real purpose of escaping from the tender inquiries of his mother. Edith seemed strangely altered, and seldom questioned him as to the cause of his anxiety; but the tender solicitude of his mother wearied him, and he could not bear to witness the bright and happy countenance of Grace. It appeared to his distempered imagination to assail him with bitter reproaches; and deeply did he deplore the part he had acted towards Edward, and inwardly resolved, if he recovered to offer no farther impediment to his union with his sister.

He had joined Edith and Grace at Ravensdale, we were saying, two days, and the third was now fast waning, during which time he had received no intelligence of Edward, which rather surprised him, as Captain Johnstone had promised to forward him the so-much-desired information; and he could only attribute his non-performance of his promise to the fact, that Edward was doubtless fast recovering from the effects of his wound.

"No news must surely be good news," he repeated, till he felt thoroughly persuaded of what he wished to believe.

It was, therefore, with a brighter aspect than usual that he presented himself at his mother's tea-table, where his wife and sister were waiting his arrival.

"Come, my dear Arthur," said his mother, smiling; "I am glad to see you returned so early this evening; we had almost despaired of enjoying your company. I think too," she continued, tenderly gazing upon him, "that the country air begins to improve your looks, for you seemed sadly out of sorts when you first came down. And Edith too, is not in such good health as before she visited London. I think, my children, you must resolve never again to quit this spot."

The earl was prevented making any reply by the entrance of a servant with a letter.

Grace sprung eagerly to her feet, and darting to his side, she exclaimed,—

"It is for me, John, is it not?"

"Yes, my lady," replied the servant, giving it into her outstretched hand.

"God be praised," ejaculated Grace, as with trembling fingers she tore it from the envelope, and glanced momentarily at the contents.

"Good God," she exclaimed, turning to her brother, and holding out the open letter, which shook and rustled in her grasp, while her lips were perfectly livid with terror. Good God! what can this mean?"

The earl's face assumed an ashy hue, but he took the letter, as it were, half mechanically from her hand, and with a boding heart, perused the contents.

MY DEAREST GRACE,—"When this reaches you, I shall have ceased to breathe. You have, no doubt, learned from your brother the particulars of our meeting. Do not blame him, Grace, for I am conscious of having acted unjustly towards you, and in a measure deserve punishment. I would have borne anything but the loss of you, whom I have ever loved (from almost the first moment that I beheld you) with a devotedness that death itself cannot estrange.

"I am too ill and weak, dear Grace, to express one half of my feelings towards you; if there is a heaven above, we shall one day meet again. Yes, comfort thee, for safe and blest we'll meet in that calm region yet."

"Farewell! dear one—forgive me—love me. No; that word is idle now, but let it go."

Grace remained motionless as a statue, calmly and intently gazing upon her brother, as with a throbbing brow and swelling bosom, he perused the foregoing lines.

Poor Grace appeared as though she were, in truth, turned to stone. Edith tremblingly approached her, and taking one of her hands, which was fair and cold as Parian marble, pressed it tenderly in her own, but Grace heeded it not; her form was rigid, and her brow contracted, and she kept her eyes immovably fixed upon her brother, as though she sought to read his very soul.

The earl was dreadfully alarmed at her appearance. Tears and sobs were indeed nothing in comparison with this silent agony; he feared for her life, still more for her reason, for there seemed an unearthly, glassy look in her large dark eyes, now opened to their full extent, and gazing, as it appeared, on vacancy; for when he earnestly spoke to her by name, and conjured her by every tender epithet, to speak to him, if only one word, she changed not the steadfast glance of her eye from the spot on which it had first fallen, nor gave the slightest token that she heard one word that he uttered.

"This is dreadful!" said the young man, turning to the countess, whose horror-stricken features told how much she was herself affected. "Speak to her, mother; she may perhaps give heed to you."

But in vain did the countess, assisted by Edith, strive to induce Grace to seat herself by their side, and listen to their soothing voices; her form remained perfectly rigid, and ringing for the servant, they had her carried to bed, and medical advice sent for.

With what bitter heart-rending feelings did Edith hang over the couch of the kind and warm-hearted Grace; she shuddered as she in vain endeavoured to close her eyes, and moisten her white and parched lips, which she bathed at once with tears and kisses.

"Dear, dear Grace!" she mentally exclaimed, "God grant that thy life may be spared."

The surgeon, who after as little delay as possible arrived, gave it as his decided opinion that she was suffering from pressure on the brain, but doubted not that with proper remedies and care she would speedily recover.

Edith's tears flowed faster, but her heart felt lighter, and she blessed God for this ray of hope.

"Go down," whispered the countess, who now entered the room, "and endeavour to console Arthur; he is the very picture of despair, and blames himself as the sole cause of the illness of poor Grace."

Edith sighed as she left the room to comply with her mother's request, for she thought that Arthur no longer wished or cared to receive sympathy from her.

On descending to the lower room, she found her husband walking, with rapid strides, across the floor; he stopped abruptly as she entered, and with a sternness on his brow, she had never witnessed before, inquired how she had left Grace.

"To all appearance exactly in the same state as when you last saw her," replied Edith, "but the doctor gives us hope of her speedy recovery."

"Unhappy girl," said the earl, in a tone of peculiar bitterness, "unhappy in having placed her affections on one so every way unworthy. Would that it had been otherwise; I thought it at least possible that he would recover."

"Then Mr. Villiers has been ill," returned Edith, faintly.

"Ill! he is dead," said the earl; "and he died by my hands. I thought to revenge an affront he put upon Grace, and I killed him."

"You killed him! oh Heaven!" said Edith, falteringly, and sinking upon her knees. "Unsay those words, my husband ι it is not, it cannot be possible that you have ever shed blood, more specially the blood of him, who is so dear to Grace"

"It is but too true," replied her husband. "I killed him, Edith, but it was in fair and open fight; he had an equal chance of doing the same by me." Then seeing that she averted her face from him in horror, he bent down and taking her hands in both his own, said with a look of more tenderness than he had assumed towards her of late,—

"My own Edith, do not hate me—do not turn from me in horror those pure eyes. There is none on earth that have not turned against me but you; I have nothing worth living for but yourself.'

Edith cast upon him a look of unutterable tenderness, as she replied,—

"Though all others forsake you, yet will not I."

"God bless you for those words, dear Edith," replied her husband. "Grace, I trust

No. 14.

will recover, and then all may yet be well; you had better now, my love, return to her.''

Edith rose from her knees with a sad and aching heart. The knowledge of her husband's crime (for to her the shedding of blood, no matter in what way it was shed, was a crime, and one of no light complexion either), we were saying, the knowledge of this wrung her whole soul with anguish. To think that he to whom she had been accustomed to look up as to the very acme of human perfection, had been capable of raising his hand against his fellow man, was so fraught with bitterness, that she turned sick and giddy, and could scarcely steady her steps sufficiently to enable her to reach the bedside of Grace. The countess observed her agitation, and took an early opportunity of inquiring the cause, and with great sorrow listened to Edith's account of the duel that had taken place between her son and Edward Villiers, and which had unfortunately terminated fatally to the latter.

"You must not allow yourself to be cast down, dear Edith," said the countess, kindly, when she had concluded. "Here is one unfortunate," pointing to the inanimate form of Grace; "do not, my love, give way, or there may be a second."

For many long days and nights, poor Grace continued insensible to all around, when suddenly she gave token of returning consciousness; she smiled sweetly, as she recognised the familiar face of Edith bending over her, and in a subdued voice inquired what had happened.

"You have been ill, very ill, dear Grace," replied Edith, kindly, "but you are better now, and will soon be quite well."

"Oh," said Grace, passing her hand over her eyes, "I remember, the excess of joy almost killed me."

"Joy!" repeated Edith, plaintively.

"Yes, love, joy. I had not seen Edward for so long a time, when he wrote, you know, to tell me that we should soon meet again. Poor girl, why do you weep?" she continued, seeing that Edith's tears flowed thick and fast. "I am so happy, for I am not ashamed to confess that I love Edward dearly, and our marriage will now soon take place; yes, I remember the very words he used,

"'Oh, comfort thee, for safe and blest
We'll meet in that calm region yet.'"

From this hour, Grace slowly but surely recovered, yet so deeply had she experienced the bitter influence of sorrow, that even her reason had sunk, blighted beneath its fatal touch, which had come to her young heart like warning ghosts, who leave the spot all withered, where they once have been.

Again she smiled, aye, brightly, as in days gone by; but the sweet, soft light of the mind, which had lent it half its beauty, was fled, alas, for ever.

The sight of his sister was dreadful to the earl. To see her thus, the wreck of her former self, wrung his heart almost to madness; for fearful thoughts constantly haunted him, whispering that he alone was the cause of the fatal change that had befallen his sister.

The countess loved her son too well and fondly to reproach him, even in the slightest degree; yet he frequently surprised her in tears, and knew too truly the cause of her grief to attribute it to aught but his own conduct.

Edith wept almost constantly, and seemed, at least he fancied so, to avoid his presence as much as possible. Grace indeed was the only one in the little circle who was not unhappy, and even her cheerfulness was such as to make others weep.

When her brother first ventured into her presence after her sad and painful illness, her mind appeared so much disturbed, and she evinced such strong symptoms of returning indisposition, that the doctor desired for the future that Grace should not be permitted to see the earl, as his presence was likely still more to disarrange her mental faculties.

And now the youthful earl seemed to concentrate all his affection upon his ill-used sister; frequently would he listen while she sang to her lute's touching strain some old ditty, whose notes sounded half extacy, half pain, yet sedulously avoiding being seen by her.

Frequently would Grace insist on being allowed to wander about the beautiful grounds of Ravensdale, wholly unaccompanied, and as she ever returned from her rambles in apparently improved health and spirits, it was judged best to indulge her. Then would her brother, with flowing eyes and aching heart, follow her fairy form at a distance; as she glided through the thickly planted shrubbery, she wended her way to the borders of the clear, glassy lake, that meandered through the grounds in such quiet beauty. Seating herself under the shady branches of the willow, Grace would remain for hours, her large dark, antelope-looking eyes fixed in mute admiration on the rich and lovely scenery that surrounded her; sometimes she would linger till the moon, fair and bright, lent its soft lustre to the scene, but she more frequently returned before the evening shades began to prevail.

CHAPTER XXXI.

" Canst thou forget the happy hours
Which we buried in love's sweetest bowers,
Heaping over their corpses cold,
Blossoms and leaves, instead of mould—
Blossoms which were the joys that fell,
And leaves, the hopes that yet remain?
Forget the dead, the past. Oh, yet
There are ghosts that may take revenge for it,
Memories that make a heart a tomb,
Regrets which glide through the spirit's gloom,
And with ghastly whispers tell
That joy once lost is pain."

EDWARD VILLIERS is dead : we draw a curtain before the closing scene. With all his faults and unkindness towards her, none more deeply mourned his loss, or wept more bitter tears, than Helen. We cannot even except the unfortunate Lady Grace. The darkening of her mind was to her a mercy, but no short eclipse even blessed the agonised feelings of Helen, when she witnessed the death of him whom she so devotedly loved.

Catherine strained her to her bosom in silence ; she respected the grief of her sister too much to attempt to mitigate it. She knew that when the heart is torn and bleeding, common-place words of condolence but lacerate it the more. Its wounds heal far better, if the anguish that caused it is allowed to have free and unrestrained vent. Without it the pent-up feelings " will whisper the o'er-fraught heart, and bid it break."

"Leave her alone," she said to Lieutenant Marston, who would have offered some words of comfort to the weeping Helen; "I know that you mean kindly, but I understand her feelings better. Time alone will stem the current of her grief, and dry her flowing tears."

It was Catherine's painful task to visit the mother of Edward, and relate to her, as gently as possible, the sad and unexpected death of her son. And no one surely could be better qualified for such an office than Catherine. With the tenderness and gentleness of a woman, she mingled none of her sex's weakness, but rather blended with it the firmness and strength of mind that more peculiarly belongs to the male character.

Still, although she readily undertook the task of being the bearer of such painful intelligence to Mrs. Villiers, she would rather, if possible, another could have been found to execute the painful errand.

Poor Mrs. Villiers! many may conceive, though no pen can describe, the intensity of her feelings on being made acquainted with the untimely death of her only son. Her husband, too, though generally of a stern, unmelting mood, drooped his head, and wept aloud. Her daughters clung to each other, sobbing as though their hearts would break. No tears came to the relief of the bereaved mother ; she could only wring her hands, and exclaim,—

" Would to God I had died for him—my son—my son !"

The strong mind of Catherine gave way before this heart-rending scene ; she could say nothing, do nothing, but weep.

After the first violent burst of sorrow was over, it was decided by the mourning family to have the remains of their deceased relative brought home—to that home which he had left but a few short days before, strong in the health of manhood.

Alas ! what a fearful extent of misery ; what an utter breaking-up of the sweet circles o endearing friends, had the uncontrolled passions of Edward Villiers caused, not only to his own immediate relatives, but to all with whom he had come in contact. How many tender and innocent hearts suffered the acutest pangs, not on account of their own, but his sins.

After the last sad ceremony had been performed towards all that remained of Edward Villiers Lieutenant Marston, always kind and amiable, proved a true friend to the sisters, and they were very speedily installed as tenants of a neat and pretty cottage in the vicinity of Hampstead.

One day, shortly after their establishment in their new dwelling, Lieutenant Marston was seen approaching the cottage ; and Catherine looked vexed, as she observed to Helen,—

"The young man, I have no doubt, means well, but we cannot admit of such constant visits. It will be better for me to tell him so, and then it cannot possibly give offence."

At this moment the lieutenant entered, and was received kindly by Helen, whose gentle bosom could not bear the thought of inflicting even a transitory pain in the breast of another ; but there was something distant and constrained in the manner of Catherine, that surprised and grieved their visitor, and he proceeded at once to make known the object of his call.

"I trust I am not intruding at an unseasonable hour," he began. Catherine bowed somewhat stiffly. "The fact is," continued the lieutenant, who was rather blunt in his manners, "I was anxious to communicate what I hope you will regard good news." Catherine bowed again. "Being a bachelor," resumed the other, "I have but few female acquaintances, but among these few, I am on exceedingly friendly terms with the lady of the colonel belonging to my regiment, who has two daughters, whom, on my recommendation, she is willing to place under your care. I have been bold enough," he added, smiling, "to improve upon the terms you named, as the lady is rich, and well able to pay."

A profusion of warm thanks broke from the lips of Helen at this pleasing intelligence ; but Catherine looked serious as she expressed her sense of the obligation. She then communicated to the lieutenant the determination to which she had unwillingly come, with regard to his visits, and satisfied the young man, in spite of himself, that it was due to their reputation that he should place this restraint upon his feelings.

He glanced from Catherine to the face of Helen, who had not once spoken, and was pleased to observe that it wore a sorrowful expression.

"Here is some relief," thought the good-humoured lieutenant ; and he accordingly prepared to take his leave with the best grace he could possibly assume.

He offered his hand to Catherine, which she received with distant politeness, at the same time tendering her thanks for the interest he had manifested in their welfare.

The young man next turned to Helen, who frankly placed her small white hand in his, and suffered him not only to warmly press it in his own, but likewise to carry it, for one brief moment, to his lips. This unlooked-for gallantry brought the rich blood to her cheeks, but she was not angry ; on the contrary, she strove to smile, and vainly endeavoured to conceal the tears that gathered in her eyes. One more long, lingering pressure of her hand, and the lieutenant was gone.

Young Marston returned to his lodgings not only grieved, but really unhappy to know that, for the future, he must be denied the pleasure of calling at the cottage.

When he seated himself once more in his own apartments, he seemed as though he had lost the great aim and object of his life, and as he folded his arms moodily across his breast, he muttered,—

"Othello's occupation's gone."

In the meantime, the object of his regard was, with her sister, busily engaged in preparing for the reception of their first pupils.

"I have not yet, dear Catherine," said Helen, "seen my little darling nephew, whom I am fully prepared to love most dearly, not only for your sake, but also for his own. When will you send for him, Catherine ?"

A burning glow sat upon her sister's cheek at these words, but she made an effort to speak calmly.

"I scarcely know, dear Helen," she replied, "whether I shall be doing right to indulge myself with the company of my child."

Helen combatted the arguments of her sister so warmly, that at length she suffered herself to be persuaded, and the infant soon became also an inmate of their dwelling.

CHAPTER XXXII.

"True happiness is not the growth of earth;
    The toil is useless, if you seek it here;
'Tis an exotic of celestial birth,
    And never blooms but in celestial air.
Sweet plant of Paradise, thy seeds are sown
    In, here and there, a mind of heavenly mould;
It rises slow, and blooms, but ne'er was known
    To ripen here—the climate is too cold."

In an elegant and cheerful apartment, in one of the most fashionable streets of Paris, at the opening of our chapter, is seated a female of middle age; she half reclines on the soft luxurious cushions of a couch, displaying a figure which, though matured by age, is of the most fair and graceful proportions. There is a soft, subdued expression on her countenance, pleasing to behold; her hair is simply arranged in thick bands on either side of her face, offering an agreeable contrast to the ivory whiteness of her forehead; she is engaged in conversation with her son, Ernest Moreton, an old acquaintance of our reader's.

"You are out of spirits, Ernest," said his mother, surveying him with a sorrowful expression. "I thought that our last conversation would have entirely banished all gloom; you know I cannot bear to see you unhappy."

"I do know it, dear mother," he replied kindly, "and deeply do I feel your tenderness, and grateful I hope I shall ever be for a generosity which I fear I cannot profit by."

"Why not, my son? When at my earnest solicitation, you confided to me the cause of your unhappiness, I declared myself perfectly willing to receive the young person upon whom you had placed your affections as a daughter, never doubting but that her worth would make ample amends for her station in society. I loved her even from your description, and her refusal to receive your addresses, on account of your position in society being so much superior to her own, greatly enhanced her value in my eyes; it proved her at once to be possessed of delicacy and refinement—two proud qualities in a woman's character."

Moreton wore a look of increased sadness, as his mother proceeded, and when she ceased it seemed with difficulty that he commanded his feelings sufficiently to answer.

"I wrote to Miss Porter, the lady with whom I told you she was living as governess to her family, in which I enclosed a letter for Miss Montravers. You know, dear mother, how tenderly I was attached to her, and therefore can judge of my disappointment on receiving the letter I had written to Catherine back unopened, and accompanied by a few lines from her late employer; but," drawing a letter from his pocket, and presenting to her, "read, dear mother, for yourself."

Mrs. Moreton received the letter from her son with a trembling hand, and with a glowing cheek perused the contents.

"This is, indeed, painful intelligence, my son," she said, turning to the young man, as soon as she had concluded; "and I trust it will convince you of the necessity of entirely forgetting the object of your unfortunate passion."

"If true, dear mother," he replied, mournfully, "I suppose I must even endeavour to do as you say."

"This letter," said Mrs. Moreton, laying her hand impressively upon it, "even asserts that she has given birth to a child, of which the earl acknowledges himself the father. After this, my son, it would be dishonour to wed with her—it would sully our family name, and be for ever a blot upon our escutcheon."

"I will never wed without your consent, my mother," said the young man; "more, I cannot promise. It is impossible for me to tear her image from my heart. I love and shall love her, as long as life or being lasts—I would even now, fallen as she is, take her to my bosom, and shield her from the cruel shafts of calumny. Methinks," he added, with increasing animation, "that she is the more to be pitied, since she has been cruelly betrayed and deserted. Oh, mother, let us judge her tenderly; much, I am certain, she has endured—and yet so noble and deserving!"

"I desire, my son," replied Mrs. Moreton, "to think leniently of her sin, and gladly would I aid her with my protection and counsel; but to bestow upon her our very name, make her part of ourselves, and thus share her sin—this is asking too much."

"I do not ask it, mother; I am only saying what my own feelings would now prompt me to do."

A long silence ensued.

"How little real, unmixed happiness is to be found on earth," thought Mrs. Moreton. "If any ever deserved to be blest, Ernest is surely among the number. I cannot see him unhappy; rather would I sacrifice my own family pride, and give my consent to his wedding the object of his affection. Fallen she undoubtedly is, but she may still be possessed of a good and virtuous heart. When we return to England, I must endeavour to become acquainted with this Miss Montravers, and judge for myself how far she appears capable of making Ernest happy. Dear, kind Ernest!" and she lifted her eyes, beaming with maternal tenderness to his face, "how many sacrifices you have made for your widowed and invalid mother; it is but meet that I should be willing, cheerfully, to make a sacrifice for you."

CHAPTER XXXIII.

" Her dewy eyes are closed,
And on their lids, whose texture fine,
Scarce hides the dark, full orbs beneath,
The baby sleep is pillowed.
Her raven tresses shade
The bosom's stainless pride,
Curling like tendrils of the parasite
Around a marble column."

NEARLY two months have drawn their slow length along since Grace received the fatal epistle of her lover. She wandered, scarcely like a thing of life, through the old park, her steadfast eyes fixed ever immoveably towards one spot, as she wandered on, perchance, scarce knowing herself why or wherefore.

An elegant white satin robe, trimmed with wide lace, that had been procured from her bridal attire, but had never received its finishing touch, was under her direction being completed by the skilful hands of her maid; and this was her sole amusement.

"I shall wear but few ornaments," said Grace to her cousin, as she entered the room, and gazed in astonishment at the splendid toilet she was inspecting.

"It is beautiful!" said Edith, surveying the rich and delicate white satin, snowy folds contrasted admirably with the rather dark complexion of Grace. "It is very beautiful, but for what occasion are you in such active preparation, Grace?"

"Silly girl, can you not guess? why, surely my wedding," replied Grace, and a softened blush sat upon her pretty features, "my wedding with Edward Villiers."

Edith sighed audibly, but made no reply.

"I sat by the lake last night," resumed Grace, drawing Edith to the farther end of the room, "till the stars were all reflected in its glassy bosom, and as I sat deep in thought, gazing down upon them, I suddenly became aware that the face of Edward was looking up into mine. Oh! you cannot guess, dear Edith, what rapture filled my breast as I beheld him."

"'You must wait a few days more, dear Grace,' he said, 'before you join me in the blessed abode I now inhabit; then those bright worlds which are mirrored in this still water, you and I, loved Grace, will wander among at will, now here, now there, just as inclination leads us. All is fair and lovely, but without you, my own love, my soul is sad and lonely.' His voice, dear Edith, was so soft and musical that I listened like one entranced, and for awhile was unable to reply; at length I recovered myself to inquire of him how much longer I must wait before I could join him in these realms of bliss. And oh, Edith, judge of my astonishment—my delight, when he answered,—

"'Only three days; on the morning of the fourth, meet me here, never again to part.' So you perceive I have but little time left for preparation; this day is nearly gone, and there are but two more for me to prepare all that I require."

"You will find them sufficient, I make no doubt," replied Edith, gently, who saw that it would be useless to attempt to reason with her unfortunate cousin.

Grace was again happy, and both Edith and the countess were too thankful to see her so to heed the cause.

At length the fourth morning dawned, a beautiful autumnal morn; the grass was wet with dew, which sparkled brilliantly in the cups and leaves of the few flowers that yet lingered out their latest day. A light breeze just rustled the foliage of the trees, ever and anon, scattering the rarest to the ground.

The breakfast parlour of Ravensdale commanded the most pleasing prospect of the lovely scenery, diversified with hill and dale. Here the countess and Edith were seated, taking their morning meal.

The youthful master of this vast domain had, accompanied by his gun and dogs, been abroad for hours. The papers and periodicals from London, were scattered on the table, and from these the pair were endeavouring to extract amusement, when they were suddenly startled by the unlooked-for presence of Grace in her full bridal costume; her lips slightly apart, she seemed breathing with impatient excitement, which tinged her cheek with a faint pink; an unusual brilliancy sat in her large dark eyes, but it was accompanied likewise with that wild, unearthly look which tells, unmistakeably, a wandering mind.

"Dear mother, dear Edith," she said, hurriedly, "I have waited to receive your farewell kiss. Be quick, there is no time to lose."

"Dear child," said the countess, embracing her, "you are dressed early, my love."

"Yes, mother, you know this is my bridal morn; I am to meet Edward on the borders of the lake, close to the spot where the clustering violets fling their soft perfume. Farewell, dear mother, now Edith, one kiss, and I must away. Forget not," she whispered as she clasped her arms round her cousin's neck, "my last injunctions. Now farewell."

"Not so," replied Edith rising from her seat, "I must accompany you."

"Oh, no, I entreat you; no," she replied, hastening from her, and hurrying from the room. The next moment they espied her from the window, darting with the fleetness of a deer along the serpentine walk, till she entered the shrubbery and disappeared.

"Had I not better follow," said Edith, hesitatingly.

"No, my love," returned the countess; "it will only vex her, and you know, she ever returns unhurt."

In obedience, therefore, to the wish of the countess, Edith re-seated herself, but it was useless to attempt even to cast from her mind the deep anxiety she felt regarding Grace. A thousand vague and undefined fears rushed through her mind, filling her heart with the severest anguish, till, unable to endure it longer, she rose, and stealing from the room, entered the garden and followed in the steps of Grace. She wandered through the grounds without obtaining sight of the fair fugitive. "Grace, dear Grace," she called, but she received no reply, "Grace love," she called, still louder as she approached the lake, "pray answer me, I wish to speak to you." Still all was silent, and Edith began to be really alarmed; her heart beat quickly, and her breath became so short that she was forced to stand still for a moment before she possessed the power to proceed; the next she darted forward and gained the spot where she fully hoped to have found Grace, but she was not there. Edith cast an anxious glance around. Her cousin had evidently been there that morning, for the marks of her footsteps were plainly visible, and the violets which grew upon the edge of the lake gave token that some had lately been torn away—one indeed had been dropped, perhaps in the hurry of departure, and now lay at the feet of Edith. She picked it up, and pressing it to her lips, in a voice whose tones breathed anguish, articulated the name of Grace, and still hearing no response, she sped onward to the house with the speed of lightning.

CHAPTER XXXIV.

"The flower that blooms to-day,
To-morrow dies;
All that we wish to stay
Tempts and then flies."

THE Earl of Clavering, filled with melancholy thoughts, wended his way towards his own ancestral seat; he had been absent some hours on a shooting excursion, and knew not of the sad and startling event that had occurred in his absence. As he neared the house, he thought there seemed an unusual bustle, while servants were hurrying to and fro with distracted looks.

"What can have happened?" was his inward exclamation, as he hastened his steps. In a few moments he entered the hall, and the sound of smothered sobs smote upon his ear; he hastily entered the room from whence they proceeded; a number of persons were gathered round a couch; he approached, and being instantly recognised by the servants, an opening was made, to admit him to the centre.

Edith was bending in anguish over the inanimate form of his mother, and the earl approaching the couch, gazed with heartfelt anguish on the face of his dead sister. Yes, it was Grace; her white satin robe, dripping with its moisture, and her long black tresses clinging in heavy folds around it, told too plainly the fearful tale. On her soft white bosom, which had once throbbed with the noblest and warmest feelings of her sex, was placed a bunch of beautiful violets, the heavy moisture caused their heads to droop, and these fragrant flowers filled the air with a soft perfume.

The earl was the first to break the silence of the chamber. Turning to the insensible form of his mother, he said " She has fainted."

The doctor, who had been hastily summoned, shook his head.

" She is suffering from a fit of apoplexy," he replied, recommending at the same time her instant removal to bed, whither she was immediately conveyed by her attendants, accompanied by Edith, when the surgeon perceiving that she manifested no symptoms of returning consciousness, considered it right to bleed her; after which, prescribing perfect quietness, he left her to the care of Edith.

In the meantime the earl learned from the domestics the particulars of the sad calamity that had befallen his sister.

It appeared when Edith returned and hurriedly related her unsuccessful search for the Lady Grace, the countess considering it right that instant search should be made for the missing lady, despatched a couple of domestics to seek for her about the park.

Wearied with a long and fruitless search, one of the men at length proposed, as a last resource, that they should look into the lake, thinking that it was just possible the Lady Grace might have fallen in. Together, therefore, they proceeded towards her favourite spot, and on stooping down, they were horrified to perceive something not unlike the white robe worn by Grace.

With some difficulty, they contrived to reach it, and on drawing it towards them, were perfectly horror struck at perceiving the well-known form of their youthful mistress. The servants wept as they bore her to the house, for they had carried her in their arms when a child, and were old and faithful retainers of this unhappy family.

Edith from her window saw them approaching with their burden, and with instinctive tenderness, would have withdrawn the countess from the room, but she refused to move; and in a few minutes the cold and lifeless form of her daughter, recovered from her watery tomb, was placed on the couch by her side.

The sight was too dreadful to meet a mother's eyes, and with one bursting sigh, she sank, in a fit, to the ground.

Whether the unfortunate Grace wilfully cast herself into the lake, or whether, in bending down to catch the imaginary glance of her lover, she overbalanced herself, and slipped in, was never known.

All Edith's thoughtful tenderness and gentle zeal were unavailing. The Countess of Clavering never recovered consciousness; but continued breathing heavily, as though in a deep, and by no means unpleasing slumber, for three days, but ere the fourth had scarcely dawned her spirit took its flight to join that of her daughter's in the skies. Edith bore up bravely, but when this second calamity was made known to the earl, he answered sternly, "Leave me alone to mourn over the fallen fortunes of my house."

The remains of the countess and her daughter were borne together to the tomb of their ancestors, and there left to repose among the honoured dead; and now there were but two left, that bore any relationship to that once large and noble family.

Edith made no complaint no noisy demonstration of grief escaped her, but she moved about pale as are the shrouded dead, and scarcely seemed a thing of life.

Poor fragile Edith, gentle, loving, and amiable, thou didst indeed bear all unrepiningly, but it was not for long, she gradually drooped day by day, the cords that bound her to earth were broken, and she longed to be at rest; each day found her more nearly approaching the tomb, but as the tired bird who has flown on weary pinion across the dark blue sea, longs to find one green spot on which it can rest, so did the tire-worn soul of Edith, who had crossed the rough sea of sorrow, long to lay down life's weary load and be at peace; she felt that

One hope was before her,
One refuge, the grave.

In less than two months from the death of the countess, she ceased to breathe; it could scarcely be said she died, so tranquil and so full of sweetness was her end.

The earl roused himself from his torpor of grief when he became aware of the dangerous illness of his wife, and during the last few weeks previous to her death, he was in close and constant attendance upon her. In his arms she drew her latest breath; a smile full of sweetness parted her lips, and the words "God bless you," found utterance, and then the earl was alone. Alone in his large mansion, surrounded by his vast domain. Alone without a relation, or a friend in the world, if we except the old and faithful retainers of his family. But the youthful earl seemed inured to sorrow, he calmly pressed his lips to the clay-cold ones of Edith, which in days

one by had warmed into ardour at the approach of his, but now still and mute in death. He saw his wife laid by the side of his mother and Grace, without shedding a single tear; he returned from the mournful ceremony, and seated himself in the library, there to brood over his anguish alone. One thought, even in this dark hour, came fraught with hope, to his dark and despairing heart; it was that of his first and earliest love, Catherine Montravers, and his child. Could he induce her to become his wife, to pardon all the past, and bless him again with her love and tenderness, he might be happy with lisping children round his knee, and might thus prevent the extinction of his family, of whom he was now the sole surviving member. In years to come he might forget the early sorrows and errors of his youth, and his heart beat again fond and

No. 15.

warm as in days gone by. His bosom expanded with joy at the very thought.   Oh, surely, surely, Catherine could listen to him if not for her own, at least, for the sake of her child, she would consent to his wishes; it would, it must be so.   And yet it was soon to think of wedding another, but if he delayed Catherine might be lost to him for ever; he would in the course of a few weeks seek her address and learn at once his destiny.

CHAPTER XXXV.

"Nothing in the world is single;
All things by a law divine
In one another's being mingle;
See, the mountains kiss high heaven,
And the waves clasp one another;
No sister flower would be forgiven
If it disdained its brother."

MADAME CHEVASSE, and her accomplice, Lawton, through the instrumentality of Moreton, met with their deserts, the former being condemned by the tribunal of Paris to perpetual imprisonment; and the other, for the long period of twenty-one years; and in consequence, the so-deeply-coveted wealth of his unfortunate cousin was forfeited to the government. Thus he was never permitted to enjoy that property which he had not hesitated to wade through crime to obtain.

Immediately after the trial, Moreton and his mother returned to England. The latter determined instantly to put her generous resolution into effect.

In the meantime Lieutenant Marston had abstained from visiting the sisters, according to the wish of Catherine, for several months, during which period he had in vain endeavoured to banish from his mind the image of the absent Helen.   At length wearied with contending with his own feelings, he resolved once more to visit the sisters.   It was a beautiful evening, and quite late in the autumn, which with its mellow tints, lent an additional lustre to the scene; the distance was speedily accomplished by the impatient lieutenant; and sooner even than he had anticipated, he stood in front of the cottage. The folding windows of the parlour were thrown open, and the young man took the liberty of entering; it was vacant, but another pair of windows opened into the little garden, in the arbour of which, he perceived Catherine in the centre of a small group of children, to whom she appeared to be relating some laughter-stirring tale, to judge of the effect it produced upon their merry faces.

At a little distance from these seated on the soft green grass, Nature's carpet, was Helen, engaged in a joyous game of play, with a rosy, lovely boy, over whose young head scarce twelve months had yet rolled.   The little fellow clapped his dimpled hands, and laughed right merrily, as Helen rolled him over and over on the grass. There is no knowing how long the young man might have stood there surveying them, had not one of the children become aware of his presence, and pointed him out to her preceptress. Catherine instantly rose and going towards him, stretched out her hand, there was a cordiality in her manner that encouraged the lieutenant, and apologising for his abrupt visit, he asked the favour of a few minutes conversation with her alone. It was instantly granted, and his errand soon made known, he loved Helen, and designed to make her his wife; would Catherine consent to plead for him, with her sister.   The tears forced themselves into Catherine's eyes as she replied:—

"Will I? oh! I shall indeed be blest if Helen accepts you, which I cannot doubt. There is but one thing which is likely to prove an impediment to your union with my sister; and that," she said hesitatingly, "rests with myself, but deep as my own humility will be in owning my sin, yet, Lieutenant Marston, as I would not have you spurn that dear girl, after marriage, I must tell you all.   You see," she continued pointing from the window, "that child she is so fondly caressing; that child," she added, "is my own, a child of sin and shame;" and the burning colour on her cheeks attested how much she felt at being forced to make this avowal. "If with the full knowledge of this, you are still anxious to wed my sister," she continued, "I will call her to your side, and tell her all; but if you hesitate to link yourself with one upon whose innocent head shame is reflected from the sin of another, go at once, and Helen shall never know that you have loved her."

"Call her, call her, instantly," said the young man. "Miss Montravers, so far from having sunk in my estimation, I admire, I respect you more for this frank avowal, and your sister is as dear to my heart as its very blood," and he stretched his hand towards Catherine. Exchanging one brief pressure, she hastened from the room to acquaint her sister with the presence of her visitor. As she did so, she was startled, at encountering in the passage a female of middle age, whose exceeding lady-like manners instantly prepossessed Catherine in her favour.

"Pardon me, Miss Montravers," she said, bowing politely, "I have called to see the daughters of an old friend, whom I am given to understand are placed under your care, and unintentionally overheard what passed between yourself and Mr. Marston. Will you permit me then, Miss Montravers to express my deep sense of the excellence of your conduct." Catherine felt gratified, and conducting the lady to a different apartment, hastened to inform her sister that Mr. Marston wished to see her. She then returned to her own visitor, whom the reader has guessed was no other than Mrs. Moreton, who had accidentally discovered from the colonel's lady, who was one of her oldest friends, that her daughters were being educated by the very young person whom she was so anxious to become acquainted with. This, then, afforded her a reasonable excuse for calling on Catherine, and the hour they spent together passed speedily away, and when she rose to take her leave, she presented her card to Catherine, and asked permission to call the following day and bring a friend with her. Consent was readily granted, for Catherine was equally pleased with her visitor; but though she recognised the name. she had no idea that she had been conversing with the mother of Moreton. Catherine then returned to the parlour, and found Marston the accepted lover of her sister. Joy filled her bosom, and the sisters retired to rest, thankful and happy. The following day, so engaged was Catherine in thinking of the contemplated marriage of her sister, that she had totally forgotten her expected visitor, till her name was announced, when hastening to receive her, great was her surprise to find her accompanied by Ernest Moreton.

"This, dear Miss Montravers, is the friend I am anxious to introduce to you," said the lady, presenting the young man.

"Dearest Catherine," exclaimed Moreton, taking her hand, and respectfully carrying it to his lips, "say that I am not altogether hateful to you. I now know and appreciate your motives for refusing my addresses whilst in Paris. Now that I know all, and still seek your hand as the dearest boon of existence, you will not, cannot refuse it."

"Dear, generous young man," said Catherine, affected even to tears, "you know not what you ask—my child—"

"Shall be likewise mine," he replied, eagerly. "I shall love and cherish it for your dear sake ; come, say that you consent to be mine."

"Alas !" returned Catherine, "if you should ever repent linking your fate with one so fallen. Your mother too —"

"Will gladly receive you as a daughter," said Mrs. Moreton, approaching and affectionately embracing Catherine. "You will consent, my love, to make us both happy ?"

Catherine could hold out no longer ; amidst tears and smiles, she gave the required promise.

Oh, what a sweet and happy party met round the tea table that evening ; what quiet, yet grateful joy filled the heart of each. It would be difficult to say who was most happy, Helen, Catherine, Marston, Moreton, or his mother.

Preparations were instantly set on foot for the celebration of the nuptials of Helen and Catherine, who found full employment in arranging their own little affairs previous to entering into the bonds of matrimony.

A week had scarcely elapsed since the mutual engagement, when Catherine was apprised that a gentleman who declined to give his name, was desirous of speaking with her. On descending to the little parlour, great was her surprise at beholding the Earl of Clavering. He looked sad, and pale, and was dressed in a plain suit of mourning. Catherine had become aware of the severe loss he had sustained through the public papers, still, though she could not do otherwise than sympathise with his sufferings; she felt greatly annoyed at his present intrusion, and expressed herself warmly to that effect.

"Wait one moment, Catherine," said the earl, "before you upbraid me with this intrusion ; hear, at least, the purport of my visit. I come, Catherine, to seek you, as my bride, to ask for the renewal of an affection that was once all my own."

"But is so no longer," interrupted Catherine ; "all love for you has long been utterly extinct in my heart. Nothing on earth could revive even one spark of it."

"Nevertheless," replied the earl, "let me entreat of you, Catherine, to accept of my proposal, for the sake at least of our child."

"Stop," replied Catherine, "I cannot allow you to proceed. Rather than become your wife, the wife of one whose character I despise, and for whom I could never entertain the slightest respect, I would submit to any hardship, and doom my child to the same, but there is no need for it; know," and she drew herself proudly up, "I am the betrothed bride of Ernest Moreton, who, fallen as I am, has persuaded me to become his wife; he knew, and made me honourable proposals while I was in Paris, at the very time you were using every art to lure me to destruction. I then, unfortunately gave the preference to yourself, but I do so no longer. I now love, respect, and venerate him, while I entertain an equal amount of averson and contempt for yourself."

"Alas!" replied the earl, who was thunderstruck at her words, "I cannot believe you will be happy in such a marriage. Moreton's proud mother will never acknowledge you."

"His mother," replied Catherine, warmly, "with kind and tender words, besought me to consent to become her daughter; she has even condescended to acknowledge my child. Under these circumstances, I could with honour receive his proposal, and in a few weeks I shall become his wife."

The earl groaned aloud, in the bitterness of his spirit, and quitting the house without another word, he resolved instantly to travel. This scheme was speedily put in effect; in less than a week he quitted England. None ever heard of him afterwards; but he must have died abroad, in the course of a few years; for up to that period, he had regularly kept an account with his bankers, through the agency of a third party. This was suddenly discontinued, and the name of Clavering became extinct.

THE END.